"I'll want more than that," Nick stated.

He grasped Karen's shoulders and forced her to meet his implacable eyes.

"Elizabeth is ill and needs us," he went on. "And you are going to play the part of a loving wife as long as I deem it necessary."

Karen knew how much Elizabeth meant to him—the woman who had been like a mother to him; who had been the only one to believe in the young incorrigible Nick. And Karen loved her, too.

She shivered as realization came of what being back in Nick's life could mean. Even for Elizabeth's sake, could she stand living a lie? But questions were futile. When it came right down to it, she really had no choice!

The Dark Side of Marriage

by

MARGERY HILTON

Harlequin Books

TORONTO • LONDON • NEW YORK • AMSTERDAM
SYDNEY • HAMBURG • PARIS

Original hardcover edition published in 1978
by Mills & Boon Limited

ISBN 0-373-2213-1

Harlequin edition published November 1978

CHAPTER ONE

I have to see you ...
Karen Radcliffe stared at the card while the words repeated themselves over and over in her brain. The familiar surroundings of her little flat receded into limbo and she was aware of nothing except shock and the message on the small white card that had been thrust under her door, awaiting her return from her hurried shopping trip. She had been gone only half an hour or so, to collect the things necessary to restock her food store for the coming weekend. He must have called during that short time.

Nick was back! He'd been *here*!

Karen sank weakly into the nearest chair. Her legs were trembling suddenly, as much as her hands, and the card almost fell from her nerveless fingers. What did he want? Why? After all this time; nearly two years of silence.

She read the three terse sentences again: *I have to see you. Imperative you contact me within 24 hours. Fiesta till nine. Home afterwards. Nick.*

They told her nothing, except a sense of extreme urgency, and anger began to burn through her shock. That was typical of Nick. No request in those stark black lines of his unmistakable hand writing. No conventional 'please'. Just an arrogant summons. He came home after two years, after all that had happened, and expected to find her waiting, ready to leap to his bidding.

She turned the card over, read the address that had once been achingly familiar, had once been home ... might still be if only ...

Karen stood up, her eyes hard. It was too late for buts, or if-onlies. She was going to ignore this—tear up the card; pretend it had never come. She walked to the window and stared down at the dusty garden and the worn patches on the square of lawn where the children jostled and tussled through their play, and suddenly she became aware that she was twisting and turning the engraved gold band on her wedding finger.

She was trembling again, not with shock, nor anger, but fear. Did this summons means that Nick had changed his mind? That he had decided to seek his freedom, despite all he had sworn? Had he met someone else?

A knock at the door brought Karen spinning round and started her blood pounding in her veins. Was it Nick? Had he come back? For a moment she could not force her limbs to carry her over to the door, then the knock sounded again and a familiar, querulous voice called: 'Are you there, Mrs Radcliffe? It's only me.'

Her garrulous, inquisitive, wily landlady! A strange weakness almost like disappointment relaxed Karen and she hurried to the door, opening it to the dark, thin-faced woman in the soiled apron who stood outside.

'I thought you was back, dearie.' Mrs Biggins eyed Karen knowingly. 'I just wanted to tell you that you had a visitor while you was out—you wouldn't have reached the corner before he called.'

'Yes, I know.' Karen kept her hand on the door, knowing that if Mrs Biggins once got in she would be there for an hour.

'Left a message, did he?' Mrs Biggins was impervious to a hint. 'I suggested he did that when he said it was very important that he see you. Gorgeous feller he was, too.' Mrs Biggins' eyes rounded and her elbow came out to nudge Karen's arm. 'Big and dark and 'andsome—with that sort of smouldering look that gets a woman feeling she'd like to'—another nudge—'you know!'

Karen gave a slight nod, unsmiling. She knew that look of Nick's extremely well, but it brought a sense of revulsion to hear it described with Mrs Biggins' knowing leers.

'Shame you missed him.' Mrs Biggins sighed as her ploys failed to raise any response from the pale, strained girl in the doorway. 'I told him he could wait in my place if he liked, long as he didn't mind the kids runnin' in and out. You know what kids are, but you can't be too hard on them. After all, they're only young once.' Mrs Biggins paused, and darted a glance past Karen, almost as though she hoped to glimpse the big dark handsome feller lurking behind Karen's slender form. But he did not seem to have eluded her vigilance and she said reluctantly, 'Oh well, as long as he left word for you. Put a note under the door, did he?'

'Yes.' Karen was striving to keep patient. 'Thank you, Mrs Biggins, it was very kind of you to come and tell me, and to offer to let him wait. And now, I've rather a lot to do . . .'

She took a step backwards, beginning to close the door, and at last Mrs Biggins retreated with a baffled look on her face.

Karen closed the door and wished, not for the first time, that she had succeeded in finding accommodation anywhere but in the domain of Mrs Biggins. The woman was kind enough, the little flat was immaculately done out, and the rent within reach of Karen's budget, but Mrs Biggins was hopelessly inquisitive, and Karen knew that her every move was watched, and the few visitors or calls she received were remorselessly monitored. However, looking for somewhere to live in London was like prospecting for gold in the pavements, and she had considered herself fortunate in finding the self-contained haven in the tall, shabby terrace house, even if the rest of the house betrayed a contrast of shabby scarred paintwork, where Mrs Biggins' two boisterous sons battled and scrapped their way through childhood. Karen could close her door on the noise and the wafts of fish and chips from below, and tell herself she was fortunate to be there, within easy reach of the Underground that took her to her secretarial job in the City each day, while she tried to rebuild her life after the most shattering patch she'd ever experienced in her twenty-two years.

The sense of shock was evaporating now, but the deep tremors of unease still chased through her body as she forced herself to unpack her carrier and stow away the groceries. Still with that unnatural calm, she set a place for one at the little table then filled the kettle and plugged it into the socket. She put a slice of bread in the toaster and whisked an egg to scramble, but while her hands worked at the preparing of the simple meal her brain was in a turmoil, seeking the answer to that small slip of white card that seemed to fill the flat with its presence.

Nick. Her husband.

The silently spoken words shattered her control, and a scalding splash of water stung her hand as she filled the small teapot. There was no question about the answer; Nick's summons could mean only one thing: he'd met someone else. Two years was a long time, time for him to meet dozens of women, even if his last big job had taken him to South America for the best part of that two years. And women had always clustered round Nick, like moths round the flame of temptation that eventually consumed them. What was it that Lisa had once said? That Nick brushed away the charred wings as casually as a speck of dust from his lapel ... Karen clenched her fists, fighting the old ache she thought she had beaten, despite all Nick had said about not making it easy for her, when he'd sworn he would put every obstacle in her path to freedom. That she would have to wait the requisite two years and then manage the whole dreadful business of the divorce herself. But surely, if he had changed his mind, he wouldn't have bothered to contact her, simply arranged to have the cold legal communication forwarded from a solicitor. Because you could have a postal divorce now, couldn't you?

Karen sat down to scrambled egg already congealing on cold toast and stared unseeingly into space. Surely he wouldn't come seeking her here, to leave a stark message that was almost an accusation because she wasn't there when he came ...

The mouthfuls of food went round and round, refusing to go down, and at last she pushed the plate away. Even the tea would choke her if she tried to drink it. What was she going to do?

She did not know how long she sat there, her emotions like a crazy see-saw. She'd be a fool even to consider seeing Nick again. It would be turning the knife in the wound. If he needed her to sign anything he could arrange it through a third party. Did he really expect her to lay herself open to renewed humiliation? No, she would *not* see him. She would write him a letter, one as cold and inhuman as the one he had written her when the dreadful affair was closed. The one that told her he had arranged for an allowance to be paid to her through his bank while he was away. She would tell him he could contact her through her solicitor. Old Mr Collins, who had handled all her father's business for as long as she could remember, would take care of things. Where was that address . . .?

Karen got up and searched through the cupboard for the black metal deedbox which had belonged to her father. The address should be in there, among the birth certificates and the old family papers she had never destroyed in case they should ever be needed.

There were the snapshots, fading now, of herself, of Mummy, of the mellowed old Georgian house in Canterbury where she had lived a happy, unchequered childhood, when Nick and Lisa and Vince Kayne had been far in the hidden future, beyond a dark cloud not even hinted at over the horizon.

Tears stung at Karen's eyes, but she dashed them away impatiently. She had done her weeping for Nick; she wasn't going to let the tears start again, no matter what happened. Through the blur she found the old address book and thumbed through the yellowing pages, only to sigh with disappointment. The address wasn't there, but she could look it up. The Kent telephone directory would have it. She would go to the post office during her lunch hour tomorrow . . .

She turned away, and the white card stared up accusingly from the table. Why hadn't Nick given her a clue? Damn him! she swore under her breath, why had he come back into her life? And to expect her to meet him at the Fiesta, of all places.

She piled the dishes into the sink, and now her eyes brimmed with the unshed tears of memory. The Fiesta, the haunt of aficionados of true flamenco, where Nick had taken her for that very first date, where less than a month later he had turned her world into wonderland by asking her to marry him ... And now he expected her to meet him there to discuss the final severance of all that began there on those wonderful enchanted evenings.

Karen dried the dishes with savage intensity and closed her heart to all reason. Then she tore the card into shreds, collected her bag and jacket, and went out into the gathering night. She spent the next hour and a half at a news cinema, had a lonely coffee at a snack bar, and returned to her flat a few minutes after nine. She had little memory of what she had seen at the cinema, or even of the journey; there was only the cold, unsatisfying knowledge that she had defied Nick.

When she let herself in she could not prevent a quick downward glance, but there was no trace of anything to betray any further untoward communication, no hurried movement from below that heralded tidings from her landlady, and she gave a faint sigh. Surely she hadn't expected him to come back!

The front door slammed, exiting Mr Biggins for his nightly pint, muffled bangs and roars indicated that the boys had settled to watch the Western, and across the road the blonde girl at Number 17 was opening the door to her mechanic boy-friend. Karen drew the curtains, and an unutterable sense of loneliness overcame her. Wearily she completed the nightly chores necessary to keep the flat from becoming too untidy, then collected together the necessities for having a bath in someone else's bathroom. Her worst fear was of forgetting her key and finding herself locked out, for the Yale latch on her door snicked shut at the slightest breath of draught, and the little locking catch didn't always function. She had never forgotten the first week, when she had had to go downstairs in her dressing gown, her hair damp and flowing, to ask Mrs Biggins if she had a spare key. Mrs Biggins had been out, and Mr Biggins and the two boys had all trooped up to see her safely back into her domain. She had felt embarrassed and foolish, although there had been nothing unkind in their amusement at her predicament, and now she always took care that it should not occur again. But with a shoe in the doorway, and the key in her sponge bag, she could relax in the warm scented water without fear.

She emerged from the steam-laden air about an hour later to find the landing outside in complete darkness. It wasn't unusual, someone had switched off the staircase light from below, and she was familiar enough by now with the house to grope her way up the three stairs and along the passage to the first doorway, which was her own, and the landing light switch.

There she paused to drape her bath towel along the banister rail, and turned to thrust open her door. Her hand froze in mid-air, and she took an alarmed step back. The shoe was gone, and the light was on inside! But she hadn't left the light on!

Karen's heart began to thump. Her first thought was of intruders, her second to dismiss that fear—no intruder would ever pass Mrs Biggins' eagle eye. Were the boys playing tricks? But they had never intruded on her in any way all the two years she had lived there.

A scream of alarm in readiness on her lips, she slowly pushed open the door and peered inside. The room was quite empty, all seemed to be exactly as she had left it, and a frightened glance at the drawn window curtains saw no trace of the feet of an intruder concealed there. Karen left the outer door wide open and went slowly into the centre of the room, prepared for instant flight. The shoe was lying about a couple of feet to the side of the doorway, and she shook her head in puzzlement. A cat? But the Biggins' household did not possess a moggie; a canary, two goldfish, and a hamster, but definitely no cat. And then she saw the bedroom door was wide open, and at the same moment she heard the sound.

A cry escaped her and she sprang back, knocking over a chair as she did so, and there was a sharp exclamation from within the bedroom. Karen's hand went to her throat as a tall figure darkened the doorway. He stood there, looking at her, and an incredulous gasp escaped her.

'You!' she choked.

'Yes, me.' Nick stepped forward, as casually as though he had every right to be there. 'Did I scare you?'

Karen struggled for words. 'What are you doing here? How dare you just—just walk into my flat, as though, as——'

'The door was open.'

As though that was sufficient explanation he moved towards her, glancing around the room, then past her towards the outer door. With a single cut of his hand he slammed it shut, and Karen spun round.

'What are you doing?'

'Closing the door.' Hands pushed deep into the pockets of his green car coat, he faced her squarely with challenge in every line of his body. 'I guessed you wouldn't turn up, so I came back.'

'Did you really expect me to drop everything and—and run to your bidding? You—you've got a nerve!'

His dark head tilted a little to one side, and a trace of cynical amusement tugged at one side of his mouth. 'So you still stammer, my lovely. You always did when you got in a paddy. In that respect you haven't changed.'

'And you certainly haven't changed!' she flared. 'You're still as arrogant and—and impossible as ever. How I was fool enough ever to fall in love with you is beyond my comprehension. You're——'

'Let's leave love out of it,' he broke in coldly. 'I didn't come here tonight to start the old roundabout going. You made a fool out of me once—and believe me, I've no intention of letting you repeat the performance.'

'Get out!' Karen's eyes sparkled with anger. 'I've nothing to say to you—ever!'

'But I have a great deal to say to you!' he gritted. 'And I'm not leaving until I've said it.'

'Then say it quickly and go!' Trembling with the force of unspent emotion, Karen backed away from the cold fury that was naked in his eyes. 'You didn't need to come here tonight to ask for your freedom—I offered you that two years ago when you made it so plain you despised me.'

'Is that why you think I'm here?' His mouth curled bitterly. 'You're contemptible.'

'Is that what you came to tell me?' Karen ran to the door and seized the handle. 'Well, you've said it. Satisfied?' She flung open the door and stood waiting, waiting for him to go.

For a long moment he stood there, his bitter gaze locked with hers, while his mouth tightened with his visible attempts to master his anger. Then he moved slowly across the room.

'I didn't come here because of us,' he said at last. 'I came because of Elizabeth.'

'Elizabeth?' Karen stared at him, and the subconscious force of intuition brought a flicker of dread. 'What's the matter? Is she . . .? She's not had an accident?'

Nick's shoulders sagged. He turned away. 'She's ill.'

Karen's hand fell away from the door. 'I'm sorry to hear that. Is it very serious?' she faltered.

'She's going to die.'

The stark words hung in the air. Karen closed her eyes. Had she really heard that appalling statement? Not Elizabeth, not the gentle, generous woman whom she had come to love almost as dearly as her own mother during the short months she had known her. The woman to whom Nick owed so much, of whom he had vowed more than once that he would sacrifice everything he possessed if it would bring her happiness. No, it couldn't be true. Then she looked at Nick and saw the anguish working in his face, threatening to break even his tough control, and she knew it was indeed true.

'What happened? When did you know?' she whispered.

'When I got back yesterday.' He straightened his shoulders. 'Have you anything to drink, Karo?'

He appeared not to notice that the old special diminutive had slipped out. She shook her head, distressed, and hurried to the cupboard. 'I've no spirits, I'm afraid, Nick. Just sherry and lime juice . . . oh, wait a minute . . . there's some Bacardi, left from New Year—somebody brought it.' She hesitated, then gestured. 'Would you like to help yourself?'

'Thanks.' He moved to her side, reaching for the glass she had taken from the cupboard. His brows went up. 'Aren't you having one?'

'No, thanks.' She became aware of his nearness, and suddenly remembered her state of undress. She drew the fronts of her dressing gown closer together and tightened the tie-belt. 'No, thanks,' she repeated rather feverishly, 'I'll probably be having a cup of something and a biscuit before I go to bed.'

He watched her edge away, and the same sardonic quirk touched his mouth again as he dashed a jigger of rum into the glass and added some lime. 'Still addicted to your bed-time cocoa?'

Her lips tightened. 'It's force of habit—we always had cocoa at home last thing. Nick, for heaven's sake tell me about Elizabeth.'

'There isn't a great deal to tell,' he said grimly, dropping into an armchair. 'Nobody told me she was ill—nobody told me a damned thing. You haven't seen her?' he asked with sudden accusing vehemence.

'No!' Karen stared at him. 'Of course I haven't seen her. I thought we agreed that it was best to let her think ... Though why we came to that arrangement is beyond me,' she added bitterly. 'It was only postponing the news. She's got to know sooner or later.'

'No, she mustn't know! Not now, after this. If I thought you would break that promise ...'

Karen recoiled from the implication of threat in his tone. 'Elizabeth will never learn the truth from me,' she said fiercely, and knew an awakening of the old agony. She turned her head away so that he should not see the pain and the bitterness in her eyes. She said quietly: 'But I'd like to visit her—I've missed her very much.'

'Have you really? You surprise me.' He looked scornful. 'It's a bit late for regrets, isn't it?'

Karen stiffened, and her head came up proudly. 'Listen, Nick. I have no intention of starting the old futile recriminations all over again. Believe me, I'm deeply sorry to hear the bad news, and if there's anything I can do you know you've only to ask. But——'

'There's certainly something you can do,' he cut in brusquely, 'and make no mistake, you're going to do it, for once in your selfish, egoistic little life.'

'How dare you! I think you'd better go, before——' Karen

stopped as his hands seized her shoulders. She winced with pain as his fingers bit into her soft flesh, and a cry escaped her as she stared up into his burning eyes. And then as suddenly she was free.

She glimpsed the whiteness scoring the lines round his mouth, glistening over the knuckles of his clenched hands as they fell to his sides, and the fear ebbed out of her as she divined the naked grief behind the harsh outburst. She stood silent, rubbing the tender places on her arms, while he crossed to the table and took up his empty glass. Then he slowly replaced it and shook his head.

'I came to call a truce,' he said at last. 'I'm not making a very good job of it.'

'A truce?' she exclaimed. 'What do you mean, Nick?'

Not looking at her, he said slowly: 'I'd better explain first. The first inkling I had of Elizabeth's illness was a couple of months ago. She wrote to me, saying she'd been feeling rather tired for some time, and she had decided to take a long holiday, with the Mitchells—I don't think you ever met them. They're old friends of Elizabeth's who settled in Marbella after they retired. They have a villa there, and Elizabeth has always had a more or less standing invitation to visit them whenever she felt inclined. The next letter came about three weeks later, to tell me she was there, and all was well, and that she was counting the days to the end of the month, when she expected we would be coming home. She sent her love, and said she was longing to see us.'

Us. Karen swallowed hard. So Nick had kept up the pretence, as he had sworn he would, all during the two years he had been in South America. Letting Elizabeth believe that all was still well with their marriage, that Karen was with him there . . .

'Oh, God!' he groaned. 'You were right—we should have told her then. She would have been hurt and desperately upset—she thought the world of you—but she would have got over it. Now . . . it's too late.'

Karen sighed and remained silent. There was an inescapable truth she would have liked to point out to Nick, but this was not the moment to retort that it had been his idea, and his alone, to deceive Elizabeth. Because he knew she would try every means within her power to bring about a reconciliation between the man she regarded as dearly as her own son and the girl he had chosen as his bride.

Karen trembled. Perhaps it was as well that Nick had gained his own way. Had he not, and Elizabeth had endeavoured to influence both him and Karen, it was possible that Elizabeth might have stumbled upon the real truth. And that would have brought even greater disillusion, perhaps even greater sorrow ... No, without knowing it, Nick had chosen the wiser course. But that had not brought much comfort to Karen.

She sighed again, and said quietly, 'Yes, it's too late now, I'm afraid. Poor Elizabeth!'

Nick's head came up sharply as she spoke. The hard glitter of determination had returned to his eyes. 'But it isn't too late to make her remaining time as happy as possible.'

'Of course not!' Again Karen was stung to indignation by what she saw as accusation in his attitude. 'As far as I'm concerned, if there's anything I can do for her, you have only to tell me. For heaven's sake, Nick, don't you believe me? I didn't know Elizabeth for very long, but in that time I came to respect her immensely. I also came to love her very much,' she said more quietly. 'Whatever happened to us and our marriage makes no difference to that, and never will as far as I'm concerned.'

'Good.' Nick got to his feet, his gaze never wavering from her face as he crossed the room and stood towering over her, his mouth grim. 'That makes it easier for me to say what I have to say.'

Karen waited, forcing herself not to be intimidated, and willed herself to remain impervious to the old quickening of the senses that he could still evoke.

'We had a long talk this afternoon,' he said at last, 'and she has expressed a wish to go back to Dellersbeck. She was born there, you know, and spent most of her married life there. It wasn't until after Uncle James died that she gave in to family pressure to come south and take the flat in Granton Place.' He paused, retrospect easing the hardness from his expression. 'I sometimes wonder if we should have let her make her own readjustment, in her own time. But Lisa was involved with her modelling nonsense, and I had too many commitments to keep me out of the country for long periods, making it impossible for me to live on at Dellersbeck. And certainly the house was too big, too lonely and too full of memories for her to carry on living there alone with only the servants for company. But I often wondered if Elizabeth was as happy and contented as she assured us she was. Sometimes, when she talked of Dellersbeck, there was a wistful look in her eyes.'

'But you only leased the house, though? You didn't sell it?'

'No—I'd never let Elizabeth sell it. We did lease it to the head of Comeche Construction while they were building the new university complex over at Beechley New Town. But they moved out when they finished the job about four months ago and there were no new takers until just a couple of weeks ago. The agents had three enquiries in one week—of course that's the way things go.' Nick took a deep breath. 'I phoned them today and told them to withdraw the house immediately. I'm driving up there tomorrow to look over the place and make any arrangements that need making. Then I hope to take Elizabeth up there early next week.'

Karen nodded. Nick hadn't changed. Once he made up his mind about a course of action he wasted no time and allowed nothing—or no one—to stand in his way. But wasn't that why Nick, a poor boy from the east end of a great northern city, was now the head of an engineering complex with contracts all over the world? Karen's face softened. She was fair enough to credit Nick where it was due without personal bias swaying her, and she loved him for his unswerving devotion to the woman who had given him the chance to make it all possible. She said softly, 'I'm glad. I think it will make Elizabeth more happy than anything else could.'

'Yes. Except for one thing.'

His voice and expression were suddenly charged with meaning. Karen caught her breath. 'And that is . . .?'

'Her family—those whom she loves—around her.'

'Isn't that natural?' Karen swallowed hard. 'You—you want me to go and see her?'

'I want more than that, Karen.'

'What do you mean?'

'I want you to come with me, to Dellersbeck, for as long as Elizabeth needs us.'

For a moment she stared at him, her natural reaction being to agree instantly, with only the thought of Elizabeth uppermost. Then the more basic implications occurred and she exclaimed, 'Yes, of course I'll come with you to see her, but I can't stay, Nick. I have a job here. But I could probably get a couple of days leave, and perhaps——'

She stopped. He was shaking his head.

'You're not with me, Karen. Or are you deliberately misunderstanding me?'

Her lips parted. 'I don't think so. I——' And then dismay choked her into silence as she thought she comprehended his meaning. 'Oh, no, Nick! You don't mean . . .'

'Yes, I *do* mean,' he said grimly. 'You are coming to Dellersbeck with me, as my wife.'

'Oh, no! I couldn't. Not after——'

'You can, and you will.' He took hold of her shoulders and forced her to meet his implacable eyes. 'You are coming to Dellersbeck, and you are going to play the part of a loving wife, as though nothing had ever come between us, and you are going to play it as long as I deem it necessary.'

She shrank back. 'You can't be serious! Do you think we can wipe out all the bitterness, all the acrimony, as though it had never happened?'

'I am serious, never more so. And don't try to persuade me that women can't deceive when it suits them.' His hands tightened cruelly. 'Listen to me, Karen. If you refuse, you'll leave me no alternative but to tell Elizabeth the truth. And if you force me to do that, make no mistake, it'll be the whole truth. Oh, yes, the truth about my so innocent little wife, and Vince Kayne! What do you think that will do to Elizabeth?'

'You—you couldn't be so inhuman!' Karen's face whitened with horror. 'You don't know what you're saying! You——' She tried to twist free of the bruising fingers, and the tears of pain welled in her eyes. 'Let go! You're hurting me!'

'As you deserve to be hurt!' With a contemptuous movement he thrust her away from him. 'Oh, for God's sake! Don't start weeping!'

She gripped the back of a chair to steady herself, fighting for control, then straightened and ran distraught fingers through her hair. At last she drew a deep, unsteady breath.

'Very well,' she whispered. 'You win. But you'll have to give me a few days to—to see if I can get leave of absence, or work my notice. I can't just——'

'I'll fix that. Who's your boss?'

'I work for Mr Drummond, at the wholesale branch of——'

'The name of the head of the firm, not an underling,' he snapped.

'How marvellous to have influence,' she said bitterly. 'Please remember that I will have to live afterwards. I like my job, and Mr Drummond is a kind man to work for. So I——' She became aware of Nick staring at her strangely.

'What on earth do you spend your money on?' he demanded. 'Surely to God you can manage on the allowance I make you?'

Her mouth compressed. 'I've never touched a penny of it, and I don't intend to.'

His brows drew together, then he shrugged, as though the matter was of no interest to him. He looked at his watch. 'That's settled, then. I'll be in touch with you in a day or so, as soon as I finalise my plans.'

She said nothing, only wanting him to go so that she could surrender to the weakness flooding her body. She heard his steps as he moved, and the slight creak of the loose board near the door, and waited for the sound that would tell her he had gone. But it did not come. Instead she heard his voice, unusually hesitant. 'Karen . . .?'

She half turned, her face still white with emotional shock. 'Yes?' she said wearily.

'This means a great deal to me—thanks.' He raised one hand, and when she made no move towards him, he sighed and let his hand fall to his side. He moved slowly to the door.

Only then did Karen glimpse all the things she had failed to read in his face before that last moment of admission—the unguarded anxiety, the forlorn hope, and the dark shadows of torment. She took an unsteady step forward, but it was too late. The door closed silently, leaving only the dead echoes of those gruff, awkwardly spoken words.

Karen sank into a chair and hugged her arms round her trembling body. She felt cold, drained and shaken, and part of her wanted to revile Nick for his arrogance, cruelty and ruthless demand. He had admitted at last that Elizabeth should have been told the truth two years ago, instead of resorting to all that subterfuge. All those lies because of his own hatred and unyielding condemnation, and because he knew that Elizabeth, once she knew, would have moved heaven and earth in her efforts to effect a reconciliation. And so he had ruthlessly prevented this, even to the extent of telephoning her, telling her the farewell meal had to be cancelled, before he slipped out of the country on the dawn flight to Rio de Janeiro. But what had he hoped to gain in the long run? Did he imagine that a two-year interval would make the breaking of the news any easier?

She stood up and paced restlessly round the room. Whatever her personal feelings she could feel no animosity at this moment. She knew too well the emptiness of pride and hostility to a heart that had experienced the depths to which love and fate could plunge a loser. Nick was reaching his own nadir of sorrow now and there was nothing she could do to assuage it, even if she admitted the bitter truth his coming tonight had revealed to her. And that was the last thing Nick would want to hear. He'd made it all too clear two years ago how little he needed her love.

Karen shivered, as though with an ague, as shock began to ebb and make way for the dawning implications of what tonight could mean. How was she going to cope with the future, back in Nick's life? Living under the same roof as a man who despised her? Hiding the truth from the man she still loved in spite of everything? Living a lie for Elizabeth...

CHAPTER TWO

For the first time in six months Karen blotted her record for good time-keeping by being nearly twenty mintes late in reaching the office the following morning.

From the moment of getting up it seemed like the start of one of those days. She found an unsuspected hole in her tights and had to change them; as she hurriedly made her modest breakfast a splash of milk marked her clean blouse and she had to change that, and then, as she ran to catch her train, she slipped and almost fell. Fortunately she suffered no ill effects bodily, but the heel came off her shoe and she had no choice but to return to the flat to make her third change of wear. This last delay resulted in missing the tube, and the quarter was chiming by the time she scrambled up to street level and scurried the quarter mile to her place of work.

She was hot, breathless and stressed when she emerged from the lift, and the sole consolation was that the chapter of small mishaps had almost succeeded in driving emotional chaos out of her mind. Until she reached the glass door of Mr Drummond's office and almost collided with her boss as he came out at that exact moment.

'I'm sorry!' she exclaimed simultaneously with his own apology, then he stepped back.

'I was wondering what had happened. I——'

'Yes—I'm late—I'm terribly sorry,' she began, 'but everything seemed to conspire to——'

'It's all right.' He smiled his old-fashioned, courteous smile. 'It's so very rare that you fail to be punctual, and I'm sure it's forgivable, under the circumstance.'

Karen stared. 'Thank you—but twenty minutes—if everyone——' she stammered, still out of breath.

But Mr Drummond was returning into his office. 'I'm very sorry to hear of illness in your family, Mrs Radcliffe.

I——' His desk buzzer interrupted him, and with a murmured indication to Karen to sit down he answered his
secretary and told her to put the incoming call through.

While he talked on the telephone Karen sat restlessly on
the edge of the chair. Had Nick been in touch with her employers already? There could be no other answer to Mr
Drummond's knowledge of this personal emergency. Nick
certainly hadn't wasted any time . . .

Mr Drummond finished his call and looked up. There was
a trace of something like disappointment on his pale, lined
face and it was unmistakable in his tone as he said briskly:
'Now I gather you need an indefinite leave of absence?'

'If that's possible—I mean, I'd like to be able to come back
here, but I realise that may not be possible.' She hesitated,
torn between loyalty to a most considerate boss and Nick's
uncompromising demands. 'Would you prefer me to hand
in my notice? I'll work as much of it as I can and forfeit
my——'

'No.' Mr Drummond shook his head. 'How can you work
the nominal notice period and help care for a sick woman at
the same time? No, take your leave, and I'm sure we'll be
able to offer you something when you're free again—you've
been a most conscientious employee, Mrs Radcliffe.' He
leaned back as she began to thank him, then added curiously,
'But why didn't you come to me yourself, my dear? We have
always prided ourselves on being understanding and
approachable.'

'I was going to.' She bit her lip, aware of anger at Nick's
precipitate intervention. 'But I didn't know myself until
last night.'

He nodded, his eyes suddenly shrewd on her face. 'You
have big guns firing for you, haven't you? I never knew you
were connected with the Radcliffe concern—or at least with
the family.'

She felt the tide of colour rise in her cheeks. 'Oh . . . I—it
never occurred to me to mention it,' she stammered.

To her relief he smiled. 'Of course not. It's purely a personal matter. After all, we have no business dealings or con-
nections with them. Well,' he gave her a dismissing gesture,

'you'll want to get away. Bad times these, when illness strikes suddenly. Let me know how things go, won't you?'

'Yes, of course I will. And thank you for being so understanding. But . . .' She realised she was free, and felt oddly disorientated. 'What about your letters, and the copies of the new report?'

He was reaching for his memo pad. 'Miss Pinkney will have to cope with all that. She'll manage until we reorganise. Don't worry.'

'Yes, Mr Drummond.' Karen was beginning to feel as though someone might pull a rug out under her feet at any moment. It seemed she was already out of a job whether she wanted to be or not. She turned and walked out of Mr Drummond's office, for once uncertain of her next move. Nick had said he would contact her, and he had also announced his intention of driving north today, so it was unlikely that she would hear from him for at least two days. Karen paused in the corridor. Really, she might as well have stayed at work until it was time to travel up to Dellersbeck, which might not be for several days.

For a moment she stood there irresolute, half inclined to go back into the office and do that report, if nothing else. She could finish it and the letters by lunch-time; Jeannie was an efficient enough typist, but her spelling was strictly her own. Karen saw the lift doors open and made up her mind. She would stay. She was turning back as she heard her name called, accompanied by a rush of light footsteps. The office junior caught up with her, breathless.

'I thought you'd gone! Here, this message was left for you a few minutes ago.' Little Sandra of the long red flyaway hair thrust a piece of paper into her hand. 'I say, is it true, Karen? You're leaving?'

Karen nodded. She stared at the telephone number she knew very well, and the scribbled line beneath. *Ring me before 10-30 this morning.* No signature, but then no signature was necessary.

'I'm awfully sorry.' Sandy looked concerned. 'We'll miss you. If there's anything I can do . . .'

'Thanks . . .' Karen forced a smile and pushed the paper

into her pocket. With a brief goodbye she hurried towards the lift. The word would have gone round the entire staff by now, and suddenly she was anxious to escape before everyone buttonholed her to ask well-meaning questions. She had always maintained a reserve with regard to her private life and although it was known she was married somehow the rumour had got round that she was a widow, and she had never denied it. It was easier to allow the unfounded surmise to stand than correct it, with the inevitable result of having to make explanations. Nick, if not exactly famous, was outspoken and often in the news, and she shrank from the curiosity that the truth would evoke if her identity became known.

Fortunately there was nobody in the ground floor lobby when she stepped out of the lift, and she walked out of the glass doors little more than ten minutes after entering them. There was a callbox at the corner of the street, and with only a brief hesitation she went into it and sorted a couple of coins out of her purse. She dialled the number and listened to the ringing tones, trying to ignore the fact that her heart had started to beat uncomfortably fast. There was a girl in a blue trouser suit just outside the booth. She was searching for change and trying to control a large excitable red setter who had spotted an Afghan hound coming out of a nearby shop with a plump woman in a red coat. The setter was winning, and the girl in blue snapped her bag shut and took a firmer grip on the dog's leash. There was a growl and a snarl, then Karen heard the phone bleeps and thrust in a twopenny piece with fingers that had started to shake.

'Karen . . .?' said Nick's deep voice before she had time to speak, and as she murmured in response he said crisply, 'I guessed it would be you.'

Karen saw the girl in blue coming back towards the booth with a chastened dog stalking at her side. Karen turned round to face the road and the blur of passing traffic. 'I got your message,' she said coldly. 'Did you have to practically take a gun to my employers like that? I seem to be out of a job already. I wish you'd waited until——'

'Don't exaggerate, Karen. It was necessary,' he broke in.

'Now listen, or the time will be up, and if I know you, you won't have any more change. I want you to go back to that —that tenement where you've chosen to live and pack your things. I'll be round to pick you up in an hour and take you home before I leave for Dellersbeck.'

'Nick, wait a minute!' Karen cried. 'I can't be ready in an hour's time—and if you think I'm coming back to—to *live* with you I'm afraid you're presuming too much. I agreed to come to Dellersbeck with you, but not——'

'You've no choice,' he said grimly, 'and neither have I. Elizabeth is asking questions already—why you weren't with me yesterday. She's coming over to see you this afternoon and you'd better be there. Otherwise we——'

The time-up bleeps hissed over the line. Karen reached for the other coin and exclaimed as it spun out of her fingers and chinked down on the floor of the booth. She cried, 'Wait, Nick!' as she stooped desperately to retrieve the coin, but she was too late. By the time she straightened and sought the slot the line had clicked back into the dialling tone. She looked at the receiver, then gave a sigh of exasperation and replaced the instrument. If she knew Nick he wouldn't answer the second time, would probably be making his way out of the house already.

With a grimace of distaste she rubbed her fingers on a tissue to remove the dirt collected from the floor of the phone box, and came out into the street. Then she hesitated, the impulse coming to telephone Elizabeth. Somehow she had imagined that Elizabeth would be bedfast, but apparently this was not so. If only she'd argued less with Nick last night and got more information . . . Abruptly Karen changed her mind. Nick had said an hour; which meant exactly that! It didn't give her much time to pack her things and settle her rent with Mrs Biggins. To say nothing of the explanations.

She was thankful to find her landlady missing when she hurried back into the flat. It would postpone the inevitable curious inquisition and allow her to get on with the hastiest packing session ever. Karen pulled her case out of the cupboard and began to fold garments quickly, but as the case filled and the minutes ticked past she began to panic. She had accumulated quite a lot of possessions during the time she had lived here, far too many to cram into the two suitcases which were all she had in the way of receptacles. Also, another thought struck her; what if Mrs Biggins had gone off for the day? Because she would have to come to some arrangement with her about storing the things she couldn't take. And she should be thinking about the time afterwards ... she could so easily find herself homeless. Would Mrs Biggins keep the flat for her, for an indefinite period? If she offered to pay some of the rent in advance? Karen sighed and straightened her aching back. That would be another problem; she wouldn't be earning. She was going to be dependent on Nick ...

Karen's nerve began to crack. She had vowed that she would never touch a penny of the allowance Nick made her, and now it seemed she would have no other choice. If only there were some other way! She crammed down the lid of the first case, fighting back tears, and then suddenly she remembered.

Sick at heart, she shook her head impatiently. God! How selfish could she get? Here she was anguishing in self-pity for her own problems while Elizabeth ... Her mouth trembled with new anguish. Why, oh, why did it have to happen to Elizabeth, dear good sweet Elizabeth, whose heart could never harbour ill or malice for her worst enemy?

Karen dashed the back of her hand across her eyes and looked at her watch. Nearly ten-thirty. He would be here any minute. She had better scribble a note for her landlady, enclose some money and say she would be in touch later.

Brief phrases of explanation proved difficult to frame. She had got as far as 'Called away suddenly. Please settle milk bill for me, and hold mail until I send new forwarding address' when the slam of a car door rang out below, and she ran to the window in time to see the top of Nick's dark head vanish under the front door canopy. Karen's heart gave a lurch and she licked lips which had suddenly gone dry.

She waited, expecting to hear his footsteps on the stairs, then at the second impatient peal of the bell she gave a small exclamation; there was nobody to let him in. She ran down the long flight and along the hall, her fingers trembling as they fumbled on the rather stiff catch.

Nick looked at her accusingly. 'For a moment I thought...'

He did not finish, and she said rather wildly, 'There's no one here—she must be out shopping. I was going to——'

He stepped in, brushing aside her flustered utterances. 'You got my message, that's the main thing. Are you ready?'

'No, not yet.' She turned to hurry ahead of him. 'I have to make arrangements—a lot of stuff to pack—and I haven't——'

'Leave it. I'll arrange to have it all picked up later.' He was close behind her on the stairs. 'Just pack a few immediate necessities.'

They reached the landing, and as she opened her door she glimpsed an expression of distaste on his face as he looked about him.

'Was this the best you could do?' He gave a gesture that seemed to encompass the entire house and its ambience. 'A shabby house in a mean back street ... God, I'll never fathom you, Karen.'

'It may look shabby to you,' she retorted, 'but it's clean and respectable, and it's convenient to my job. As far as I'm concerned that's all that matters.' She looked at him coolly, once again in possession of the mask of calm. 'You seem to forget I was supposed to be out of the country these past two years. Doesn't it occur to you that if I'd stayed anywhere near our neighbourhood I'd have risked meeting someone we both knew?'

'You didn't need to come to the East End. London's a big place.'

'And the world's a small one.'

His mouth was still hard. The corners went down in the cynical twist she remembered so well. 'Would you really have been lost for an excuse? The climate could have driven you home, even if I didn't.'

She thrust past him into the flat. 'Maybe, but I hardly think this is the time for a discussion of the merits of my present home.'

He shrugged and followed her inside, watching as she

went through into the bedroom. She lifted the heavy case off the bed, and its weight dragged her slender body momentarily into a curve, but the fierce pride of independence made her carry it towards the outer door, until he gave an exclamation and wrested the case from her hand.

'All right!' Sparks of anger glittered in his eyes. 'I thought we made an agreement last night. I'm trying, Karen, but don't try me too hard or I'm liable to forget.'

For a long moment she met that burning stare, then she forced herself to nod and say soberly 'I'll bring the small case.'

In silence they went down to the car. While Nick stowed the cases in the back she propped the note on the hallstand where her landlady would be sure to notice it and then slammed the heavy door shut. There was a strange sensation in being back in the passenger seat, next to Nick, with all the small remembered familiarities suddenly beginning to happen. The automatic reminder, 'Fasten your seat belt,' the twist of his body as he reversed to clear the vehicle parked in front before he pulled away from the kerb, the way he flicked down the indicator with that chopping movement of the edge of his palm, and then the faint smell of hair stuff and after-shave coming momentarily with his nearness, all combining to awake sleeping memories . . .

With an abrupt movement Karen turned to stare out of the window, determined to maintain her detachment; the past was past, and her hard-won peace of mind demanded that it remain that way.

If Nick noticed her deliberate withdrawal he gave no sign and made no attempt to break the silence until his route approached a supermarket with parking space. He swung into the turning, straight into a vacant place right beside the check-out exit, and said briefly: 'Come on—the cupboard's bare.'

The very routine of trailing along the aisle, steering the skeletal, jangling trolley to the accompanying banal flow of piped music, while Nick tossed foodstuffs into the trolley, brought a renewed sense of unreality. It had all happened so quickly; for two years she had lived alone, shopped alone, and managed her own life, and now those two years had vanished in less than a day. It couldn't be true; life didn't happen like that. Nick's muttering that coffee seemed to cost a hell of a lot more and giving a faint whistle when the check-out girl gave him the tally failed to evoke the obvious response from Karen—that the cost of living had risen somewhat during the two years of his absence—and instead induced a feeling of hysteria. On a see-saw of emotion those two years had become the unreality; suddenly she felt married again ...

But you are still married, and Nick is still your husband, a small taunting voice whispered in her brain as Nick loaded the box of foodstuffs into the car and they set off again. The whisper persisted, and tremors began to chase down her spine. The tautness of tension made her sit stiffly, and when landmarks she knew began to appear and she recognised the familiar roads that led to Valentine Grove she had to clasp her hands tightly over her bag to control their trembling. She saw the scarlet flash of the pillar box on the corner, and the heavy green of the avenue of tall trees that lined the quiet road and partly screened the imposing old Victorian villas set back in their long gardens. As though it were yesterday, she was back in time to the day two and a half years ago when the car brought Nick and herself back from their honeymoon, to slow at the fifth gate and crunch over the red gravel drive, to stop before the threshold that awaited a bride.

There had been laughter and bantering voices to welcome them home, warmth and music and food and drink amid the chaos of alterations, and then tactful departures ... Now only a sparrow rose in protesting flight, to watch from an overhead branch as his little grey crumb vanished under the wheels of the invading monster, and the front door swung inwards to silence and a chill, lost air, as though the house itself waited uncertainly, waited to return to being a home.

Nick stood back, giving a small gesture that betrayed impatience, and Karen entered slowly. The dark oak dower chest still stood in the hall, near the little oak and glass telephone niche that Nick had built himself. The door at the end of the hall stood partly open, and through it Karen could see the row of gleaming black and white units that lined the big modern kitchen. Automatically she moved towards it, while behind her Nick picked up and glanced at a couple of letters on the hall table, muttering 'They don't waste much time,' before he followed her into the kitchen. She noticed the fridge door standing ajar and glanced into its cold, newly cleaned blue and white interior.

'How have they left the place?'

She looked round. 'Who?'

'The Gilburns.'

Karen's expression still held no comprehension, and he said, 'Of course—you wouldn't know. I let the house to them on a two-year lease. Americans, a nice couple. His firm sent him over here for a year at first, then his senior was moved to their new Italian branch and Gil was promoted here. His wife didn't like the flat they were in and couldn't stand the thought of another two years there. John Bain put them in touch with me.' Nick walked round, glancing cursorily into cupboards, then added, 'I'll bring the stuff in —you'll want to stow it away.'

'Nick . . .?'

He halted.

'There's nothing here at all—didn't you stay here last night?'

'No—I went back to the hotel.'

'But . . .' she frowned, 'in your note, you said at home?'

'Once I'd seen you it wasn't necessary.' He gave her a direct look. 'I'd told Elizabeth we were at a hotel for a couple of days because the Gilburns couldn't leave until today.'

'But why?'

'Oh, for God's sake! Use your loaf, Karen!' His mouth compressed with impatience. 'Elizabeth would have been on that phone within five minutes of our due arrival time, and wanting to talk to you. Yesterday I told her you'd gone to the shipping office to see about a missing trunk we'd shipped home in advance—just another in the tissue of lies I've had to tell to explain why you were not with me yesterday and all the rest of the time.'

Karen's face whitened. 'Don't look at me so accusingly,' she flashed. 'It was never my idea.'

'I know that. I just want you to get used to the idea,' he said grimly. 'And while we're on the subject, I've made a note of some things you'll have to remember.'

Karen stared at him while he pulled out his pocket-book and took from it a piece of paper. He handed it to her. 'The address we were staying at—at least the address *you* were supposed to be staying at in Sao Paulo. The names of some of my colleagues, the site of the project, and a few other details. I've also got a guide book in my luggage, when I get unpacked. You can study it in quiet and I'll clue you in as much as I can when I get back. You'll have to look as though you had some recollection of the places and people that are bound to crop up during conversations once we all get together again.'

Full comprehension of what Nick meant began to flood over her and bring dismay into her eyes. 'But I've never been anywhere near South America, I don't know the first thing about it,' she stammered. 'How am I going to talk about a city and a country as though I'd just *lived* there for two years? I can't, Nick,' she added desperately.

'I don't expect you to,' he said curtly. 'Keep quiet and nod agreement to whatever I say. I'll make it as easy for you as I can. But you've got to go through with it, for as long as Elizabeth needs us. Afterwards ...' his shoulders rose and fell heavily, and he turned away, 'I'll make it worth your while—and you can go to the devil for all I care.'

Karen gasped, recoiling from the cruel words. Yet the tears that instantly smarted in her eyes were not entirely from the wound Nick had inflicted. 'How can you?' she choked. 'How can you talk about afterwards? As though you were measuring the time that Elizabeth has!'

'Why not? It's the truth. It has to be faced.'

'You're inhuman!' she cried. 'And to talk of making it worth my while. As though you're buying my time! It's——'

'Yes, that's also true,' he cut in. 'If you prefer to put it that way. I'm prepared to buy your time. Another man could, why not your husband?'

'*Nick!*' Shock drained every vestige of colour from her cheeks. 'How dare you!' Without knowing how she got there she **had** crossed the room and risen a hand like a flail.

The crack of her palm against his face rang out like a shot, then left a dreadful silence. Like a man in the daze of slow motion Nick raised one hand towards the white imprint slowly filling with red across his cheek. Then halfway to its aim his arm checked and shot out.

'You vixen! You vile little bitch! I——' His fingers made a grab at her throat and his eyes burned with violence. 'I could kill——'

The shrill of the phone rushed into the room, imperative, cutting across the charged atmosphere and bringing a slow ebb back to sanity. Nick's hands fell away, and Karen took a trembling step back, putting shaking fingertips to the bruised tenderness of her throat. The ringing went on, and Nick jerked away and out into the hall. Karen heard his voice, rough and unsteady, then coming under control, and then the words, 'Yes, we're here. We've just arrived ... Yes, darling, she's here...'

From the doorway Karen watched him turn, look at her, and silently hold out the receiver. Her legs felt weak as she went towards him, and she had to steady herself against the table as she took the instrument from his hand. 'Hello,' she whispered.

'Karen—my dear. At last!' came Elizabeth's soft voice. 'How wonderful to hear your voice again. How are you?'

'I'm very well.' Conscious of the tall sombre presence of Nick at her side, Karen had to grope for words, something she had never had to do before when speaking to Elizabeth. 'How are you?' she asked, then too late cursed herself for allowing the stilted phrase to slip out. But Elizabeth seemed not to have noticed.

She said brightly, 'Much better after my long holiday, but

your homecoming is the best tonic I could have. Are you glad to be home, darling?'

As though he had heard, Nick moved, and it was like a warning. 'Oh, yes, I—I've missed you so much,' Karen said in the same choked whisper. 'I'm looking forward to seeing you, and—and so is Nick.'

'Bless you—but I'm not going to keep you,' Elizabeth said abruptly. 'I know you'll have masses to do, unpacking and getting the house going again. Actually, this is why I rang. Nick is so impetuous, this idea of his, sweeping us all up to Yorkshire. It doesn't seem fair to you, having to take off again before you've had time to get your breath back. Tell him it isn't necessary to have all this rush—he won't listen to me!'

'Won't he?' *He certainly won't listen to me*, Karen sighed under her breath. She swallowed hard. 'Don't worry—we're going to look after you and try to relax ourselves for a while. So why not leave everything to Nick?'

'Yes, dear,' there was a faint note of protest in Elizabeth's tone, 'but I can't get him to understand that I don't need looking after. I'm fine now—and one doesn't have to take as gospel every word the doctors say, you know. They themselves are the first to admit that they aren't always infallible. I know they warned me that things weren't quite right, but I'm certainly not going to let it worry me, and I want you and Nick to promise me that you won't worry. After all, it's how I feel that really matters, isn't it?'

Karen's mouth worked, and she could only nod and make a small, muffled assent.

Elizabeth said more sharply, 'Are you sure you're all right, Karen? You sound rather strained. Is something wrong, dear?'

'No-no, nothing's wrong. I—I——'

Nick's arm came across her and pulled the phone from her hand. 'Mother Beth, the only thing that's wrong is that you'll have a phone bill as high as a steeple if you don't stop the girlish gossip.' His voice softened. 'Karen will come over to see you as soon as she's unpacked, and I'll see you in a couple of days or so. Okay?'

Through a haze of tears Karen saw his mouth curve in a whimsical grin at something Elizabeth said, then he said goodbye and replaced the receiver. He turned to Karen, saw the tears she made no attempt to conceal, and groaned softly.

'Don't, for God's sake. You mustn't give way.'

She shook her head wordlessly and made to move away, and then felt his hand on her shoulder. She tried to shrug free of its pressure, and he said, 'No—no, Karen,' and pulled her roughly to face him.

'I'm sorry, I shouldn't have said what I did—before. It's just—all this—and——' he stopped, and the torment was back in his shadowed eyes as he stared down at her.

Karen's mouth trembled. She whispered, 'I'm sorry too—sorry I hit you. I didn't——'

'Don't say any more.' His grip hardened on her shoulders. 'We've got to try to forget our differences. It won't be easy, but we've got to try, for Elizabeth's sake.'

His hands fell away and he turned with an abrupt movement, going with heavy tread to the outer hall. Karen stood there, seeing through a haze the outline of his tall figure as he opened the front door and passed through on his way to the car. When he returned a few moments later with the first of her cases she had regained a measure of control. But inwardly she was in turmoil. For a few moments, back in the telephone niche, she had thought Nick was about to take her into his arms. But he hadn't, and the surge of sudden longing had been totally unexpected. She had been so near, it would have been so easy just to sway forward . . .

With an effort she fought down the disturbing thought and rushed feverishly to help bring in the things from the car. It didn't take long, and the need for activity made her rummage through the box of groceries in search of the coffee and the carton of milk. Nick came into the kitchen, betraying no trace of the emotional storm that had passed so short a while before, and saw her striving to turn on the water main under the sink unit.

'Let me.'

She straightened, while he turned the stiff tap with strong fingers. 'I thought I'd make some coffee,' she ventured.

'I really haven't time.' He dusted his hands and settled his tie. 'I'd like to make Dellersbeck by four, to give myself time to go over the place and make any necessary contacts before everybody shuts up shop for the night.'

'What about lunch?'

'I'll get a sandwich on the way.'

He seemed anxious to be gone, and she yielded reluctantly. The instinct to offer to pack a snack lunch was uppermost in her mind, but something kept her silent; perhaps the reluctance to permit a quickening of any encroaching intimacy. It was too soon for that—or too late, she thought with a flash of sorrowful reflection.

He said, 'Anything you want before I leave?'

She shook her head. 'I don't think so.'

'No?' His brows lifted sardonically. 'How about this lot? Spare keys—in case you no longer have your own. Money. Dellersbeck number—they changed them recently. And that guide book.'

She looked at the little collection on the pearly white expanse of Formica and picked up the wad of notes. 'I don't need this.'

He shrugged. 'Shove it in the bureau, then. It'll be there if you do.'

There seemed nothing else to say, and again she was painfully aware of the need for a touch of understanding, a slender bridge on which to meet in this strange new divided relationship into which fate had chosen to thrust her. But there was none, not from Nick.

With a prosaic reminder that she could contact him at the Dellersbeck number should anything crop up he strode out to the car. Now that he had completed the first stage of his plan he appeared indifferent to her feelings and misgivings.

But why shouldn't he? Karen closed the door and slowly turned to face the empty silence of the house that had been her home. Caring and consideration came of loving, and Nick had made no pretence whatsoever regarding his present feelings for herself. Nick no longer loved her. Sometimes she wondered if he ever had.

CHAPTER THREE

KAREN returned to the kitchen and made herself a cup of coffee. Reaction was setting in, and the stormy scene with Nick had left her weak and shaken. She perched on one of the two yellow stools at the breakfast bar and cradled icy fingers round the beaker. How was she going to face the ordeal which lay ahead? Living a lie for Elizabeth's sake; pretending that she and Nick still shared that wild, ecstatic happiness they had known for so short a time. Guarding every moment lest it brought a betrayal of their shattered marriage.

The heat of the coffee burned through to her fingers, and she set the beaker down to cool, staring with remote eyes at the greys and greens and yellows in the patterns of the wall tiles. They were the only part of the beautifully fitted kitchen that she and Nick had not chosen, and the only part she did not like. There were eyes hidden in the strange whorled patterns, and a hint of evil in them. But Lisa had chosen them as her contribution towards the home, and Nick had liked them because they blended perfectly with the carefully worked out colour scheme. There hadn't been time to search any longer for the elusive pattern that would be just right for the section above the breakfast bar. And so when Lisa had called that morning, triumphant with the sample tile and insisting that they would be her gift if they were right, Nick had said yes, adding they would never find a better match.

If only time could roll back to that morning. Three days before their wedding day ...

Karen shivered and took a gulp of coffee. What was the use of going back over all the 'if onlies', and the bitterness? Of hoping that somehow a miracle would resolve the tragic misjudgement fate had chosen to enmesh her in? She had given her promise. But if she had known what that promise of silence would lead to ...

Abruptly Karen slid from the stool. She rinsed out the beaker and determined to close her mind against useless retrospect. If she was going to spend the next few days alone here until Nick's return she would have to organise a room for herself and see what jobs had to be done after two years of occupation by strangers.

At the foot of the stairs she felt a strange reluctance to ascend. The ghosts of past joys and the spectres of unhappiness lay in wait for her in this silent house, and every step revived a memory. There was the silvery dolphin they had brought back from their Florida honeymoon, enshrined for ever in its sphere of blue and green glass, and the little corner bracket shelf on which it stood, reminding her of the day Nick had fixed the shelf himself—and managed to gash his hand with the chisel. Panic! There had been blood everywhere and Karen had not known whether to rush to the phone for the doctor or try to dress the wound herself. She'd bound a towel round it and hauled Nick down to the car while he protested all the way, and the doctor had put three stitches into Nick's hand. She'd been worried sick when they got home, remembering all the old wives' tales about getting lockjaw from a wound at the base of the thumb, and Nick had laughed at her. She had been indignant, and Nick had pulled her down to him: '*I can still make love to you with one hand ...*'

Karen wrenched her thoughts back to the present and made herself continue her tour of inspection. The tenants had left the house spotless, and the only chore they had left behind was a neat bundle on top of the linen chest consisting of two pillow slips, the cover of the continental quilt, and a couple of towels. There was a note pinned to the corner of the top towel, with a folded pound note tucked inside. The note read: 'Many thanks for trusting us with your home, we have tried to leave it as we'd like to find our own. Sorry about leaving these, hope this will cover laundering cost. Sue Gilburn.'

Almost thankfully, Karen took the things downstairs and loaded the washing machine. There was little for her to do, for there was no point in putting the house into full running order when it was going to be shut up for an indefinite period. Most of their personal things, Nick's clothes and the things he had not taken to South America, and those possessions Karen had left behind, had been packed up and stored in the small boxroom. Karen decided they could stay there; the task of sorting them out would be too great an emotional strain.

When the covers and towels had been hung out in the drying space down at the end of the long back garden she made herself a light lunchtime snack and then returned upstairs to sort out blankets for the divan in the small spare bedroom in which she had decided to sleep. It faced north, and was the chilliest room in the house—even the central heating didn't seem to cope with that chill—but in it she would at least be spared the memories of the main bedroom, and the big guestroom which Nick and she had shared during the weeks while their chosen room was being decorated and fitted with its vanity unit and built-in wardrobes.

She sighed, unable to resist opening her mind to the flood of recollection.

Theirs had been such a whirlwind romance. They'd scarcely signed the contract for the house before their wedding day, and consequently returned from their honeymoon to a chaos of plastering and rubble, electrical cables festooned everywhere, water taps that no longer functioned and new crystal and gold ones not yet connected. And in the midst of it all they'd thrown a housewarming party!

Nick had had caterers to bring in all the food and glasses. They'd danced on bare boards in the dining room, which was furnished by a paper-hanger's trestle table with the record player on it. One of the guests had accidentally walked through the newly laid cement at the side of the garage and come indoors wondering why it was so muddy when there had been no rain for weeks. And then the main fuse blew, and in the resultant milling around in the dark somebody tipped over a two-litre pot of paint. They'd been so deliriously happy they'd just laughed. Even in the cold light of the following morning she and Nick had laughed—and fallen laughing in each other's arms again . . .

The shadows darkened in Karen's eyes. If only she had known what a prelude to disaster that party was to prove! For that was the night they met Tony Foster, the stranger jollied along by a friend of Nick's to make the numbers even. But how could they have guessed that Tony would forge the first link in the chain that led eventually to Vince Kayne, the famous artist, a meeting that began the long slide down to tragedy and the shattering of an innocent girl's happiness.

Mine! whispered Karen.

Her eyes stung with tears and she knuckled angrily at them. Stop thinking! she almost shouted aloud as she stuffed the pillow into its case. It's all over. It's too late. But how did one stop thinking, stop remembering, when one's heart cried out in anguish and bitterness against the injustice of fate? Why should she have to suffer the destruction of all her dreams and illusions?

With the stiff movements of an automaton Karen unfolded the candlewick bedspread and stretched it across the divan. Why couldn't she see that it was better to have had her illusions destroyed then than later, perhaps after a child had been born? Because hadn't it proved how little trust Nick had in her? When he had been ready to believe the worst, scarcely giving her a chance to defend herself before he accused . . . That had hurt most of all, more than the harsh, wounding words he'd flung at her when——

The abrupt summons of the doorbell rang through the silent house, wrenching Karen back to the present. Who could it be? Had——? suddenly she stiffened. Had Nick returned?

Karen completed the final tuck-in of the bedspread, despising herself for the crazy little tremors of excitement the thought evoked, and sped downstairs. It would be somebody selling something, or the man to read the meter—nobody knew she was here. She saw the blurred outline of the caller beyond the opaque panel of glass as she slid the catch, and then she exclaimed aloud as she remembered . . . It was Elizabeth.

For a long moment she stared incredulously at the slim,

attractive form of Nick's adoptive mother, and then Elizabeth opened her arms.

'I hope I'm not interrupting anything, but I had to come and see you.' Elizabeth hugged Karen tightly. 'If you're busy, please say so, darling.'

'No! It's just that I—I——'

'You didn't expect me,' Elizabeth laughed. 'Oh, I'm still mobile, thank heaven.'

Karen drew a deep breath. She was not sure what she had expected at the first meeting with Elizabeth after two years' lapse; certainly not to see Elizabeth looking scarcely any different from the woman she remembered. A little thinner, perhaps, and the soft fair hair was almost white now, but that was all. The blue eyes were still clear and bright, the delicate pink and white skin still smooth-bloomed and unblemished, and the warm personality that drew everyone to her was still as lively as ever. It was only when one looked more closely that the shadows of pain were discernible beneath her eyes, and the air of fragility was more pronounced than formerly.

'I thought there might be something I could do to help—it's quite an upheaval in one's life to be away from home for two years. Oh, it's wonderful to have you back again,' Elizabeth exclaimed with emotion unashamedly betrayed in the eyes searching Karen's face. 'This has been the longest two years in my life!'

Karen felt her throat constrict, but she managed to smile as she disengaged herself gently and drew Elizabeth indoors. 'It's wonderful to see you again—come on in and I'll make some tea.'

She ushered Elizabeth into the sitting room and then hurried to fill the kettle. The small, mundane actions gave her an opportunity of regaining her composure, and when she carried the tray through to the sitting room she was able to say in a commendably casual voice: 'Nick hasn't been long gone —a little while earlier and you'd have seen him.'

'I didn't want to see him.' Elizabeth accepted the cup of tea and shook her head at the biscuits Karen proffered. 'I wanted to talk to you—that's really why I came.'

Karen's heart gave a lurch. What had happened? *Did Elizabeth know?* She sat down in the chair opposite and looked anxiously at the older woman. 'But why—is something wrong?'

The moment the words were out she realised their unfortunate connotation and gave a small exclamation of distress. But Elizabeth did not seem to have noticed.

'No, darling, not exactly.' Elizabeth helped herself to sugar and stirred her tea thoughtfully before she looked up. 'But I'm rather worried about you and this proposed upheaval.'

Karen frowned, unsure, and Elizabeth went on:

'I'm not altogether happy about this arrangement of Nick's; of us all moving up to Dellersbeck. Of course I expect you don't need me to tell you what he's like once he gets an idea into his head—nothing short of an explosion will shift it. But the last thing I want is for you to feel you're being coerced into this move.'

Karen relaxed with an inward sigh. She said hastily, 'Of course not! I think it's a marvellous idea.'

'Do you? Well, I don't,' Elizabeth said bluntly. 'I think it's most unfair. He's scarcely given you time to get off the plane before having to pack up and get on the move again.'

'*That* is the least of my worries,' Karen said firmly. 'Please don't give it another thought. I shan't.'

'I'm afraid Lisa won't agree with you,' Elizabeth sighed. 'You know as well as I do that Lisa will be bored stiff before she's been five minutes at Dellersbeck, and it means that Clifford will have to commute to Yorkshire at weekends, which is terribly inconvenient for him, and he's going to have to go home to an empty flat during the week. But Nick just refuses to listen. I wonder . . . could you talk him out of it?'

'Me?' Karen wanted to laugh hollowly. If only Elizabeth knew! That through Nick's coercion she herself had given up her flat, lost a perfectly good job, and, into the bargain, was embarked upon a course of deceit which held the ever-present threat of disaster. 'I doubt it,' she said wildly. 'Nick's made up his mind.'

'Yes, I was afraid of that.' Elizabeth's voice held resigna-

tion and a note of annoyance. 'The trouble is, I'm not sure
it's for the best. Oh, I know Nick's doing it all for my sake,
and I appreciate it very deeply, but it doesn't seem to have
occurred to him to probe a little deeper into this business of
making Mother happy.' Her usually sweet mouth curved
with irony. 'Let's face it, if you were me, would you feel
enthusiastic about having all your family gathered about you,
waiting for you to die?'

'Oh, no!' Karen's hand went to her throat. 'I'm sure
Nick doesn't . . .'

'Doesn't he?' Elizabeth's tone was dry. 'But it's the basic
fact, isn't it? Only Nick can't or won't see it that way. He
fondly imagines it as a lovely cosy family reunion, all closing
around Mother, trying to make her remaining time in this
world as safe and secure and happy as possible.'

Elizabeth paused, her blue eyes unclouded by false senti-
ment. A faint smile touched her lips as she looked at Karen's
expression of distress. 'Don't look like that, my dear. I have
no intention of admitting to such a cold and negative future,
now that I know what I have to overcome. My chief worry
just now is trying to convince people that I feel perfectly
well, far better than I did a couple of months ago. And I
have no intention of allowing myself to be wrapped in cotton-
wool by anyone, even my own darling family. They may
find themselves wearying of it long before their worst fears
are realised!'

Karen did not know what to say. In the face of Elizabeth's
indomitable courage it was difficult to suppress the sudden
flare of hope; was it possible that the doctors could be
wrong? Yet it would be cruel to suggest this, for, according
to Nick, his mother had demanded to be told the truth, and
the verdict had been a tragic negative prognosis. If Elizabeth
had chosen her own way of coming to terms with fate the
least they could do was to respect her wishes.

Elizabeth calmly helped herself to a second cup of tea.
Then she looked up. 'I've told Nick that I love Dellersbeck in
spring and summer, even autumn, but if he imagines I'm
going to spend next winter there he's in for a rude disabuse-
ment. I'm going back to Marbella in November—if that

should be the will of my Maker,' she added wryly.

Karen bit her lip. 'Nick thinks you're not truly happy in the flat,' she ventured.

'Well, I'm not *unhappy* in town,' Elizabeth shrugged, 'and I won't pretend I didn't experience a sudden tremendous longing to see Dellersbeck again, but I'm beginning to rue that I ever voiced it so carelessly. Nick took me up on it like a flash, and within hours he had set everything in motion.'

Yes, Nick would, thought Karen, with a trace of bitterness. But despite this she softened. However brutal he had been towards herself, however ruthless he was in business, he held a reverence and an utterly selfless devotion for the woman who had given him love and care at a time when the whole world seemed determined to break his spirit.

Not for the first time Karen experienced a flicker of curiosity about the secret, closed part of Nick's early life. He would never talk of it, even in their most intimate moments of closeness, and she knew only that he was an orphan and that Elizabeth and her husband had taken him into their home when he was eleven years old, that this was the first time in his life that anyone had given him love and—more important even to a lonely child—they'd given him the priceless gift of two-way trust. Abruptly Karen stood up and went to Elizabeth. She stooped and put her arm impulsively round her shoulders.

'Please, Elizabeth,' she begged, 'try not to worry about it and just leave everything to us. And I promise, I'll try to make Nick let you have things the way you want them. You'll see, it'll work out, I'm sure.'

'Bless you.' Elizabeth gave a tremulous smile. 'I'm a fortunate woman to have such a wonderful son and daughter-in-law. And now'—she began to gather up her gloves and handbag—'I'd better get back or Magda will be fussing like an old hen.'

'Magda is still with you?'

'Yes, of course.' For a moment Elizabeth stared in puzzlement. Then she smiled. 'It's really time she retired, but she flatly refuses to leave me.'

Karen walked to the door with her. She had nearly given herself away then with the careless question about Magda, the housekeeper who had been in service with Elizabeth's household since the time of Elizabeth's marriage nearly thirty-four years ago. Karen shivered; so many traps for a deceiver. She almost started with guilt when Elizabeth turned suddenly.

'By the way, dear, I do want to thank you for all those lovely long letters you wrote while you were away. It was such a joy to have regular news—Nick never wrote a letter in his life if he could help it! And so beautifully typed,' Elizabeth went on. 'I don't know why some people say they think typing makes a letter impersonal. I think it makes a letter flow far more clearly and crams so much more into an airmail—quite apart from being so much easier to read. Some people's handwriting . . . !'

Karen felt more and more uncomfortable, aware of shame at being the recipient of appreciation she did not merit. What *had* Nick put in those letters?

She watched Elizabeth drive away and closed the door slowly, at last able to allow the guarding mask of care to fall. The meeting with Elizabeth had made real all the doubts and fears Nick had scarcely given her time to consider. She had now had her first experience of the pitfalls dug by deception which lay in wait for her unwary footsteps. And by this time next week it would be even more dangerous. They would be at Dellersbeck, all together, with the spectre of Elizabeth's illness ever present, and the fragments of a shattered marriage to conceal. To say nothing of Lisa . . .

Karen's heart grew cold with foreboding. But there was no escape. She had given her promise, and deep inside her she knew she had no desire to break it. For however much she tried to tell herself she no longer cared for Nick she knew it wasn't true. That would be just another lie . . .

The next three days were the most uneasy she had ever known. There was no word from Nick—but then he never wasted time on phone calls unless for a definite reason—and no approach from Lisa, which did not really surprise Karen as she had always been conscious of the fine, imperceptible barrier which prevented them being sufficiently drawn to one another to become close friends.

Elizabeth rang a couple of times, the second time to say that Lisa and her husband were coming to dine with her that evening and would Karen come over as well. An unreasoning panic rose in Karen at the prospect and she pleaded an arrangement already made to visit another friend. Elizabeth was instantly understanding, commiserating over the rush Karen must be having to fit everything in before Nick carried them all off to Dellersbeck.

When Karen rang off she felt her cheeks hot with the now familiar guilt, yet she was aware of relief that the reunion with Lisa was to be postponed for a little while longer. It was quite ridiculous to feel like this, she told herself. She had no reason to avoid Lisa. But she could not imagine Lisa being concerned . . .

With an effort she pushed the past into the background of her mind, and seized the opportunity of making a journey over to her own little flat. There she finalised her arrangements at a more leisurely pace with her landlady, managing to sidetrack the more probing questions of that inquisitive lady and leaving with a somewhat easier mind.

Mrs Biggins had offered to store the rest of her things in the boxroom at the top of the house and promised faithfully to 'fix something' in the way of accommodation for Karen when she eventually returned. As Karen had feared, the word had got round the neighbours that Mrs Biggins' tenant was going and the hopeful enquiries were rolling in. 'So I've promised to give first chance to Jenny's niece—she's just got married and desperate for somewhere to live, but he's expecting to be sent up to Manchester in a couple of months time, so it might work out dandy for everybody,' Mrs Biggins said hopefully. 'You see, I need the little bit extra money, and with not knowing just how long you're going to be away . . .'

Karen understood, and had no doubts about Mrs Biggins keeping her word. At least she would have a bolthole to come back to when she needed it.

On the way home she did some shopping, browsing a little

longer than she realized, and heard the phone ringing as she put her key in the door.

She knew before she ran to it that the caller was Nick, and heard him say impatiently, 'Where on earth have you been? This is the third time I've tried to reach you.'

'Sorry—I've been shopping,' she said breathlessly. 'But I expected you to ring later in the evening. Is everything going to plan?'

'More or less. I'll be back tonight, and I see no reason why we shouldn't take Elizabeth up there tomorrow.'

Karen frowned into the phone. 'That isn't giving her much time to prepare, Nick. It's gone seven now.'

'We can leave the start until after lunch,' he said crisply. 'Now listen, Karen, I'm in a service station and I'm in a hurry to get back—I've an appointment at eight. Don't wait up for me, I'll be eating out, and I'll be late. So get your own stuff packed tonight so that we can get over to give Elizabeth a hand in the morning. Okay?'

'Yes.' There didn't seem much else she could say.

'Oh, and will you ring Elizabeth right away and tell her? It'll save me a few minutes.'

'Yes,' Karen said again, and heard his laconic 'So long,' and the click as he rang off.

When she had passed on the message as promised she unpacked her shopping, made herself a light meal, and began to get together the things she would need for the journey. As she folded clothing her mind returned to the phone call. Who was going to keep Nick out late? Probably a woman, she thought, and found she did not care for the answer her imagination had suggested. But wasn't it logical? Nick was unlikely to have spent two years in a monastic seclusion from the opposite sex. Then she remembered that he had been home less than a week—hardly time in which to form a sudden attachment, considering that three of those days had been spent in Yorkshire preparing the house for Elizabeth.

Karen's emotional see-saw went up to comfort, then plummeted as quickly back to zero. Two years was a long time— plenty of time for making any number of new relationships, wherever Nick happened to be. Oh, why argue with herself? she thought impatiently. Nick was still her husband—but in name only. This partial resumption of their relationship was for Elizabeth's sake, and for that only, and the sooner she got that fact firmly into her sights, to the exclusion of all else, the happier would be her stress levels.

But sleep refused to come, once the light was out and the house lay dim and silent outside her door. At last, at midnight, she gave in to wakefulness, switched on her bedside light and began to read. At ten past one she finished the book and rubbed her tired eyes; surely she should sleep now. She settled down again, and then heard the sound she had to admit she had waited for. The soft swish of the car entering the drive, the door closing, the scrape of the garage door as it swung down, and then the key in the door.

Karen's body tensed and her eyes strained towards the strip of carpet beneath her door, where the chink of light should show when Nick put on the stairway lights. But there was nothing, no light, no sound, nothing, except the knowledge that she was not alone in the house. Fifteen minutes ticked by, then five more, and Karen's nerve began to crack. Why did Nick make no sound? He had had ample time in which to make himself a sandwich and a nightcap, which, if her memory did not play her false, was unlikely. Nick had never cared for food after the conventional eating times were past. So why didn't he go to bed and settle down, then she could sleep in peace?

Abruptly Karen sat up and swung her limbs free of bedclothes. She switched on her light and shrugged into her wrap, then went slowly down into the empty hall. No light in the kitchen, or the dining room, and after a moment of hesitation she crossed towards the thin shaft of amber spilling through the partly open door of the sitting room. Gently she pushed it open, the uncertain 'Nick ... is that you?' hovering on her lips, and then she saw him lying back in the armchair, his features sleeping in the shadows by the table lamp. There was a whisky tumbler at his elbow, still almost untouched, and his hair had fallen into a heavy curve above one eye.

She stood there for a moment, caught by indecision. Should

she leave him to sleep there? But she couldn't do that. He might sleep until daylight, to awake cramped and cold, in no state to face another long drive north. Yet she felt a reluctance that was near to fear. He could be drunk. She had no way of knowing. He had not been an intemperate man, but he had a tough job and two years could change a man. She took an uncertain step forward, then jumped with pure shock as she saw his eyes were wide open, staring straight at her with the small reflections of light mocking from their depths.

'Well, Karen.' His teeth glinted in a hidden smile. 'I didn't expect a wifely welcome at this time in the morning.'

'I—I thought you'd fallen asleep,' she stammered.

'I had—until you drifted in like a zombie and I realised I wasn't dreaming. What's the matter? Feeling a little wifely concern?'

She ignored the sarcasm in his tone. 'Nick, do you know what time it is? If you intend driving up to Dellersbeck again tomorrow hadn't you better get to bed?'

'Ah, so you're worried!' He sat up, wrenching carelessly at his tie until the knot hung low beneath his opened shirt neck. 'Or could it be you have other ideas?'

'Ideas?' For a moment she stared at him, then comprehension came and she took an indignant step back, instinctively drawing her wrap closer about her slender form. 'You flatter yourself!' she exclaimed hotly.

'Why not? You're still my wife.'

He stood up, and his movements were incredibly swift. His hand shot out and seized her wrist, halting her retreat towards escape. Suddenly he was very tall, very strong, and overwhelmingly close.

'Tell me, Karo,' he said silkily, 'what would you say if I told you I'd suddenly rediscovered desires I thought were dead concerning yourself?'

'I—I'd tell you to forget them!' Her heart began to thud painfully. His mouth in the shadows, his breath warm on her face, his touch and his arm pulling her close until her body contacted his through the thin billowing transparencies of her wrap, all evoked remembered intimacy, remembered promise ...

She tried to pull back. 'Nick, for heaven's sake be sensible! This wasn't part of the bargain, and you know it!'

'Do I?' He showed no sign of releasing her. 'I thought we had a truce.'

'Yes.' She fought for control. 'For Elizabeth's sake, remember?'

She heard his sudden indrawn breath, and then abruptly she was free. He turned away, pulling off his tie. 'Yes, I remember,' he said in a dull voice. 'God, I'm tired.'

'You're not the only one.' Shakily she refastened the tie belt of her wrap. 'Would you like me to make you a drink? Chocolate or something? There's plenty of milk.'

'Milk! Oh, God, spare me the dutiful little wifely details.'

'If that's how you feel ...' Her mouth compressed. 'I thought it might help you to unwind.'

'I can do without that sort of unwinding.' He picked up the tumbler of whisky and gulped down half of it, standing with his back to her. He held the tumbler for a moment, then took a deep breath and downed the rest of the spirit. He set the empty glass on the mantelpiece, ran his fingers through his hair, and swung round. When he saw her still standing there with the worried expression in her eyes his own eyes narrowed darkly.

'Just go to bed and leave me alone, Karen,' he muttered thickly, 'or else ...' He stopped, and let his hand drop heavily to his side.

Karen licked lips that had suddenly gone dry and taut. There was no mistaking the meaning in his voice. Tension stretched between them like a thin brittle wire, and with a choked little murmur she reached blindly for the door, slipping out and tugging it shut to block out the sight of him. When she reached her room and fumbled out of her wrap, to seek the cold sanctuary of her narrow bed, she was trembling uncontrollably from head to toe.

What a fool she had been to go down to him like that, so that he thought she ... But what else could she expect if she behaved with the impulses of a naïve child? Nick hadn't been drunk, but he had obviously wined as well as he had dined, and then the advent of herself like a boudoir apparition invading his semi-stupor ... Fool! She pummelled her fist angrily into the pillow and tried to deny the tears squeezing between her closed lids. At least she had one meagre consolation. That pride and willpower had won over that wild, feverish urge to give in, to stay silent until Nick kissed her, until it was too late to recall sanity.

It would have been so easy.

Dry-eyed now, she stared into the darkness and waited for the ague of desire to ebb from her body. Once again pride had intervened, but was it worth it? she asked herself bitterly. Pride could be many things, a source of anger, arrogance, or pain. At best it brought the emptiness of self-righteous satisfaction, at worst the torment of all illusion lost. But debased pride was the cruellest of all, as she was finding to her cost. Was there no end to its destruction?

CHAPTER FOUR

THE drive north next day seemed endless. They set off in bright sunshine after an early lunch, but less than forty miles north of London the skies clouded over and the first big drops splashed against the windscreen. Almost immediately they were into a grey torrent that slowed their speed and gave no indication of being a band of rain they might soon pass through.

The strain of driving against such adverse conditions kept Nick silent, but fortunately did not appear to depress Elizabeth and Magda in the rear of the car. Magda, a plump, energetic little woman in her sixties, was animated with the prospect of returning to her native Yorkshire, and she and Elizabeth chattered happily, oblivious of the mud and murk outside. Karen huddled down in the front passenger seat, a prey to the lonely misery of her thoughts. Breakfast that morning had been a strained and edgy affair with Nick curt and herself wretchedly aware of the miasma of the previous night hanging over them like a sullen cloud. She was thankful that there had been so much to do; load the car with luggage, check round the house to make sure everything was left secured and the Chubb alarm set, then drive over to collect Elizabeth and Magda. By the time the same routine was completed at Elizabeth's flat it was time for lunch.

Karen found herself stifling a yawn. The warmth of the car was making her realise how tired she was physically as well as low in spirits. She glanced through the side window and noticed that the rain was lessening and a watery, metallic copper colour was lightening the northern horizon. The weather was clearing at last. She surrendered to weariness and let her eyelids droop, only for moments it seemed, until a crackling roar of sound jerked her back to startled wakefulness.

Elizabeth was saying, 'Don't be so obstinate, Nick! You can't go on in this!'

They had run into a violent thunderstorm. The skies were as dark as night, split by great jagged slits of lightning and punctuated by ominous rolls of thunder.

'I can't stop here,' Nick retorted. 'Put your hands over your ears for another couple of miles.'

The motorway had become a grey rushing river glistening with the gashes of headlight reflections. Karen and the two women stayed silent, thankful they weren't driving, and a few minutes later the service station lights came into view. Nick pulled into the slip road, and they dashed for the shelter of the café. There they drank tea and nibbled biscuits and waited for the storm to abate.

'Karen looks tired,' remarked Elizabeth.

Karen scarcely heard her, but she came back to the present in time to hear Nick say carelessly, 'She's all right, aren't you, Karo?'

'Just like that—Nick, you are heartless! She's as pale as a ghost,' Elizabeth rebuked her adopted son.

Nick grinned and threw a casual arm round Karen's shoulders. 'Were you scared of the thunder, sweetie?'

Karen wanted to wrench out of his arm. But she had to play the bitter charade and force a smile. 'No, Nick—only your driving!'

Elizabeth laughed, and Nick withdrew his arm rather abruptly. 'Time to get moving. Any of you ladies want to make calls?'

But none of them needed comfort stations and they moved out to face the squally rain. The storm proved only the first of their delays. A diversion soon after leaving the motorway added to the journey, then Magda persuaded Nick to make a short cut which proved anything but, with the result it was almost five by the time they got back on to the right road.

'I did this run in three hours on my own,' Nick said somewhat bitterly when the old white signpost to Dellersbeck loomed up on the moorland road.

'I'm sorry,' said poor Magda, 'but I'm positive that turning should have brought us out on the Helmsley road.'

'Instead of which we landed in a network of lanes and

found ourselves nearly back to York. Women and their short cuts!'

'Oh, Nick darling, what does it matter? We've got all day.' Elizabeth attempted to soothe. 'We're not on a rally—although it felt like it at times,' she added feelingly.

As though to mock them, the sun burst forth as the car topped the rise at the head of the dale and Dellersbeck lay verdant and peaceful below. The winding grey road wove through a patchwork of fields and the dark green clumps of copse, past the mellow stone houses with blue slate roofs and the whitewashed cottages that dotted the valley, and down into the village that clustered about the ancient black and white timbered inn and the hump-backed bridge over the river.

Elizabeth's face was rapt as she stared at remembered places she loved, pointing out the square grey Georgian house where she had been born, and when the car turned into the narrow lane at the far side of the bridge she said eagerly, 'Oh, stop, Nick, please. Let me look.'

Without speaking Nick braked to a halt. Elizabeth exclaimed softly, 'It's so beautiful—how could I ever have left it?' Abruptly she opened the car door. 'You go on, Nick. I want to walk up the path past the weir.' She scrambled out as she spoke.

'No, I don't think you should,' he protested. 'Wait till tomorrow.'

She stooped and looked back into the car. 'I'm not going to get lost—it's only ten minutes' walk at the most!'

Karen had glimpsed the flash of real concern in his eyes, and without stopping to think she grabbed her bag from the glove compartment and fumbled for the catch of her seat belt. 'I'll go with Elizabeth.'

'Will you? Thanks, Karo.'

She saw the first warmth for her that day in his face as she closed the car door, and it brought a stab of bitterness that only an indirect courtesy gesture could break through his indifference to her feelings. But she had known it would be this way; she might as well resign herself to his attitude.

She shrugged away the thought and hurried after Elizabeth, who was already striding away along the narrow path to the river bank. The sound of the car moving off masked Karen's footsteps and she called out in case her sudden over-taking should startle the older woman. Elizabeth turned, her smile surprised, then rueful.

'Don't tell me he made you get out!'

'No—I was getting stiff in the car.'

'Yes, it's a long time to sit.' Elizabeth moved on, sniffing at the sweet, sharp clean smell of the air. 'I had to come this way—a kind of first time, first way, again.'

Karen murmured, not following Elizabeth's meaning but aware of some significance behind her words.

'This week is the anniversary of the first time I ever came to Dellersbeck Hall, and this is the way we walked, leaving the car as we did just now.'

'We?' Karen turned her head. 'Your husband?'

Elizabeth nodded. 'It was a March day then, with the same pale fresh green tipping the branches and the wonderful newness of nature beginning a new life with the retreat of winter. I'd met James for the first time only a few weeks earlier, but we both knew that it was "it" for us. We were supposed to be going for a run to York, then suddenly he said, "Come home with me", and he turned the car and drove back here. When we got to the lane end down there he said he wanted to show me the weir path.' Elizabeth paused. 'It's just a little way further on.'

She was silent, leading the way as the path became very narrow and rose steeply under the arches of the trees. The water below was becoming turbulent and the rushing sound of the weir more pronounced. Then abruptly the path entered a small, hilly clearing. There was a tiny rustic bridge, weathered grey and green with moss, spanning the stream, almost immediately above the wide rocky brink where the water gushed over into the foaming pool beneath. Ferns fringed one side, and a willow draped forlorn arms over from the far bank, and a little farther down a row of stepping stones dotted the narrow end of the pool.

'It was on this bridge that James asked me to marry me, and then we walked on up to the house to tell his parents.'

Elizabeth rested her hands on the gnarled rail, her eyes remote with memory. 'We were so happy.'

Karen was silent. There was nothing to add.

'Six years after our marriage James's father died and we made our home here. His mother was very sweet, she had her own part of the house and there was never any of the friction one tends to find with in-laws. But it's such a happy house.'

Karen looked down at the swirling water. This was her first visit to Dellersbeck. In the early months of her marriage she had heard the family speak of it often, and Elizabeth had shown her photographs of the house and of her husband, James, who had died a year before Karen's meeting with Nick. She said slowly, 'Has it been in the family for a long time?'

'Nearly three hundred years.' Elizabeth moved her hand along the knotted timber of the rail. 'While I realise that in today's changing age it isn't possible for Nick to live here, I hope he won't sell it after I'm gone.'

'Oh, I'm sure he won't!' Karen bit her lip, wishing she could speak with more authority. 'Nick loves Dellersbeck.'

'Yes, I know.' Elizabeth stared at the winding vista of sparkling stream and wild greenery. 'It's so strange that Nick, who is not my born child, should take on a greater sense of kinship with Dellersbeck than ever Lisa did. Lisa will never live here. She could scarcely wait until she was eighteen and we let her escape to the fleshpots of the city. Yet right from the start Nick grasped the idea of how an estate is run, and the responsibility it entails. When James had his first stroke Nick was a tower of strength during the two years that followed. He wanted to give up going to university and come home for good, but we had to insist that Nick complete his education. He needed it, and if ever there was a classic example of latent brains and talent lying fallow Nick was that.'

Karen would never dispute that fact, and despite the bitterness that had destroyed their love she could still feel regret and compassion for his chequered boyhood when she recalled her own secure childhood with loving parents. She said slowly: 'Yes ... I suppose no one who has belonged to a happy family unit can truly comprehend what it must be like to be brought up in an orphanage, having nobody who is completely one's own. Even though they are terribly kind to the children and do everything possible to give an orphaned child a good start in life it can never be the same.'

Elizabeth had turned her head as Karen spoke. She exclaimed, 'Orphanage? But, my dear, Nick was never in an orphanage.'

It was Karen's turn to stare. 'But I thought ... I always assumed ...'

'You mean he never told you?'

Karen shook her head. 'I knew he was an orphan, and he had a very unhappy childhood until you and James adopted him when he was eleven. And I know that he thinks so much of you he'd give anything for you. But he would never talk about his life before that.' Karen paused. 'Once, just after we were married, I asked him about those early years, but he changed the subject quite abruptly, and when I tried to persist he just closed up and said he didn't want to talk about it, ever.'

'Yes,' Elizabeth took a deep breath, and her eyes were sombre now, 'he tried to cut those years out of his memory, as though they never existed. He begged us not to speak of his childhood experiences, and knowing what we did we could understand that it was a nightmare he would want to forget. Even Lisa was never told the truth. But I'm surprised to hear that he never confided in you.'

The truth! What truth? Karen felt a shiver of fear. What did it mean? She gave Elizabeth an imploring look. 'I don't understand—what did happen to Nick? I mean, to cause him to——?' she hesitated, afraid of forcing a confidence Elizabeth might be unwilling to give, yet suddenly aware of an overwhelming need to know the secrets Nick had withheld, not only from his adoptive sister but even his own wife.

Elizabeth sighed. 'It was sad, in fact more than sad; it was tragic. Sometimes I suspect that even we didn't learn all of it. You see, Nick never knew his own parents or the circumstances of his birth. He was told only that his mother had gone away when he was a baby and his father was a naval officer who died at sea. It wasn't until he was about eight that he learned, in the cruellest possible way, that his mother was a seventeen-year-old girl who abandoned him immediately after his birth and disappeared into London, and his father a casually picked up sailor whose second name was never even known. The girl's parents brought Nick up, and as far as we can tell were reasonably kind to him, until his grandmother was widowed and then remarried about a year later, after which she moved to a different part of the city. Nick would be about six or seven then, and from that day onward poor little Nick's childhood was a nightmare of brutality at the hands of his new step-grandfather.' Elizabeth paused, her eyes clouding with remembered worry. 'By all accounts he was a dreadful man and his new wife was soon terrified of him. Remember that although the term "grandmother" may give the impression she was old, this was not so. She was still scarcely forty and soon pregnant again, and she had taken on three great louts of stepsons who all showed every sign of following in their father's footsteps. There was little she could do to protect Nick, and at last he ran away.'

Elizabeth paused again and gave a sad little shake of her head. 'They found him in Durham, where he was caught stealing an anorak in a supermarket, and brought back. One can only guess at the thrashing he received, for two weeks later he took off again, to Leeds this time, where a policeman found him curled up asleep in a bus shelter at midnight. Poor little pet, he fought and screamed when they told him he was being taken home, and fortunately one of the young police constables at the Leeds station became suspicious. He and a welfare worker examined young Nick and were appalled at the weals and bruises on his body. There was a court case, the grandfather was fined heavily, threatened with gaol, and there were the usual defences that Nick was a bad child but it wouldn't happen again.' Elizabeth sighed. 'But of course it did, and Nick was taken into care a few months later.'

Karen looked aghast. 'I never dreamed there'd been anything like that. I thought . . .' She stopped helplessly, trying to imagine the Nick she knew as a small, hapless boy at the mercy of an unloving world, alone and friendless. Why hadn't he told her?

Elizabeth sighed. 'By then Nick felt the entire world was against him, and the pattern began: truancy, vandalism, petty theft, until the child welfare authorities were in despair. No one could get through to him, and my husband, who was on the bench at that time, was warned somewhat ironically by a colleague that trouble was on its way once Nick reached the age of criminal responsibility, that obviously the boy was destined for crime. Anyway, just before Nick's ninth birthday they found foster-parents for him, and we began to hope that Nick's problems might be solved. We heard nothing more of him for about three months, then we heard he was in trouble again.

'I was on the local N.S.P.C.C. committee at that time and we were keeping tabs on him as quietly as possible. We went to see the foster-parents, who swore they could do nothing with him, he was a young tearaway beyond all control. Nick was mutinous. He said he didn't want to live with them any more, that they hated him and were cruel to him. The foster-parents were horrified at these accusations and quoted the cases of the three children they'd previously fostered, all girls now happily settled in jobs or back with their own families. My husband, who by this time was puzzled and interested in Nick's case, always had an uncanny flair for judging character, and he was completely baffled. He swore that Nick was not a wilful wrongdoer at heart, that to the contrary the boy was extremely intelligent with a tremendous untapped potential of skill. But how to redirect those energies into the right channels, instead of mutinous lawlessness?'

Elizabeth watched a floating log bob over the weir and nudge into the bank of the stream. She took a deep breath, her sweet face still remote with memory. 'It seemed a hopeless problem. We talked to Nick. We talked to the foster-parents, we talked to Nick's headmaster, and we hoped. And then suddenly the scandal broke. Another boy, a year younger than Nick, was put into the care of the same foster-parents.' Elizabeth smiled wryly. 'I often wonder if Nick remembers young Rickie and what he owes to him.'

Karen frowned, catching her breath, but remained silent, waiting.

'He was a most winsome child,' Elizabeth went on reflectively. 'One of those wide-eyed angelic-looking children whom teachers promote to monitor duties and old ladies smile fondly on. Of course he was a young rip as well, but he had an unblemished record—not like poor Nick!—and everybody believed him. He put up with his new foster-father for exactly one week, then he marched into the child welfare office on his way home from school and made a complaint.'

Karen watched the log edge out again. 'There was something wrong?'

'Something wrong!' Elizabeth exclaimed. 'There most certainly was. In all my years of experience with child care I never heard of a case like it. Usually it's the other way round, foster-parents do a tremendously good job in trying to make a happy home life for the children entrusted to them, and we have those heartbreaking scenes when the child has to leave them to return to its own family. But someone had made a monstrous error of judgement when this man and his wife were selected. He was a positive monster.'

'Oh no!' Karen breathed. 'How dreadful!'

'He didn't ill-treat them in the physical sense; his methods were much more horrific. The stories Rickie told of the sheer psychological tortures that man devised if those children did not obey his every dictate hardly bear thinking about. Of course he was off balance mentally, and after the enquiry there was a tremendous shake-up. Nick and Rickie weren't the first to suffer his sadistic methods of child-character formation. The three girls were traced and questioned, individually, and once they were convinced that they weren't going to be punished for telling the truth, three stories emerged that were too similar to be unfounded. But all of them were like Nick in the respect that they had records of being very difficult children with bad environmental backgrounds, so nobody would take their word.' Elizabeth's mouth tightened. 'And all that time that man was presenting the façade of an upright pillar of society while subjecting those poor children to what amounted to a blasphemy of God's laws.'

Karen felt the numbness of horror spread through her. How Nick must have suffered, to have reached the point where he gave up all hope of finding anyone to believe in him.

'Apparently the favourite initiation into the hell that awaits badly behaved children was to lock the child for a day and a night in a tiny, windowless boxroom with only dry bread and water and no light. It was like a Victorian horror story,' Elizabeth said vehemently. 'Can you imagine it? Nick was scarcely nine, and had no memory of what love and happiness should be, of a secure, loving home. Imagine the nameless terrors in the dark, the isolation and the fear. Imagine being made to sit at the meal table and watch the others eat, because you'd had a sickly tummy and could not eat the fat on your meat the previous day. Can you imagine your feelings if you brought home a tiny stray puppy, only to see your foster-father fill a bucket of water and plunge the poor little scrap into it, and hold it down until . . .'

Karen groaned and closed her eyes. She felt sick, and wanted to cry out to Elizabeth to stay silent, not to tell her any more.

As though she sensed Karen's horror Elizabeth said slowly, 'Yes, it seems unbelievable in this day and age, because even though it all happened over twenty years ago we prided ourselves then that we had found the new approach to child care. The thought of Nick haunted us for weeks. We knew he'd gone to a holiday home by the sea for a month, where he *would* be cared for, and that other arrangements were being made for his future, and then one evening after dinner James said suddenly, "You're still worrying about that boy, aren't you?" and I said, "Yes," and he said, "I know, I can't get the poor kid out of my mind either." Then the next morning at breakfast he asked how I would feel about adopting Nick. I wasn't really surprised, and once we'd made the decision we could hardly wait for all the legal procedures to be over, trying to trace his real mother and dreading that she would turn up and suddenly decide she wanted him . . . Listening to our friends warning us that it might not work out, that we had

Lisa to think of—she was about four at the time—and that the doctors might just be wrong about my being unable to have another child. But we didn't listen, and it did work out, and we thank God in all our prayers that it did.'

Elizabeth fell silent, and Karen stared unseeingly into the gathering dusk. There was so much she wanted to say, but the words eluded her, and she could only think of Nick in the light of this new knowledge; of Nick and the might-have-been had his destiny not brought him to the faith and understanding of the woman at her side. Then Elizabeth moved, drawing her jacket collar closer about her throat.

'I—I think it might be as well if you're discreet about all this—I'd hate him to think I'd betrayed his trust,' Elizabeth said slowly. 'But I think you should know. It may help you to understand when—when he has those withdrawn moods of his.'

'Yes.' Karen bit her lip. 'Thank you for telling me.'

'Because I know it left a scar,' Elizabeth said, as though Karen had not spoken, 'and it's the reason for Nick being so slow in bestowing his trust. Nick has always had lots of friends, but he has always kept people out of his heart. Even Lisa, who adored him when she was a child—he was so protective towards her—never succeeded in getting close to him. But no one can go through life isolating their emotions and their trust for fear of betrayal, and that's why I've told you, because when I go Nick is going to need you more than you realise. There will only be you.'

Karen felt a lump gather in her throat. She was aware of Elizabeth waiting, waiting for the sign of reassurance she sought, and Karen gulped. Reality was coming back, bringing its grim awareness of the falsity of making that reassurance. Yet what could she say, other than what Elizabeth wanted to hear? Wasn't that all part of what Nick was trying to achieve? Then she saw Elizabeth's thin hands clenched on the rail, the fragile bones showing white under the delicate skin. And she felt Elizabeth tremble.

Impulsively she put her arm around the older woman. 'Will it help if I tell you I've never loved any other man but Nick? That all I wanted was to go on loving him and caring for him? For as long as he needed me?'

She held her breath, knowing she spoke only the truth, yet not daring to put the fervent little reassurances into the present tense, where they ought to be. Had Elizabeth noticed? Then she saw Elizabeth nod tremulously and felt pitifully cold fingers close over her own in a mute gesture of gratitude.

'You're frozen!' Karen exclaimed. 'Hadn't we better be moving? It's nearly dark.'

Despite this, Elizabeth seemed reluctant to move, almost as though she were still caught in the limbo of the past and the moment was not yet nigh to break free of its bond. Then she looked up and smiled.

'It's so clear, that beautiful dark country sky,' she said softly. 'So infinitely vast in its heaven, it brings peace to the soul. Here, one can almost believe that time can stand still. Oh, I'm so happy to be back.'

'Yes—but you won't be happy for long if you catch pneumonia standing here communing with the night. Come on,' Karen forced a jocular note into her voice as she urged Elizabeth towards the dimly seen path beneath the trees, 'or Nick will be furious. And you know who'll get the blame! Me! For not looking after you!'

Elizabeth began to laugh and linked a friendly arm within Karen's as they began to make their way along the narrow winding path. But beneath her pretence at lightheartedness Karen felt the leaden weight of sadness. The shock of Elizabeth's confidence was still acute, and she knew it would be a long time, if ever, before her imagination ceased to recoil with sick pity from the thought of what Nick had suffered as a child. Inevitably this new knowledge must bring a fresh insight into Nick's character, and in the light of it could even affect their relationship—such relationship as remained to them, she emended bitterly to herself.

If only she knew how it was all going to work out!

CHAPTER FIVE

KAREN's prophecy proved not to be unfounded.

Nick was out on the gravel forecourt at the front of the house, some ten minutes later, when Karen and Elizabeth finally reached the end of the path where it rejoined the main driveway. Even though it was completely dark now, there was enough light spilling from the porch lamp behind him to reveal the taut lines of worry in his face. He hurried towards them, and Karen's heart sank.

'Where the devil have you been?' He glared at her accusingly. 'I was on the point of sending out a search party.'

Elizabeth laughed. 'Nonsense—did you think we'd got lost? We were talking on the little bridge—oh, dear, I did want Karen to have her first sight of the house by daylight.'

Nick had seized her arm and was ushering her into the wide stone portico. 'She can see it tomorrow—you must be frozen.' He turned his head and snapped, 'Really, Karen, you should have more sense than to keep her standing around talking in this freezing wind. Why didn't you——?'

'Nick!' Elizabeth stopped and swung to face him. 'It isn't Karen's fault! It's mine. I don't know what South America has done to your temper, but it certainly hasn't improved it!'

Karen bit her lip, the familiar sense of despair and injustice pervading her heart again. Already the tension between herself and Nick was threatening the joy of Elizabeth's homecoming. Then she remembered, and her instinct to retort died. Forcing herself to meet the cold anger in his eyes, she said hastily, 'Let me go and make a hot drink for Elizabeth straight away.'

'Magda has already made tea—it's in the sitting room, but stone cold by now, I imagine,' he said, unmollified. 'You've been nearly an hour out there.'

'I told you, darling!' Elizabeth sighed. 'I started reminiscing about old times and didn't even notice the cold.' She turned and touched Karen's arm. 'Come on, let's have that tea, even if it is cold, and then perhaps we'll be forgiven.'

She led Karen through a lovely old spandrel doorway at the right of the panelled hall and into an oak-beamed, chintzy sitting room where a log fire blazed in a wide basket grate. A scrolled silver tray stood on a low table at one side of the mellowed stone fireplace, and it had obviously been set with loving care by Magda. There were tiny sandwiches, buttered scones, pink and white marshmallow biscuits, dainty fragile china with gold rimmed cups, and blue forget-me-nots embroidered on the snowy traycloth. Karen saw the pot under its cosy on the hearth, but as she bent to it Magda came hurrying into the room.

'Leave that—here's a fresh pot.' Magda busied herself at the tray, a smile of satisfaction hovering on her pleasant face as she did so. Imperceptibly she had become a countrywoman again, happy to be back at Dellersbeck in her native county. When she had poured the tea and pressed her mistress and Karen to start on the sandwiches, with apologies because it was 'only shop-bought stuff today, but we'll be back to home made from tomorrow,' she straightened and said, 'Now about dinner . . .?'

'Dinner?' Elizabeth relaxed back and regarded the housekeeper with wry amusement. 'But it's nearly seven. Are we having dinner tonight, Magda?'

'Well, Master Nick thought a bit of roast beef and Yorkshire . . .'

Elizabeth shook her head. 'I don't think you should be toiling over the stove tonight, after such a long day. For myself, I just want to laze in front of this gorgeous fire. Besides, we've to unpack yet.' She glanced at Karen. 'How about you, my dear? Are you ready for a big meal?'

Karen shook her head. 'I'm not hungry—certainly not after this.'

But still Magda looked rather uncertain. 'You haven't been in the kitchen yet, Mrs Radcliffe.'

Elizabeth frowned. 'No. Is something wrong?'

Magda sighed. 'No, nothing's wrong. But there's a new

deep freeze—a huge thing—packed with stuff. I've never seen so much food outside a shop. And the pantry's stacked up as well. He must have——'

'Laid in for a siege?' Elizabeth's mouth quirked. 'I'm afraid Nick does tend to be rather wholesale when he does things.'

'I'll never be able to find anything.' There was an aggrieved note in Magda's voice. 'And there's a new mixer—big enough for an hotel, by the look of it. He says it'll halve my work,' she added disbelievingly.

Elizabeth laughed. 'If you don't approve, you know what to do! You've chased Nick out of your kitchen on more than one occasion in the past. Don't be afraid to let him know you're still boss there.' She slipped her feet out of her shoes and curled still slim and shapely legs up on the cushions of the chesterfield. 'Now do sit down, Magda, and have some tea yourself.'

After a moment's hesitation Magda obeyed, and for a little while the two women chatted desultorily about the house, being home again, and the expected arrival of Lisa and her husband Clifford the following afternoon.

Karen sat silent, staring into the fire and wondering where Nick had gone. Should she offer to cook something for Nick? Obviously Magda would be tired, and Elizabeth would probably have an early night, perhaps with a light snack on a tray. But Magda might not welcome an intruder in her domain, no matter how well-meaning. Karen put her cup and saucer back on the tray and sighed. Suddenly she was aware of a desperate tiredness stealing over her, and the warmth of the fire made her long to relax back and just close her eyes. She suppressed a yawn, and at that moment Nick came into the room.

Before he could speak Elizabeth sat up. 'Nick, what's this about dinner? We're all so tired, I don't think we should——'

He raised one hand. 'But I do. If you lot are content to stoke up today on cups of tea and motorway buns I'm not.' He strolled across the room. 'Don't worry, everything is under control. We dine at eight-thirty, and I want no interruptions in the kitchen. Understand?' He shot a mock look of

severity at Magda, who apparently forgot her previous annoyance and giggled.

'What are we having, then, Master Nick? Beef charcoal
and singed spuds?'

'I'm surprised at you, Maggy.' He pretended to threaten
her. 'Don't you know that jealousy gets you nowhere?'

'Me? Jealous? What of?'

'Come off it, Maggy, all the best cooks are men.' He
brushed past Karen's knees and bent to toss another log into
the heart of the fire. He straightened and grinned down at
the affronted housekeeper. 'I'm really looking forward to
some decent nosh at last.'

'What about the reckoning afterwards?' Elizabeth asked
weakly.

'Maggy will soon knock that off.'

'Oh, no!' said Elizabeth firmly. 'Not the mountain of dirty
dishes *you* leave after you've amused yourself in the kitchen.'

He shrugged. 'We can leave it all until tomorrow for
Timsy.'

'Timsy!' Elizabeth's eyes widened, while joy and disbelief
vied on her face. 'Nick, you don't mean——?'

'Yes.' Plainly satisfied with Elizabeth's reaction to his
casual suggestion, Nick nodded. 'She's coming out of retire-
ment for you. She would have been here today to welcome
you home, but her fourth grandchild was being christened
this afternoon, so of course she had to be there.'

'Dear Timsy—I can't believe it! Now I know I've come
home!' Elizabeth sprang up impulsively and flung her arms
round her adopted son. 'I think that's the nicest surprise you
could have given me.'

He held her gently for a moment, then said wryly, 'I
suppose I'm forgiven now?'

Elizabeth's eyes were unnaturally bright. She smiled and
shook her head. 'What for?'

'For being such a boor when we arrived.'

'Blame the storm—I think it made us all edgy.' Elizabeth
slipped back into her seat and glanced across at Karen. 'Now
go and see if Karen's forgiven you—she looks so tired, bless

her heart, she can scarcely keep her eyes open.'

For the first time since he had entered the room Nick turned and looked directly at his wife. She did look tired, her eyes wide and dark-shadowed against the flush induced by the heat of the fire, and the contours of her mouth tremulous with doubt as she waited for his reaction to Elizabeth's command.

He moved towards her, his dark face unreadable, then sat on the arm of her chair. He slipped his hand behind her head, his fingers tangling in the soft silky strands at the nape, and then pulled her against his side.

'Tired, darling?'

Sudden anger made her want to drag herself away from his caresses. Did he think she was a toy, to be picked up or ignored as the mood took him? Then, her body stiff with rejection, she saw Elizabeth watching them, and she mastered the bitter impulses. 'Yes,' she whispered, 'a little. But it'll pass. Who is Timsy?' she added on a note of desperation.

'The backbone of Dellersbeck,' he replied, continuing the unnerving caresses. 'She was Lisa's nanny, then housekeeper —Magda was our cook in those days—but when we moved to London she didn't want to leave her family. Rob, her husband, looked after my father's horses for years.' Nick's fingers stayed their motion, and Karen sensed a sudden tension in him. Then he laughed, looking at Elizabeth. 'Do you remember that day when he caught me trying to ride Lucifer? He was going to horsewhip me.'

'I'll never forget it.' Elizabeth bit her lip. 'It was fortunate that I happened to be on my way down to the stables that day. I don't know who was the more affronted, Lucifer at the indignity of a child daring to try to mount him, or Rob being thwarted in his attempt at administering discipline. But I couldn't allow that. You'd . . .'

Elizabeth stopped, and the unspoken words formed in Karen's mind. *You'd been punished enough* . . . Was that what she had almost said?

'That horse was a fiend,' Elizabeth sighed reminiscently. 'I never had a moment's peace of mind when James was on him.'

'Yes.' Nick's voice was clipped. He stood up. 'I must inspect the steak. Excuse me.'

He was moving away, and scarcely realising it Karen got up and followed him. She caught up with him at the door. 'I'll help you.'

'I thought you were tired.'

'Oh, for goodness' sake . . .' She closed the door behind her. 'Stop needling me, Nick. I'm trying to do what's best.'

'I'm sorry,' he said in a perfunctory tone. 'I suppose we're all a bit edgy.'

'And it'll be easier for me if you don't play the charade quite so convincingly—when you remember!' she added bitterly.

'You not exactly making a very successful effort yourself.' He pushed open a baize door and led the way into a big square kitchen. 'It takes two, you know.'

'Does it?'

'What do you mean?' He shot her a cold glance.

'It only takes one to quarrel—your way,' she returned bitterly.

'I said I was sorry—for goodness' sake have a look at that meat—how anyone copes with that antiquated contraption is beyond me,' he exclaimed impatiently.

The 'antiquated contraption' was the large, admittedly rather elderly solid fuel stove that perforce had had to serve the Dellersbeck cooking needs for many years in the absence of a gas supply and the dislike of Elizabeth's mother-in-law for the idea of having an electric cooker installed. Karen went to the stove, bracing herself for the blast of heat as she opened the heavy iron door, and cautiously withdrew the tin holding the meat.

She basted it, turned it over, and returned it to the oven. 'It's all right,' she said, straightening, 'but the oven's too hot. Can you turn it down, or something?'

Nick swore under his breath. 'How the tenants managed with it I do not know. The electricians should be here tomorrow to install a split level, thank heaven.'

Karen sighed. 'Actually, these are supposed to be very

efficient—one has to get used to them. Perhaps we'd better ask Magda . . .'

Nick's mouth tightened obstinately. 'I said I'd fix this evening meal, and I meant it. I've never been bested by a bit of mechanical metalware in my life and I don't intend to give way now.' He turned from the offending oven and frowned. 'Can you fix something for afters?'

She began a survey of the cupboards for suitable ingredients of a cold sweet which would, she hoped, cool and set in the fridge in the hour which remained before it would be required. Fortunately Nick had laid in ample supplies of everything, and soon she had made an apricot cream, which with the addition of a dash of Cointreau would make an attractive and luxury dessert. Nick was sorting vegetables out of the big deep freeze which stood in one corner, and Karen could not help a wry smile as she remembered Elizabeth's remark about Nick's wholesale methods. He had not wasted much time during the few days he had spent at Dellersbeck prior to their arrival.

Besides the obviously new deep freeze chest, which was packed with frozen food and an assortment of meats and poultry, there was a large food mixer with various attachments, some of which were still in their cardboard packing, a modern washing machine, and a run of de-luxe fitted units in black and pale green along the length of one wall. The big old scrubbed kitchen table had been banished to the corner near the door, along with the old-fashioned glass-doored kitchen cabinet and a washing machine which had obviously seen many years' service.

Karen put out biscuits and cheese on a platter, measured coffee into a jug and milk into a pan ready to heat later on, checked the meat again, then looked at Nick. 'We've about a quarter of an hour or so—I'd like to wash and change. Where is my room?'

Nick was stacking plates to warm. He did not turn. 'Upstairs, first door to your left. There's a bathroom adjoining. I took your cases up,' he added.

She found her way along the corridor to the main hall and went up the old, carved oak staircase, appreciating the age-worn smoothness of the banister rail beneath her hand. There was wainscoting to shoulder height, beneath a mellowed heavy wallpaper of Adam green embossed with velvety fleur-de-lys motifs, and gilt-framed paintings from a bygone age. At the head of the stairs a gallery ran round three sides, from which at least six doors opened and two passages led off to parts of the house as yet unknown to Karen. She opened the first door to her left, groping for the light switch and seeing first her cases standing just inside the door. With a little sigh of relief she closed the door behind her and looked curiously round the room.

Like all the rooms she had seen so far it was high-ceilinged and spacious, with an ornamental plaster frieze and big circular centre rose. There were two tall windows with curtains of pale blue velour falling from ceiling height to floor, topped by fringed and embossed pelmets of a deeper blue that matched the background hue of the Chinese carpet. There was a fireplace painted white, as was all the woodwork, with an embroidered fire-screen before it, and the furniture was white Regency style, with gilt handles and gilt-touched beading edging the oval inset panels. Karen touched the pale-blue satin stripes of the wallpaper almost absently; she was suddenly reminded of her own family home in Kent. Not that it had remotely approached Dellersbeck Hall in size or antiquity, but it had held the same quiet, restful atmosphere of a country house which had aged graciously. Here, as there, the only concessions to modernity were the central heating radiators—which would certainly be essential when the northern winters seized the house in their grip—and a rather ancient fitted washbasin in the corner beside the left-hand window.

A rush of nostalgia for the warm, safe haven of her childhood home, now no longer waiting for those times when she needed it, made her eyes mist. There had been times when she had not appreciated it, or the unselfish love of her parents, until it was too late and she realised just how much she had lost. Karen shook her head, realising she did not have much time, and opened her big case to delve in search of her sponge bag and towel. Quickly she stripped off her sweater and skirt, throwing them on the end of one of the twin beds, and turned on the tap, hoping that Dellersbeck would yield hot water. Then a scarcely registered fact about the room struck into her mind with sudden significance and she frowned. Such a large bedroom, and twin beds . . .

She swung round, an exclamation hovering on her lips and suspicion flooding over her. She ran to the wardrobe, to fling open the double doors, and knew the wild suspicion was grounded in fact. Yes, there were Nick's clothes. And in the dressing chest were his shirts, socks, ties . . . Karen ran to the other door, saw the bathroom Nick had mentioned, and all the signs of a man recently in possession; the navy towelling robe, shaving kit, a flagon of lotion and a toothbrush in the rack, while the warm imprint of masculine toiletries on the air stole faintly into her nostrils.

'Oh, no!' she whispered, dismay draining her cheeks of their colour. Surely he didn't imagine . . . surely he didn't believe that she was prepared to carry the charade through to this extent?

Her mouth tightened, then anger brought the need to confront him, and she ran blindly back into the bedroom. All thought of changing for the evening had fled and she snatched at the garments so recently discarded. Then a movement and a shadow darkening the blue carpet made her start with shock. She spun round, and the sweater dropped from her hands.

Nick was standing by the window.

His brows went up. 'Seen a ghost in the bathroom?'

Karen found her voice. 'What are you doing in here?'

'Turning off the tap you left running—and drawing the curtains,' he said coolly, suiting the action to the words. When she continued to stare at him a frown deepened between his dark brows. 'Is something the matter?'

'The matter!' Karen's anger erupted. 'Get out!'

'What? Out of my room?'

'*Your* room?'

'I've occupied it for the past week.'

'Then why did you bring my cases in here?' she demanded, incensed by the arrogant assumption in his tone.

'Surely that should be obvious.' He moved to the other tall window and pulled the tasselled draw cord.

Karen took a step back. 'What is that supposed to mean?'

He turned to the dressing table, stooping slightly to adjust the set of his tie and his gaze swinging in search of her through the mirror. 'Isn't it usual for husbands and wives to share the same bedroom?'

'Not in this case! That wasn't part of the bargain when I agreed to this—this pretence,' she cried hotly.

'I don't recall this particular question being discussed.' He turned to face her. 'I took it for granted.'

'You—you had a nerve! How dare——'

'How can you be so crass!' he broke in. 'What do you think Elizabeth—to say nothing of everybody else—is going to think if we occupy separate rooms?'

She saw the implacable hardness back in his eyes and she felt cold. She raised her hands to cradle her shoulders, and felt her bare skin chill under her own touch. With an exclamation she bent to snatch up the fallen sweater and started to struggle into it. Anger made her clumsy and the sleeves elusive, and cynicism touched Nick's mouth.

'Need help?'

'Not from you.'

The corners of his mouth turned down. 'Why not? Afraid I might glimpse too much of your charms?'

Flushed with mortification, she dragged down the folds of the sweater and seized her skirt. 'Should I be—after the scorn you professed regarding them two years ago?'

'Perhaps my memory of them has grown a little hazy over the two years for me to care much now,' he said brutally.

'But not your scorn! Well, I've no intention of allowing you to refresh your memory!' With the convention of clothes a safe cloak about her body again Karen could face him and match him with the determination of anger. 'I mean it, Nick. I want another room.'

'That's not possible, and you know why.'

'I don't accept reasons from you any longer.'

'You've no choice, I'm afraid,' he said flatly.

'Nick! I am *not* going to sleep with you!'

His mouth compressed into a tight line. 'You're making that very plain, Karen. But you——'

'I'll make it plainer! I'm not going to have sex with you.'

'I wasn't aware that I'd asked you to. Will you hear me out, for God's sake?'

'There's nothing I want to hear!' she flashed angrily. 'If——'

'Oh, but there is—and you're going to hear it!' He seized her shoulders. 'Do you think I brought you here to force you into bed with me? After what happened two years ago? Do you think I've forgotten so easily?'

'Nick——! Let me go!'

He seemed not to hear, his features set in a dark mask of bitterness as she struggled to free herself. But his grip only bit harder into the soft flesh of her upper arms.

'How do you think I've felt these past two years?' he gritted. 'Continually reminded of the whole rotten affair. Even in South America I couldn't escape. The day I walked down a street in Sao Paulo . . . Once in somebody's house, a stranger's . . . the last place I expected to see that—that——'

'Hello . . .?'

From a long way off Karen heard the light, tentative voice, and the tap on the door. Nick's hands fell from her arms, and the muscles along his jaw flickered in a spasm as he swallowed hard.

'Yes . . .? Come in.' His voice was uneven as he moved to the door, while Karen raised a trembling hand to her throat.

Elizabeth walked in, the smile on her sweet face faltering as she looked from Nick to Karen's deathly pale countenance. But she made no comment and glanced back to her son. 'I came to tell you that everything is ready—we smelled something burning—I'm afraid the potatoes have had it! But Magda rescued the meat, and she says if you don't hurry the Yorkshires will be ruined.'

'I thought I told her we would manage the meal tonight,' Nick said in a distracted voice. 'We——'

'I think it's just as well we didn't take you at your word,' Elizabeth said gently but firmly. 'Will you be much longer?'

'Karen's just coming.' Nick ran his fingers through his hair. 'We'll follow you down.'

Feeling as though she had emerged from a tempest, Karen had seized a comb and was trying to repair the ravages of her hair. Desperately she pushed the thick silky lengths behind her ears and said quickly, 'I'm ready now.'

She hurried towards the door, knowing she could not bear to be left alone with Nick again until she had had time to rehabilitate her shattered resources. Elizabeth was silent as they went down the stairs, and Nick's dull, heavy footfalls as he followed seemed to communicate his anger to Karen. As though Elizabeth sensed the antagonism in the air; as though he accused ...

To Karen it was one of the most strained and miserable meals she had ever endured. She wished bitterly she could be like Nick, able to hide her true feeling behind the suave and conversable manner he seemed to don without regard for his real mood of the moment. But she had to admit that he made conversation easy for her, by recounting anecdotes of the South American job in a way that required only a yes or a no from her in response, and then steering the topic away from himself and encouraging Elizabeth towards the subject of plans for the garden at Dellersbeck.

Elizabeth had always been an enthusiastic gardener, and she was diverted instantly into wondering how the garden had fared during her long absence. 'I shall be up at the crack of dawn tomorrow for a tour of inspection,' she said eagerly.

'You will not!' Nick eyed her sternly. 'You will have your breakfast in bed and not get up until the morning is decently aired.'

'Oh, Nick!' There was a definite trace of impatience behind Elizabeth's apparently wry tone. 'If you think I'm going to stand for being mollycoddled like a helpless old woman ...'

Karen seized the chance offered by this not altogether teasing exchange to escape to make the coffee, sending a checking gesture towards Magda, who also rose and then subsided.

Karen's sympathy was beginning to lie wholeheartedly with Elizabeth; while undoubtedly Elizabeth's frail health must be closely guarded, Nick's overbearing concern could do more harm than good. For Elizabeth was the kind of person who would want to fight her grim battle with illness in her own way, and Nick's interference could easily undermine her confidence. But try to get him to see reason once he got an idea into his head ... Karen sighed; he had a streak like steel in his character, which had helped him to win the place of power he now held in a very tough man's world, and that power in its turn had forged the steel even stronger. And after Elizabeth's confidences earlier in the day Karen had a fresh insight into what had gone into the founding of Nicholas Radcliffe. It was not going to make her own battle with him any easier.

When the coffee was made Karen took the tray through into the sitting room and switched on the standard lamp, then put another log into the heart of the richly glowing embers. The others were still in the dining room and she was crossing the hall to summon them when the phone rang. She hesitated with the brief moment of indecision as to whether to answer it, when it wouldn't be for her in any case, or hurry to tell Elizabeth and Nick. She turned back and lifted the receiver, quickly giving the unfamiliar number on the dial without adding her own name.

'Who is that?' asked the caller.

'It's Karen here,' she responded quietly, instantly recognising the puzzled, little-girl voice at the other end. 'How are you, Lisa?'

'Oh, all right.' Imperceptibly Lisa's tone had altered. 'I didn't recognise your voice.'

'It's a long time since you heard it,' Karen returned, with more calm than she was feeling. 'Hold on, I'll call your mother.'

'Yes—just a moment!'

Karen waited.

'Is—is everything all right?'

Was it fear that had roughened Lisa's voice? Karen stared across the empty hall, her eyes unseeing. 'Your mother seems very happy to be home, and apart from being tired she managed the journey very well.'

'Oh, good.' A hesitation, then, 'Is Nick there?'

'Yes, do you want to speak to him?'

'N-no, not just now.' It was almost possible to see Lisa all those miles away, her brow furrowed and her small white teeth biting into her lower lip. 'I think if you would ask Mummy, please—I won't keep her long if she's tired.'

'I think she's coming now.' Karen heard the murmur of voices as the dining room door opened. She turned and held out the phone, saying, 'It's Lisa,' as Elizabeth came across the hall.

Karen went slowly into the sitting room and poured out coffee for Magda, Nick and herself, then retreated to a chair that lay beyond the pool of light shed by the standard lamp. Weariness and depression had settled again and she longed for nothing more than to be alone. Already she felt as though she had been at Dellersbeck for a long, long day instead of a mere few hours. It was still only a little after nine, far too early to excuse herself, even to the understanding Elizabeth. And there still remained the problem she dreaded. Somehow it had to be settled tonight, her way. Nick had to understand that the masquerade must stop short of resuming the intimacies of marriage. Too much pain and bitterness and recrimination, to say nothing of a two-year separation, lay between them, and those two years had done nothing to blunt the edges of a marriage irretrievably destroyed. Sometimes she wondered if those first months of sheer enchantment had been a dream, a dream through which she and Nick had drifted hand in hand, intoxicated with the joy of discovering one another, until suddenly, unbelievably, the dream was shattered by a force beyond her control. When she wakened to a Nick she scarcely knew emerging from the lover she loved with every atom of her heart, mind and body. A Nick without trust, bitterly accusing and hardly giving her a chance to defend herself. Until shock and disillusion banished even the desire to try to defend herself. Now, as then, she faced the dreadful realisation that Nick had never loved her. For if he had truly loved her surely her word would have been enough. He would not have demanded the explanation she could not give ...

The fire flames misted before her eyes, the heat causing a dry, burning sensation under her lids, and she blinked hard, looking up to meet Nick's gaze. Something in it made her heart lock for a moment and then bound painfully at the intensity in his darkened eyes. It was as though she met a deep plea for communication, but then he moved and the old hardness, unreadable, came back like a shutter closing. But it had been there all the time, she thought bitterly. Only the twin reflections of the warm firelight had brought an illusion of that warm intensity into his eyes, that wonderful secret message that once dwelled there always for only herself to read ...

He stood up, and at the same moment the door opened and Elizabeth came in. She apologised ruefully for letting the coffee go cold, but her expression held a tinge of worry. 'That was Lisa—she can't make it tomorrow after all. A very important business associate has arrived from New York and naturally she has to help Cliff entertain this visitor and his wife. But she hopes to be here Friday afternoon.'

Nick had remained still while Elizabeth was speaking. Now he gave a non-committal murmur then went from the room. Elizabeth sank into silence, cradling her cup of coffee in her two hands as she stared into the fire. Since the phone call from her daughter her mood had changed and all the happiness of homecoming that had glowed in her all day had faded. Studying her, Karen felt concern. It was possible now to see the effects of Elizabeth's illness. Her face was drawn and pale, the blue eyes heavy with fatigue, and tension showed in the grip of the slender fingers round the cup. But how much of this loss of buoyancy and spirit was due to something Lisa might have said? Or was it simply disappointment that the family reunion was not yet to be completed?

Karen said gently, 'Why don't you have an early night—it must have been a long, tiring day for you.'

'Yes,' Elizabeth smiled faintly, 'I do feel rather whacked. Do you mind if I leave you?'

'Of course not. Is there anything I can do . . .?' Karen made to rise, but Magda was already on her feet, taking the half-drunk coffee from Elizabeth.

'I'll bring you a nice nightcap as soon as you're in—I always think coffee sends sleep out of the window!'

Magda took over firmly, shepherding the frail Elizabeth to the rest she badly needed, and when they had gone Karen stood for a moment, uncertain in the big quiet room. There was no sound or sign of Nick, and with a sigh she remembered the reckoning still awaiting in the kitchen and dining room.

But it did not take her long to clear the table and wash dishes for four, and she decided that while she was busy she might as well set out the places for breakfast next morning. She was just finishing this task when she heard footsteps outside. But it was only Magda, coming to heat the milk for Elizabeth's bedtime drink and full of reproaches because Karen had not waited until she could help.

'You will have enough to do,' Karen returned, closing the wall hatch, 'and I would feel happier if I made myself useful.' She hesitated. 'Just tell me if I tread on your toes, Magda.'

For a moment she thought her plain speaking had offended the housekeeper, then Magda's face relaxed and she began to laugh. 'Thank heavens for that! Do you know, I was wondering how I was going to manage on my own with all the family here, and maybe no help. It's a big house, you know, and Miss Lisa isn't all that keen on lending a hand. The other way round, in fact—though I suppose I shouldn't say it! She always did like being waited on hand and foot. A proper little lady. And of course since she's married an Honourable . . . I suppose we must expect it.' Magda smiled fondly, turning to rescue the milk pan before it boiled over and thus missing the shadow that crossed Karen's face. 'Yes, Miss Lisa's made a very good marriage, I must say.'

Karen stayed silent. Her thoughts of Lisa's 'good marriage' could not be voiced aloud to anyone, least of all to Magda, so close a confidante of Lisa's mother.

Magda glanced up as she spooned malted milk into a beaker. 'But then what does it matter who you marry, an earl's son or a farmer's lad, as long as you're happy together?'

Karen forced a smile. 'That's true. I wonder ... I'd better go. Nick may be wondering where I am.'

'Oh, he went out a little while ago. He always used to walk around at night in the old days,' Magda recalled. 'He would take one of the dogs. Just in case anybody was prowling around. Then he'd lock up for the night. Look, I think that's him now.'

Karen followed the direction of the housekeeper's gesture and saw the shadow outside moving into the dim radiance from an unseen light somewhere. But from within the brightly lit kitchen it was not possible to make out features, and suddenly she was glad she was not alone. What if it should be an intruder? Then the lobby door opened and Nick stood framed there.

'Come on, Karo,' he ordered, 'join me for a breather before I lock up.'

Refusal leapt to her lips. Then he held out one hand, and she realised Magda was hovering nearby, the beaker in her hand, watching. Reluctantly Karen moved forward. 'But I haven't a coat or anything—it'll be cold.'

'There's an old one of mine here. Nobody's going to see you.'

'Yes, go on,' Magda urged. 'A bit of fresh air blows the cobwebs away.'

Karen was to discover that Magda had a fund of ancient country clichés, one for every occasion, no matter what. Nick had reached up to take an old anorak from a peg in the lobby, and he held it out, ready to drop it round her shoulders.

The last thing Karen wanted at that moment was to go out into the darkness with Nick. But there seemed no escape, especially while the housekeeper continued to stand there watching.

Slowly Karen went towards him.

CHAPTER SIX

NICK dropped the old blue anorak about her shoulders, his hands pausing to clamp its folds firmly to her contours. To an onlooker it must have appeared a gesture of husbandly love and care, but to Karen it only underlined the whole sham of their present relationship.

He did not speak as he closed the door behind them and walked her out of the radius of yellow light cast by the big old coach lantern above the lobby's outer door. The night was cold and blustery, with a hint of late frost in the air, and the black and amber shadows of the shrubbery were anything but inviting. But he steered her along the lee of the house wall until a high thorn hedge loomed out of the darkness, its thickness providing a break against the chill invasion of the northeast wind.

Nick stopped. 'I won't keep you out here long, but I have to talk to you where we're not likely to be overheard or interrupted.'

She huddled closer into the anorak and looked up at the shadowy blur of his features. 'Hasn't it all been said?' she asked wearily. 'There's only one problem to be settled, and you know perfectly well what that is.'

His shoulders moved with a sigh. 'We're not making a very successful go of our truce, are we?'

Karen stiffened. 'I warn you, Nick, don't try to blame me for that. You're not making it very easy for me,' she said quietly.

'And you're not making it very easy for me!' he retorted. 'Surely you realise——'

'Just a moment,' she broke in, 'let's get this straight. I didn't come out here to start another argument—or listen to more accusations. I—I can't take much more, Nick. I——' Despite her attempts at control her voice broke as the never far distant sense of despair threatened its attack. 'For God's sake try to understand and be reasonable, Nick.'

'How do you think *I* feel?' he demanded. 'Do you think it's any easier for me?'

'I don't know,' she said hopelessly. 'I only know that it's proving far more difficult than I imagined. In fact, I'm not sure it wouldn't be better if I went away again. Once the reunion is over, Elizabeth will understand, and we——'

'No!' He almost spat the denial with his vehemence. 'No, you mustn't leave. It would ruin everything I'm trying to do. Listen, Karo—we've got to thrash this thing out, before it gets any worse and Elizabeth discovers the truth.'

'She's more likely to discover it if I stay,' Karen said bitterly.

'Not if we try to forget our differences. And not if you forget this stubborn insistence on separate rooms.'

'No—I'm prepared to keep my promise, but not——'

'Karo——' he seized her arm, 'hear me out. I know what you're thinking, but we have to solve this problem. Now listen, I'm only here for two more days—or should we say nights,' he interjected with a touch of grim irony, 'then I have to go back until next Tuesday. And I'll probably have to go away again the following week, so my time here is going to be limited in any case. Remembering that, will you leave the arrangements as they are, and I'll endeavour not to intrude on your privacy. I promise.'

She was silent, unable to decide how much trust she dared put into his promise. His tone was sincere enough, and she had an inkling of how much such a promise was costing his pride. But instinct warned that it wasn't as easy as that. How could a resumption of close propinquity work? When so much bitterness lay between them, ready to erupt at even a word? She remembered the scene the night he returned late, when she'd made that foolish move downstairs to him, an innocent attempt at friendship, to make the truce genuine. And earlier this evening, before Elizabeth unwittingly interrupted. How could Nick imagine they could share that most intimate of all places, a bedroom, as though they were two strangers?

He had sensed her doubt instantly, and his hand fell from

her arm. He said heavily: 'Listen, I know it's all over for us, that anything we once had going is dead beyond recall. So will you trust me?'

There was the slump of despair in his shoulders as he stood looking down into her troubled face, and for a wild moment she experienced a surge of longing to soften and yield to him. She wanted to cry: *Don't let it be over!* and reach up to touch his face, to voice the crazy, urgent plea: *Can't we try again . . .?*

But then he moved and straightened, drawing himself to his full height, and she felt the chill of his implacability emanate from him as he said grimly: 'If it'll make it any easier for you I can at least promise you one thing. When it's all over I'll do everything I can to help you get your freedom quickly. And I'll make sure you don't suffer financially.'

'You don't have to bribe me with payment,' she said coldly. 'I don't want anything from you.'

'I'm not doing it for you—or myself. I'm doing it for Elizabeth.'

The whine of the wind and the stirrings of the leaves suddenly ceased. She and Nick were enclosed within a dreadful silence in which echoed the final death knell of her marriage. Karen felt the ice form round her heart and heard her own voice, curiously remote, say stiffly, 'I too. I thought that was clearly understood.'

She turned away quickly, knowing she couldn't take much more, and began to stumble along the dark, uneven path towards the light. Nick's steps crunched behind her and she increased her pace almost desperately. He caught up with her just before she reached the door.

'Just a minute, Karo. It isn't enough.'

'What do you mean?' she asked in a low voice.

'You can't go rushing in there looking as though—as though I'm the man you hate most in the world. For God's sake remember Magda!'

'Magda?' Karen stared at him blankly.

'Don't you realise what kind of a woman she is?'

'I—I don't understand. What is it to do with us?'

'Karen, are you blind?' he exclaimed impatiently. 'Magda

misses nothing. She's alone in the world, and you know what that means.'

'But I don't follow you. What does it mean?'

'That she has no emotional involvement of her own apart from that which she has with us. We're the only substitute she has for a family. She's totally devoted to Elizabeth, and everything that happens, everything that might remotely concern the family, is duly and faithfully reported.' Nick bent forward, and the amber light caught his face, illuminating his tense features. 'Do I have to spell it out? You of all people, Karen, ought to know! Surely to God you haven't forgotten!'

The intensity of meaning in his tone only bewildered Karen more. Yet something in his tone and his whole demeanour brought a flutter of fear. 'But what have I forgotten?' she faltered.

The light cast harsh hollows round his eyes, but no darkness could conceal what was in his expression and Karen recoiled. 'You mean . . . Magda *knows*?' she whispered.

'I hope not,' Nick said grimly. 'I did a pretty good job of persuading her that it wasn't you in that photograph. But she——'

'*The photograph!*'

Nick stared at her, his mouth a hard line. 'Oh, come off it, Karen, for God's sake. Don't try to sound as though you didn't know which photograph. I can take so much, but not——'

'Yes,' she cried wildly, 'but where does Magda come into it?'

'Magda saw that photograph,' he said savagely. 'She actually rang me up to ask if it was you!'

'Oh no!' Weakness and shock brought Karen to the verge of collapse. She swayed forward, and Nick gripped her shoulders with hands that felt like steel. 'But I didn't know!' she whispered desperately trying to hold on to consciousness. 'I never thought anyone would recognise me. The print was so blurred, and . . .'

'Karen, pull yourself together!' His hands slid under her elbows, supporting her against him. 'I'm simply trying to

warn you.' He shook his head despairingly. 'That morning
was such a nightmare—you'd flown into your room like a
zombie—and then Magda ringing . . . I couldn't believe it all.
I told her she ought to take more water with it . . . There
were thousands of girls in London with long hair that blew
across their faces, and coats with big fur cuffs. I know I convinced her at the time. But I knew.' Nick gave a shuddering
sigh. 'Though your features were blurred, that clasp on your
bag stood out. That's how I knew. Because it was the new
handbag I'd given you only a couple of days before—and the
fancy shopping bag you'd treated yourself to at the same
time. Thank heaven Magda hadn't seen those! *"Stephan Esse
and the Mystery Girl outside Vincent Kayne's studio
today . . ."* ' Nick quoted bitterly. 'All I could think was that
Elizabeth mustn't find out.'

A wave of sickness rose in Karen. Was she never to escape
the consequences of that dreadful day? She made a desperate
effort to regain control and pull back from Nick's hold. The
anorak fell to the ground and she swayed as she turned to
stoop and grope down for it. But Nick moved more quickly.
He snatched it up and thrust it round her trembling shoulders.

'Better get inside—you're shivering.' He thrust open the
door. 'And remember!' he hissed. 'Be on your guard.'

She stumbled blindly into the lobby, fumbling for the coat-
hook and hearing the harsh rasp of bolts as Nick locked the
outer door. There was light shining through the glass panels
of the door leading into the kitchen, and she saw Magda
standing at the sink, rinsing out Elizabeth's beaker.

Was it her imagination, or was Magda giving her a meaning, speculative look? Then Magda smiled, and the illusion
vanished.

'It's turned very cold, hasn't it? Of course it's always a bit
colder up here than it is in London. Like me to make you a
cup of something hot?'

But Karen wanted nothing but escape. She shook her
head. 'No, thanks, I—I'll have to finish unpacking.' She
glanced round and found Nick watching her closely.

'Don't wait for me if you're tired, darling.' He touched

her shoulder lightly. 'I've a few things to see to and they'll take me a while.'

His tone and expression were as casual as his words, but the message in his eyes was unmistakable. It said *I'm playing my part, I expect you to do the same*. She nodded mutely, still aware of the housekeeper's sharp-eyed attention in the background, and forced herself to smile and wish Magda goodnight.

But she was still shaken by the time she finished a hasty unpacking some half an hour later and crawled wretchedly into bed. What if Magda remembered? What if the fact of seeing Karen again jogged her mind into reminiscence, back to the wedding, back through all the events of the six months that led up to the dreadful prelude to Nick's departure for South America. *What if she'd even kept the cutting?*

Karen tossed restlessly, trying to tell herself she was imagining the worst. If Nick had not reminded her, in fact told her something she did not even know, she would never have given Magda another thought. Because of it, the housekeeper seemed suddenly to have taken on a sinister aspect Karen would never have dreamed of prior to this night. Anyway, even if Magda did remember, what did it matter? Nick would take care that it never reached Elizabeth's ears. Wasn't it all for Elizabeth?

As for herself, what had she to lose? She had lost everything that mattered most two long years ago. Nick's love, his trust, and his respect.

Lying there, a prey to the agonies of emotion freshly revived, it was all too easy to give way to the old, useless folly of 'if only' . . . If only she had kept to her original plan that fateful morning and gone shopping despite the rain she would have missed that telephone call with its frantic plea for help . . . and if only she hadn't let Stephan Esse delay her with that drink she didn't want she'd have escaped before that reporter and press photographer arrived on the scene. Instinct had made her rush away, and her very flight had caught their interest, convinced them she must be the mystery girl whose identity still intrigued the media, and the art world in particular. But what else could she have done? She had promised her silence, totally. How could she break that promise?

It was a long time before Karen fell into a troubled sleep. At least Nick kept his promise. She had left the lamp switched on beside the other bed so that he did not blunder in into darkness, and he came in quietly, making no sounds beyond the light movements as he shed clothing and went through into the adjoining bathroom. When he returned she thought he paused briefly as he passed the foot of her bed, but he did not speak and she gave no hint of being aware of his presence. A few moments later his light clicked out and there was stillness, broken only by the faint, regular rise and fall of his breathing.

The very closeness of him made it impossible for her to relax into sleep. How often in her dreams had she gone back to the times of happiness? Reliving them waking or sleeping, wishing, longing . . . and now fate had, in part, made the dream come true, but in a form nearer to nightmare. She had never imagined herself sharing a night again with Nick, not this way, with the heartache and the gall still an immeasurable rift between them. So near and yet so . . .

Hours later, it seemed, she drifted down into darkness, to awake to the touch of a hand on her shoulder. She sat up with a start.

It was daylight, the clear March sunlight streaming across the blue quilt, and Nick was sitting on the side of her bed, fully dressed. There was a cup of tea on the bedside table.

'Magda brought the tray a few minutes ago,' he said. 'But I told her not to wake you because you were very tired. I thought it was best that way.'

'Yes, I suppose so . . . thank you.' She sank back against the pillows and drew the coverings up over her bare shoulders. She felt at a disadvantage, defenceless almost, in the filmy, revealing folds of her nylon and lace nightdress, still disarranged by sleep. But his next words dispelled that fear instantly.

'You look dreadful,' he said bluntly.

Her hand trembled in the act of picking up the cup. She set

it down again unsteadily. 'I—I didn't sleep very well,' she defended.

'Were you crying in the night?'

She caught her breath. 'Crying?'

'Yes. Why?'

'I—I wasn't crying.' She picked up the cup and sipped at it carefully. 'You must have imagined it.'

'My imagination woke me up, then. I nearly got out of bed and came to you, in case you were ill, or anything. Then,' he hesitated, 'I thought my concern might not be exactly welcome.'

'Were you concerned?' She avoided his eyes.

'I'm not entirely without feeling, you know.'

Her mouth hardened. 'Well, don't run away with the notion that I was shedding tears on your behalf.'

He stood up and gave an ironical nod. 'Yes, it's a bit late for afterthoughts, Karen. Drink your tea before it goes cold,' he added in the same even tones. 'I'll see you at breakfast.'

The tears scalded and overflowed as he walked out of the door without a backward glance. If only she could armour herself against Nick's cruelties! She gulped down the tea and slid out of bed, aware of an unwillingness to face the day ahead. In the bathroom she recoiled with shock from the reflection that stared back from the mirror. No wonder Nick had been so caustic. Wan white face, eyes still tear-drenched and lost in dark-shadowed hollows, and her mouth scarcely less pale than her cheeks.

Somehow she fought the temptation to crawl back to bed and plead indisposition when the inevitable queries came. But the concern she would arouse from the rest of the household would be too embarrassing. She would feel such a fraud. And it would worry Elizabeth. Karen felt a quick rush of shame. How could she give in to such self-pity? And where was her sense of pride? Hadn't she convinced herself during the past two years that Nick was not worth breaking her heart over? For her conscience was clear. She had told him the truth; that she had never met Stephan Esse before that day, and was unlikely ever to meet him again. That she had never even met his famous artist friend and protégé, Vincent Kayne, so

tragically killed by a hit-and-run driver. But Nick had not believed her . . . And the one person who could corroborate her
statement could not, dared not speak . . .

She was thankful to find that Nick had finished breakfast
by the time she got downstairs and had driven into the
nearest town to buy some plants Elizabeth particularly
wanted for the garden. Karen breakfasted alone in the big
dining room, and had almost finished when Elizabeth came
in, looking extremely well and happy, and kissed her affec-
tionately.

'I'll join you for a second cup of coffee, I think, and I'm not
going to be pressured into having breakfast in bed after
today. There's far too much to be done!'

She launched into a list of things she had already decided
were in need of attention; the sitting room covers were
desperately shabby, the dining room curtains faded, a damp
patch threatening to shed its wallpaper near the door in the
hall, and a sash cord had broken at one side of her bedroom
window. 'I must have that repaired before Lisa arrives.'
Elizabeth smiled fondly. 'My daughter is so accident-prone
she'd be bound to get her hand caught in it sooner or later!'

Karen was silent. From snippets of family talk heard at one
time or another Lisa did seem unable to stay out of trouble
for long. She'd taken more than the average quota of tumbles
while riding, she'd broken her leg skiing, the new car given
to her by her father for her eighteenth birthday had its
elegance marred the very first time Lisa took the wheel, and
judging by the long procession of childhood predicaments
from which Nick had extricated her his advent into the
family when she was four years old must have added con-
siderably to Elizabeth's peace of mind. But then there always
seemed to be someone to hand to rescue Lisa from the results
of her foolhardiness, Karen thought with bitterness.

'So that must be the first job this morning,' Elizabeth was
saying.

'I beg your pardon,' Karen said contritely. 'I—I was daydreaming.'

'Thank heaven I'm not the only one who does that,' Elizabeth laughed. 'I was saying I must get my things moved out

this morning so that we can get the room prepared for Lisa and Cliff.'

'Room? Your room?' Karen stared.

'Yes, I'm moving into the smaller bedroom, next to yours.' Elizabeth lowered her voice. 'Nick probably forgot when he had my old room made up for me, but it's the bathroom problem. We can't expect Cliff and Lisa to share a bathroom with Magda and Timsy—to him they're servants. And Lisa won't like having to use the ghastly old bathroom on the second floor. On the other hand, I don't want Magda and Timsy to have to climb all those extra stairs. So the easiest way out is for Lisa and Cliff to have our old suite, you and Nick have the guest suite, Magda, Timsy and I will have the three small bedrooms and share the main bathroom. That way we needn't open out the top floor at all. Besides, I don't need a dressing room now, and——'

'But you mustn't!' Karen leaned forward to interrupt, having listened to this allotment of rooms in a house of which she did not know the layout and experienced the dawn of dismay. 'I didn't realise . . . Why can't Lisa and her husband have our room? I don't mind sharing the communal bathroom, and I'm sure Nick won't want you to to move out of the room you've always had. No, Elizabeth, we'll move to make things more convenient.'

Elizabeth shook her head. 'No, my dear, I wouldn't dream of pushing you and Nick into a room without even a washbasin, and poor Nick having to queue up with three women for the other bathroom.'

'I think Nick will have objections to your plan,' Karen protested.

'No,' Elizabeth gave a determined smile, 'I think Nick will see that my idea is the most sensible. He——'

At that moment there was a prolonged jangle from the front door bell, an excited exchange of voices, and then the sensation of an invasion in the dining room. Timsy had arrived.

Timsy belied her name, which to Karen had suggested someone small, fragile and Pucklike. Timsy was none of these things. The woman who was caught in a joyous embrance of reunion with Elizabeth was large and solid and noisy. Her hair was white and straight and cut short, her cheeks ruddy from a lifetime of no make-up to counter the effects of the north-country winds, and her portly form upholstered in an uncompromisingly plain tailored suit of navy serge and a heavy tweed coat. Surely no child throughout Timsy's reign with the Radcliffe clan had ever defied that booming voice and commanding gesture, Karen thought as Elizabeth drew her forward to make the introduction.

But Timsy's unfaded blue eyes were kind, her smile warm and friendly, and her handshake not quite the crush of a millstone that Karen was prepared for. Magda went to make a pot of tea, Elizabeth and Timsy adjourned to the sitting room, and Karen quietly excused herself. Somehow, she didn't think that Elizabeth would get much done during the next hour or so, until reminiscences were exhausted. But at least she could try to forestall an upheaval and inconvenience she felt Elizabeth should certainly be spared. This was one point on which she and Nick would be in perfect agreement, she decided as she made her way upstairs.

Their room was still as she had left it before going down to breakfast, and no one came to disturb her as she set to work. An hour later she had returned all her small possessions, as well as Nick's, to her suitcase, taken her clothes out of the wardrobe and laid them across the armchair ready to carry to another room, and she was stripping the beds when Nick walked in unheard.

'*What the hell are you doing?*'

'Nick!' She spun round with shock.

He advanced with a couple of quick strides and seized her shoulders. 'What's the meaning of this? Don't tell me you're going back on your word! You——'

He was shaking her, deaf to her cry of alarm. She thrust her hands against his chest. 'Nick! Listen! I'm not going—let me explain!'

His grip slackened by only a fraction, and his eyes still blazed. 'Then why are you packing? Karen, I thought we'd talked this out! Are you trying to ruin everything?'

Suddenly she went limp. 'When you've finished ranting I'll tell you.'

The weariness in her voice got through to him, and the taut muscles of his jaw relaxed. He stared down at her, his own shock still betrayed by the whiteness round his mouth. 'I don't understand, Karen. Why this?' his glance slid to the disarray of the room.

She explained, and saw the anger and tension ease out of him, to be replaced by a different kind of annoyance. His grip slid from her shoulders. 'So that's it!'

'I feel that Elizabeth is the last member of the household who should be disturbed just as we've got her here.' Karen turned away, rubbing the tenderness left by Nick's unmerciful hands. 'I felt sure you would agree.'

'I most certainly do. Although I can see her point,' he said slowly. After a moment he added, 'But don't you mind?'

'Sacrificing the luxury of a private bathroom? Not at all. Until we married I'd never known it,' she returned flatly, 'so I'm not going to miss it.' She picked up a pillowcase and folded it, remembering the gaunt old bathroom in her girlhood home. It had been converted from a bedroom about half a century before her parents bought the property and there had never been enough money to improve it, let alone install another one. It had been so terribly cold that bathing was perforce a purely functional affair, sybaritic extras like heated towels, delicious warmth and endless hot water a dream while the old geyser clanked and gurgled and allowed one exactly three inches before giving way to ice . . .

Nick was frowning. 'The trouble is that Dellersbeck hasn't been fully modernised, not by today's standards. Come on, we'd better see what there is to offer!' He inclined his head as he spoke, then glanced back at her. 'But I'm forgetting—you haven't seen the rest of the house, have you?'

'No, not yet.' Karen stacked the sheets and blankets into a neat pile on one of the beds and then moved to the doorway where Nick waited with a hint of impatience.

There were six bedrooms on the first floor of the house, and as Nick showed her round Karen began to realise why Elizabeth was concerned. The two principal bedrooms overlooking the front of the house had once had dressing rooms attached, which had since been converted into luxurious bathrooms en suite, but the other two double bedrooms were high and stark and musty, betraying every sign of disuse.

'They've never progressed past the washstand stage,' he said flatly. 'Just look at that wallpaper!'

'It was probably very attractive when it was first hung,' Karen said politely, eyeing the festoons of Victoriana that were now sadly faded. 'A lot of people are trying to reproduce just that today.'

'You can keep the trendy fashions for me.' Nick cast a disparaging glance at the heavy carved mahogany bedroom suite. 'This is the twentieth century. One should live in it accordingly. You can't go back.'

'No,' she said sadly, painfully aware that the flat statement was a summing up of Nick's philosophy in more ways than one. At least she had no illusions about that. She drifted over to the window and stared out at the unbroken vista of green countryside stretching to the horizon. 'It's a beautiful view,' she said almost to herself.

'Yes, better than from the front. Let's see if we can let some air in.'

Nick reached across her to the window fastening, and she moved aside, suddenly conscious of the man beneath the grey suit and the green striped shirt. The window gave to his strength, with a shower of dust and paint particles that swept in with the gust of wind. A sharp pain stung Karen's right eye and she turned away with an exclamation of distress.

'What's the matter?' he gave her a sharp look.

'Nothing—just something in my eye.'

His hand caught her shoulder. 'Let me see.'

Almost unwillingly she obeyed, steeling herself against the moment of intimacy as he put one hand under her chin to tip up her face and peer down into her eyes.

He saw the reddening, streaming right eye and pulled the lids apart with firm fingers. 'I can see it—keep still.' There was a moment of sharp agony as he tried to remove the black grain with a corner of his handkerchief, succeeding at the second attempt.

'Better?'

'Yes—I think so.'

His breath was soft against her cheek, his fingers still a cradle round her chin, and the warm hardness of his thigh still a pressure against her own. She took the handkerchief to mop the moisture from the watering eye and took a deep breath prior to turning away. But he kept a light grasp on her arm, persuading her to look up at him.

'Karo, I'm sorry I blew up at you, before.'

Surprise parted her lips. 'Oh, it doesn't matter.'

'Perhaps not, but . . .' he sighed, the line of his mouth softening for a moment, 'I realise that all this isn't any easier for you than for me. To be honest, I was never sure if you would agree to—to come here with me.'

'You didn't give me much choice,' she said quietly.

'No, I'll admit that. But you haven't known Elizabeth for very long, and you can't know just how much she means to me. If you did I think you would understand.'

Karen looked down, to hide the traitor weakness and the unbearable longing ever ready to betray itself. She did know, and she did understand since Elizabeth's confidences, but none of it could make any difference to her relationship with Nick. It was better to remember only the true motive for Nick's seeking her out, to steel herself against the dangerous knowledge of Nick's mouth, his arms, the whole essence of him the merest ace away, while every instinct of her woman- hood clamoured with temptation. She had only to yield, to look at him in that certain way . . .

But to give way to the treachery of moments like this could only lead to more disillusion, more heartache.

For Nick would take her, the sudden glimpse of naked hunger in his eyes told her that, and her own need would sweep away the cold dictate of pride like a slender sapling before the storm, but afterwards, when the ecstasy had ebbed and their bodies lay quiescent, Nick would remember . . . He would turn from her, despising himself and hating her . . .

A shudder ran through her limbs and she eluded his hands,

to stand by the window with her back to him, willing her own weakness to subside. She swallowed hard and said in a low voice: 'I think I do understand, and—and thank you, for apologising to me.'

Close by her shoulder, he said slowly, 'When I came in, and saw the cases, and—and everything all over the place, I thought . . .'

'Yes, well, don't worry.' She kept her gaze steadily in front of her. 'I would not go back on my word in that way, without warning.' He was still too close for peace of mind and she turned quickly, hurrying from the room. 'But show me the rest of the house. What's up there?'

'The old schoolroom, the traditional nursery—and a row of miserable little attics that were the abodes of the skivvies in the bad old days.' Nick paused, his hand resting on the time-worn newel post at the foot of the stairs to the second floor. 'Want to go up?'

'Yes—in a moment.' She looked along the big landing. 'Which was your room?'

'Oh . . .' his foot stepped down from the lower stair, 'this one. I thought Timsy could have it—if Elizabeth doesn't have other ideas.'

Karen walked through the door he had opened and looked round the long, narrow room which still held traces of the youthful Nick whose domain it had been. As she might have guessed there were no frills. There was a divan with white-painted shelves and compartments behind it, a desk-cum-table with drawers and niches above and beneath stretching the full width of the end wall and linked to a wardrobe and more unit fittings which continued along the wall under the window, and brown and cream curtains of the same heavy material as the divan cover. The walls were lime green, and the carpet the colour of warm beech leaves.

'Did you build all this yourself?' she asked.

'Yes.' He reached up to rip down a couple of posters and grinned. 'I doubt if Timsy would approve of these.'

Karen was riffling through the heap of old singles on the desk, and as his movement distracted her she noticed a rather unusual carved plaque of wood set in the wall behind the divan. There was a little ledge at its base on which rested a small polished hammer that looked like rosewood. 'What's that?' she asked curiously.

'Oh . . .' Nick gave a somewhat unwilling shrug and his mouth curved one-sidedly. 'I fixed that up when I was about thirteen. Its mate is on the same spot on the other side of the wall—in Lisa's room.'

Karen stared, waiting for him to go on.

He reached over for the hammer and turned it over in his hands. 'I think it was an auctioneer's hammer originally—we found a couple of them up in one of the attics, years and years ago—I've no idea where they came from.'

'They're odd ornaments, surely?'

He nodded. 'Lisa used to get nightmares and wake up scared stiff—usually about three in the morning. Sometimes she used to cry . . . So I got this idea one day. I told her to rap three times, and I'd wake up and knock back, and she'd know everything was all right. Gradually we worked out little tattoos and next morning she'd say she'd guessed my tune and had I guessed hers.' Nick put the hammer back on the ledge. 'Kid stuff . . . but it helped when she was scared, and eventually she grew out of them. But she would never let me take the plaques down.'

Karen was silent, her mouth betraying a sadness. Then she forced lightness into her tone. 'Didn't this—tom-tom lark in the middle of the night disturb the rest of the household?'

'I don't think so. These rooms are at the back of the house and the walls are pretty solid. I think Elizabeth was so thankful that something calmed Lisa and gave her confidence that we could have marched a band round the house as long as it worked.' He paused, the expression in his eyes far away. 'I've never forgotten my first experience of Lisa's nightmares—they started when she was about seven. She'd dreamed she was trapped in a fire, and she wakened up screaming, and ran into her parents' room crying that she was on fire and still trying to beat the flames out of her nightdress. We had to sit by her bed for ages afterwards, after she'd had warm milk, until eventually she settled down.'

Nick turned and led the way to the room next door, once

Lisa's and now Magda's, and Karen followed silently. She had known the dreaded realm of nightmare, but never as badly as that recounted by Nick. She stood in the doorway of the spotlessly tidy room, and saw that there was no trace left now of the young Lisa—except the small polished panel on the wall with its beaded frame and ledge beneath.

'Anyway, if Timsy or Magda suffer from bad dreams they have the cure,' Nick remarked with a return of his old irony.

But Karen could not smile. She was experiencing a sudden rush of fantasy, of sleeping in that narrow bed, with Nick on the other side of the wall, tapping out their messages of appeal, comfort, and childish affection—or love ...

It gave an insight into tenderness buried deep in Nick's heart, despite the scars inflicted by life on his young nature. Try as she might, Karen could not repress the welling of bitterness.

Why did everything always come back to Lisa?

CHAPTER SEVEN

In one way it was fortunate for Karen that the day proved a busy one, leaving her little time to dwell on her own unhappy thoughts. The domestic help Nick had engaged failed to arrive, sending a message saying she was unable to come until the following Monday, so much of the work fell to Karen. However, Nick had none of the male scruples which dismissed any form of household tasks as below his dignity and he set to work with Karen to clean out the bedroom and rearrange the furniture more conveniently. Magda was already ensconced in Lisa's old room, and it did not take long to prepare the one next to it for Timsy, who after her tea and reminiscence session with Elizabeth had adjourned to the garden with her old friend and former employer.

Nick could see them from his vantage point at the window as he repaired a curtain track stiff from long disuse. He paused, balanced on top of the step-ladder, and frowned through the dusty glass. 'I hope she doesn't get chilled through out there,' he muttered, then gave a small exclamation. 'God! She's down on her knees now, weeding!'

Karen switched off the vacuum cleaner and went to look. Elizabeth was indeed getting down enthusiastically to tackle the new young weeds that reared among the lifeless-looking rose bushes in a circular bed at the far end of the lawn. Timsy stood by, examining the rose bushes and obviously offering advice to the kneeling Elizabeth.

Nick watched silently for a few moments, then looked down at Karen. 'Will you promise me something, Karo?'

'If I can,' she said quietly, still uncertain of this latest mood of truce.

'I know the last thing Elizabeth will thank me for is cosseting,' he said slowly, 'but I can't help worrying about her. Will you try to make sure that she takes care of herself and doesn't overdo things while I'm away?'

'Of course I will—you don't need to ask. But do you think it's wise? I mean, we don't want her to feel she's being continually protected,' Karen ventured. 'After all, she is the best judge of how she feels and how much she can take. I think you have to realise that, Nick, or risk undermining not only her confidence but her very great courage.'

Nick sighed. 'She's been talking to you, hasn't she?'

'Yes.'

'I thought so.' Nick descended the steps and shifted them abruptly. 'Well, I won't force you to break any confidences she may have made, but remember ... I'm relying on you, Karo.'

There was a note of warning in his tone, and the same warning was in his eyes next morning just before he left. He kissed Elizabeth, then turned to Karen.

She tensed, knowing he had to make the pretence of a loving farewell while Elizabeth stood there and Timsy loomed in the background. But as though he divined her thoughts he switched his briefcase into his other hand and grasped her arm, edging her nearer to the car.

'You won't forget my instructions,' he said in a lowered voice.

She nodded. 'Try not to worry.'

'I'll ring you tonight,' he said, 'they'll expect it—and they'll also expect this ...' He bent his head, drawing her close into the circle of his free arm, and kissed her on her mouth, hard and deep and without haste.

The self-defence of pride made her strive to immunise herself against the dangerous pressure of his body and the warm masculine fragrance of his skin. When he drew back she stared fixedly at the maroon and silver knot of his tie and repeated, 'Don't worry, we'll look after Elizabeth.'

He tossed his briefcase into the car. 'I'll be back Tuesday at the latest,' he added as he slid behind the wheel.

A moment later he was driving away, and Karen, her mouth warm and disturbed from his kiss, watched the car vanish down the drive while she gathered composure about her before she turned back towards the house.

She felt the emptiness within Dellersbeck the moment she

set foot indoors, and the strange sense of loneliness now that Nick had gone persisted the rest of that day. Karen tried to tell herself she could now relax, that several days of peace lay before her in which to accustom herself to these new surroundings and settle in without the goad of Nick's bitterness ever present in her flesh. But some perverse part of her wished he had not gone, at least not until Lisa had arrived and the first meeting in two years with her sister-in-law had taken place.

Karen tried to subdue the unease which possessed her as the hours drew nearer to late Friday afternoon. She told herself she had no cause to dread this reunion with Elizabeth's daughter; Lisa knew nothing of the rift in her adoptive brother's marriage, and even if she did there was little likelihood of her ever betraying the fact to her mother. Whatever faults Lisa might have, lack of love and respect for her mother was not one of them. She adored Elizabeth and the last thing she would wish would be to cause her hurt. And although Nick had not said so he might well have confided in Lisa and advised of the need for discretion.

So Karen tried to reassure herself, yet despite this her hands felt cold and her limbs shivery with suppressed tension when the big white Mercedes rolled up the drive shortly after six o'clock on Friday evening.

Lisa's husband was first out of the car.

Cliff was a tall, leanly built man with smooth silver-fair hair and a thin, sensitive face. He was walking round the front of the car as Lisa scrambled out, and he stood there, watching his wife as she poised for a moment, her arms opening wide in a gesture of extravagant joy that embraced the entire house and those who hurried out to welcome her home.

'Mummy—darling!' she cried. 'And *Timsy*! Oh, darlings!'

She was still as breathtakingly attractive as ever. Tall, lissom and slender in a fine wool scarlet suit and a snow-white polo-necked sweater, the latest cuff-top bootees in white buckskin, huge matching gauntlets, and a scarlet leather cap atop her short blonde hair, all worn with the grace and panache of a successful model.

Karen had scarcely repressed her initial start of surprise; at first glance she had hardly recognised Lisa. Not that Lisa had changed so much during the past two years. The oval features with the high wide cheekbones and the slightly pointed chin were as vivacious and elfin as ever, betraying no hint of her twenty-seven years, and the curving red mouth with the full, sensuous lower lip, the wide blue eyes with their bold, direct stare still held the hint of arrogance that dared all challenge, but there was still a startling change.

Up till two years ago Lisa's hair had been a dark, lustrous chestnut colour, almost the same tint as Karen's own, falling thick and straight to well below her slim shoulders. Now it was pale gold, cut short and beautifully shaped to her head, with smooth wisps feathering her brow and cheekbones, and it transformed her completely.

'Hullo—Karo darling! How wonderful to see you again!' Lisa ran forward, stretching out both hands and leaning forward to proffer an alabaster-smooth cheek for Karen to kiss. 'We were beginning to wonder if you'd got lost in the jungle or something, weren't we, darling?' she laughed over her shoulder towards her husband.

Thus appealed to, Clifford nodded and gave that thin smile of his. He was a reserved kind of man, almost austere in his manner, and Karen had always found it rather difficult to make trite conversation with him on the few occasions they had met. Although he would discuss at great length subjects which were of especial interest to him, one did not make small talk with Clifford. Now, returning his conventional phrases of greeting, Karen could not help wondering, not for the first time, what had drawn him and the volatile Lisa to one another. Chemistry, she supposed with a wry inward shrug, and dismissed the thought as they moved into the house.

Lisa exclaimed excitedly as she looked round the old hall, now mellow and warm in the cheerful glow from the fire, which was only lit on special occasions. She ran towards it, holding out her hands to the blaze, and cried, 'Oh, I'm so glad Percy is still here!'

'Percy' was a somewhat fearsome suit of armour that stood to the right of the great stone fireplace, his mailed fist raised threateningly, and his visored gaze directed towards the entrance.

'Do you remember the day I crawled inside to scare Nick, and the whole lot toppled over, and I couldn't get out?' Lisa giggled.

'Indeed we do,' Timsy chuckled with fond remembrance. 'Your poor father came running—he thought the house was collapsing.'

'And it took all four of us to disentangle you.' Elizabeth shook her head, happy with reminiscence. 'The scratches on the hall chest are still there to this day.'

'And Nick said it would have served me right if I'd had to stay a prisoner in armour for the rest of my life. Shades of the mistletoe bough!' Lisa bit her lip in a secretive little smile. 'Where is Nick, by the way?'

'He had to go back to London,' said Karen, when nobody else seemed disposed to answer.

'London! Until when?' Lisa looked at Karen as though it were her fault. 'How dare he be away when I've come home?'

'He thought you'd be here earlier in the week,' Elizabeth said placatingly. 'He'll be back Tuesday, didn't he say?' She glanced at Karen.

Karen nodded confirmation, and said hastily, 'Hadn't we better help Clifford with the luggage?'

'No—he's a big strong man. We haven't got such a lot, anyway,' Lisa said carelessly. 'Cliff's only going to be here weekends.'

Despite this assurance, Karen felt sceptical. She went to the glass-paned inner hall door and looked out, to see Clifford coming across the forecourt burdened with two large cases. By the opened boot of the car stood a further collection: a small scarlet soft-top, a large canvas tote bag with the word 'Karachi' stencilled in big black letters round it, a bulging Harrods' carrier, a Chinese straw basket, and what was obviously Lisa's fitted make-up case. Karen ran out and picked up a couple of items, to be halted by Clifford as she re-entered.

'It's awfully kind of you, but please leave them,' he told her firmly.

'But I'll have to show you your room, so I may as well carry something.' Karen began to lead the way upstairs.

'That's right.' Timsy had arrived on the scene. 'No sense in going up empty-handed.'

Clifford's mouth tightened. At the first landing he halted and leaned over the balustrade. 'Lisa, you'd better rescue the rest of your stuff. It looks like rain out there.'

The directive sounded affable enough, but Karen knew he was displeased. Apparently Lisa realised it too, for she left the fire and ran outside, to come hurrying up with the rest of her things. 'It isn't raining,' she said accusingly, dropping her burden. 'Where are we?'

'In here.' Karen gestured to the open door.

'Oh, goody!' Lisa danced into the beautiful bedroom Karen had given up. 'I've always wanted to sleep in here —it wasn't done up until after I left home, and then the place was let.'

'Well, darling, we had to make the old place look a bit more inviting to justify the phenomenal rent the agent suggested.' Elizabeth had followed them upstairs. She leaned against the wardrobe, her breathing visibly laboured, and smiled at her daughter. 'But it is rather attractive, isn't it?'

'Super—but I chose the colour scheme and the bathroom suite, remember?' Lisa, after a glance at herself in the mirror, was already moving doorwards again, obviously intent on a further nostalgic exploration of her old home. 'Look, Cliff,' she called, 'this was my teeny den. Goodness, I'd forgotten how teeny it is!'

Crowded in the doorway of the narrow room, they watched Lisa look out of the window and then turn, to exclaim, 'Oh, it's still here!'

She leaned across the bed and picked up the little gavel. 'Listen,' she began to rap on the panel, 'this is our secret code. Nick and I used to talk to each other through here in the middle of the night.'

She knelt on the bed, a strange, childlike secretiveness on

her enrapt face. 'Nick always did have wonderful ideas.'

'Aren't you getting a bit old for that nonsense, my pet?' Timsy asked fondly, smoothing the rumpled counterpane as Lisa stood up.

Lisa replaced the gavel on its ledge and for a fleeting moment her gaze crossed Karen's. 'There is some nonsense one is never too old for—but I doubt if Timsy quite appreciates that, do you, you old darling?' She hugged her old nanny briefly and whirled out of the room as quickly as she had entered. 'I suppose I'd better start unpacking.'

Timsy bustled away in the direction of the stairhead, announcing to no one in particular that she had better go and give Magda a hand with the dinner. Elizabeth called out to Lisa to let her know if there was anything she wanted and then excused herself before going into her own room to change before dinner. Clifford stood still for a moment, then turned away but not before Karen had glimpsed the expression in his eyes. She had seen it flash there as Lisa recaptured the memories of those childhood nights long ago, and the haunted expression was still there as he moved slowly towards the opposite room. An expression of despair, and dark, brooding suspicion . . .

*   *   *

For Karen it was an uneasy weekend.

On the surface it was a time of family reunion and a celebration of the return to Elizabeth's beloved Dellersbeck. Lisa sparkled happily enough, basking in the warm affection from her mother and Timsy, and Clifford gradually emerged from the somewhat chill restraint that had been so noticeable the night he arrived. Timsy, in a way that seemed perfectly natural, had imperceptibly taken charge, seeming always to be there at a moment when stress or responsibility threatened Elizabeth. This was a relief to Karen, which she duly reported to Nick when he telephoned again on the Saturday evening.

'Good,' he said. 'Everyone else okay?'

'Yes.' After a hesitation, she added, 'Lisa seemed very disappointed that you weren't here when she arrived.'

'Oh, I didn't have time to let her know,' he said casually. 'Is she around now?'

'No, she and Clifford have gone over to Longdale for a drink.'

'Lisa getting restless already?'

'I don't think so. She seems very happy to be home.'

'Good. We can close the report book,' he said on a note of finality. 'So long till Tuesday.'

And that was all. Karen put down the receiver. Her own feelings were of no consequence to Nick—and he didn't have to pretend over a telephone, she thought bitterly. But then it would be foolish to expect him to, wouldn't it?

On the Sunday morning the weather changed. Rain and wind blustered in battle for supremacy and both had the bitter sting of the north-east. Despite this, Elizabeth insisted on going to church, vowing that nothing, least of all the elements, was going to keep her away on her first Sunday back at Dellersbeck after so many years. No one had the heart to try to dissuade her, and so Clifford drove them over to St Stephen's, the fifteenth-century church of weather-pitted stone that guarded the head of the dale some three miles from Dellersbeck. Here Elizabeth and James had been married, Lisa had been christened, Nick had taken his first communion, and Lisa's wedding had been the event of the village's year. Now there were happy reunions and Elizabeth was showered with invitations from old friends and neighbours.

'We heard you were home—oh, my wife will be so disappointed she's missed you. She had to go to York on Friday to nurse a sick relative.' The vicar was almost overcome as he grasped Elizabeth's hands after the service. 'But you're not rushing back to London for a while, are you?' he asked earnestly.

'No—I'm too happy to be home again.' Elizabeth introduced Karen, invited the vicar to bring his wife to lunch, accepted an invitation to dinner with a Major Carson, who had a tall, scholarly-looking German called Herr Lindner in tow, and promised to go to a coffee morning in aid of the

N.S.P.C.C. before being persuaded to return to the car for the drive home.

'That German chappie seemed to take a liking to your mother, didn't he?' Clifford remarked later that afternoon, after Elizabeth had gone to lie down for an hour. 'His eyes lit up when Major Carson asked her to dinner.'

'Did they?' Lisa frowned. 'I don't think Mummy should have made all those arrangements. Somebody should have stopped her.'

'I fail to see how anyone could,' Clifford said mildly.

'Nick would, if he'd been there.'

Clifford flung aside his newspaper. 'Really, Lisa, how can one interfere with an adult's decisions? Besides, why shouldn't your mother entertain her friends and be entertained by them in turn? She isn't an invalid!'

'But she's going to be.' Lisa stared through the rain-streaked window, watching the sway of the shrubs outside and the daffodils striving to keep their golden heads high. 'Isn't that why she's here? Why we are all here?'

Clifford shook his head and sighed. Karen could find no answer, and the silence stretched morosely. Then Lisa put up her hand to trace long finger trails down the misted pane.

'Karen, do you think she's going to die?'

The question robbed Karen of breath. 'I—I don't know,' she said helplessly. 'I hope and pray not.'

'I didn't think so, not even when I heard what the doctors said.' Lisa's voice was dull and toneless. 'But now I'm afraid. I believe it now.'

'Oh, for God's sake ...' Clifford was shaken out of his calm. 'Must you be so morbid, Lisa?'

'But it's true.'

'You can't be sure!' Clifford sprang up and went to his wife, putting his hands on her shoulders and turning her to face him. 'Listen, Lisa. Nothing is true until it happens. And it hasn't happened. You have to remember that. It's all we can do.' His hands dropped from her shoulders. 'Would you like a drink?'

'No, thanks.'

'You, Karen?'

'No, thank you.'

'Well, I'm going to find one for myself.'

He strode from the room, leaving Lisa staring at the closing door like a stricken ghost. Karen felt a twinge of alarm at the sight of Lisa's wan face, and she rose from her fireside chair. 'Are you all right . . .?'

Lisa seemed to snap back from her haunted mood. 'Yes, I'm fine. Don't take any notice of me,' she said with a return to her more usual manner. 'I—I think I'll have that drink after all.'

With the words she was across the room and gone, leaving Karen with a sudden strange realisation. This was not the first time since her arrival that Lisa had made a hasty exit the moment she realised she was alone with Karen. In fact, Karen thought, Lisa seemed to be avoiding her, almost as though she were afraid . . .

Karen sank back into her chair and stared into the fire. Surely she was mistaken. Lisa couldn't be avoiding her deliberately. It must be coincidence. Surely Lisa did not imagine that after all this time Karen would . . . Abruptly she picked up the paper Clifford had left on the settee and shuffled its pages into manageable order. She was allowing the situation to get the better of her nerves and starting to imagine things.

But before another day had elapsed Karen was forced to conclude that she had not been indulging in idle fancies. Two more occasions had left her alone with Lisa, and each time Lisa had suddenly remembered something that needed her presence elsewhere. Lisa quite definitely was avoiding her.

Karen sighed and told herself to dismiss the fact from her thoughts. After all, from the first time of meeting Lisa she had been aware of a faint, invisible barrier which would always prevent them from being drawn sufficiently close to one another to become close friends. Lisa could be very sweet and sparkling when the occasion demanded, and she could be equally appealing when she wanted something, but there was little true warmth in her for another of her own sex. Lisa was strictly a man's girl. Men adored her, and she was Elizabeth's one completely blind spot. Elizabeth could see no wrong at all in her only child, and probably because of her inability to have any more children Lisa had become doubly precious. From Nick, Karen had learned that Lisa's birth had almost cost Elizabeth her life, and it was then that Elizabeth and James learned that the son they both longed for was never to be—until the day they took a small, miserable, unwanted boy into their hearts and home.

For the first time it occurred to Karen to wonder at the child Lisa's first reaction to the strange boy thrust suddenly into her world all those years ago. Had she resented him? Resented the intrusion which forced her to share the love and favours which had been hers alone? But whatever the wilful and capricious Lisa had thought of having an adopted older brother as a permanent feature in her life, she had soon come to accept him as yet another subject in her domain; one to offer her yet more spoiling and protection. And even after her marriage, shortly before that of Karen and Nick, Lisa invariably had some problem on which she needed Nick's advice or help, advice and help which it seemed even her husband could not supply. Looking back to those few brief months, Karen could recall several occasions when Lisa had breezed in, to 'steal back my brother for a little while' and she seemed to hang on his words and judgment as though he were infallible. Nick in his turn had always treated her with a warm indulgence and air of protectiveness, as though he had never been anything else than her real, true-born brother. And yet . . .

Was Lisa's feeling for Nick something deeper? A feeling whose truth she did not even recognise herself?

A shiver coursed down Karen's spine. But no, it was unthinkable. Desperately she tried to subdue the fantastic idea that in the heart of her Lisa loved Nick, not as a brother, but as a man.

But the wild thought refused to be dismissed. For was it so crazy? There was no close relationship of blood to prohibit such a love. And if it were so, it could explain much that had puzzled Karen in the aftermath of those bitter days two years ago . . .

And what of Nick himself? Had such a thought crossed his mind regarding Lisa's feeling for himself? Karen shivered again, yet some deep instinct told her that whatever Lisa might feel for Nick its ultimate answer did not echo in his heart. For he had undoubtedly loved Karen herself, passionately enough to make her his wife, even though that love had been so short-lived.

A log collapsed amid greying embers in the low-burning fire, spattering glowing fragments across the stone hearth and wrenching Karen back to the present. She sprang up and seized the fireside tongs, kneeling to transfer the smoking pieces back into the fire. Intent on the action, she failed to hear the door open, and she spun round sharply at the sound of Timsy's voice.

'Thank goodness there's someone still in the house. Have you any idea where I'll find some aspirins?'

'No—but I think I have some upstairs.' Karen looked up into Timsy's healthy-looking features and saw traces of alarm there. 'Have you got a headache, Timsy?'

'No, but I'm afraid Mrs Radcliffe is developing a severe chill.'

Karen's face paled. 'Oh, no! When did——?'

'Just now. I thought everyone was out—with Magda gone down to the village to see Jessie Collins and Lisa's husband taking her through to York to hire a car for her to use when he goes back tomorrow—she doesn't want to be stuck here without a car during the week if Master Nick is going to be often away as well. And it was so quiet I thought you had gone out as well. So as it was almost four I thought I'd go up and see if Mrs Radcliffe was ready for her afternoon tea.' Timsy paused and drew a sighing breath. 'I found her all flushed and feverish, and her voice almost gone. Do you know,' Timsy added grimly, 'I thought she sounded husky at breakfast, but she wouldn't have it, said she was fine.'

'She was rather quiet at lunch, too,' Karen said reflectively. 'I'll go and look for those aspirins right away. Shall I take them in to her?'

'No, bring them down to me—I'll be in the kitchen.'

Karen hurried upstairs and quickly hunted out the little glass bottle, thankful to see that there were still several tablets left. She returned downstairs and found Timsy rummaging in the vegetable racks.

'I want to make her a hot lemon drink—with aspirin it's the best thing for bringing down fever—but I can only find one fresh lemon, drat it!' Timsy heaved herself up stiffly. 'That won't go far.'

'Will I get lemons in the village?' Karen asked.

'May do. Would you slip down for me?'

'Of course.' Karen hesitated. 'Shouldn't we call the doctor?'

Timsy frowned. 'She'll be furious if we do. We'll give her a little while, see how she is by tonight. Oh, will you bring a packet of barley as well?'

Uneasily, Karen went to get her jacket and bag and set off down the long winding drive. Ten minutes later she entered the one shop the village possessed, which was post-office and general store combined and sold practically everything from paraffin and postcards to peas and pet-food. She bought the last four lemons in stock, the packet of barley, and added a bottle of Lucozade. When she got back to the house Timsy had brewed up the first hot lemon drink, and Karen accompanied the older woman up to Elizabeth's bedroom.

Already Timsy had persuaded her to undress and get into bed properly, where she was now partly propped up, with a pink lacy wool shawl round her shoulders. She managed a wry smile when she saw Karen, but her voice was indeed thin and husky, and her cheeks burning with two great circles of high colour.

'You got this standing talking outside church yesterday morning,' Timsy said sternly. 'That was a bitter cold wind, and freezing rain into the bargain.'

Elizabeth slipped tiredly against the pillows. 'I'll probably be all right in the morning.'

Watching her, Karen wasn't too sure of this. She touched the back of her hand to Elizabeth's hot, paper-dry forehead, and then circled the fragile wrist, checking the pulse rate against her watch.

'You do that very professionally,' Elizabeth whispered. 'I

didn't know you were a nurse, darling.'

'I'm not, but my mother was, and she taught me a little first-aid. I think you have a temperature, Elizabeth. Is your throat sore?'

'A bit,' Elizabeth admitted. 'It's probably a bug going round.'

'I'd like to have the doctor check you,' Karen hesitated, then added candidly, 'if only to forestall the wrath of Nick when he gets back tomorrow and finds out we haven't!'

Elizabeth gave in to this argument, as Karen had guessed she would, and the local doctor came to Dellersbeck shortly after six. He was an elderly man, according to Timsy the much-loved village practitioner for nearly thirty years, and he, arrived like an old friend, chatted up Elizabeth as he examined her, and then took Karen back with him to collect the prescription from his dispensary. As she turned to leave he shook his head at the unspoken plea in her eyes.

'I can't say, my dear. Her records have just come through.' He held the door open for Karen. 'These tablets will deal with the infection she has picked up, and I'll see her again tomorrow. But otherwise ... we can only take care of her as best we can. Goodnight, my dear.'

They were all subdued at the evening meal, and no one had much appetite for yet another of Magda's delicious menus. Elizabeth's gaiety during the previous few days had lulled them into a kind of false security; now that gaiety was suddenly dimmed, and the shadow of fear lay darkly over Dellersbeck.

Lisa, who had returned in high glee, driving a jaunty scarlet Saab, had been shaken when she heard the news.

'But she was all right this morning—she asked me to bring her some seeds and a length of chintz to recover the window seat cushion upstairs.' Lisa had dropped all her parcels just where she stood and gone running up to her mother's bedroom.

She spent the rest of the evening wandering up and downstairs between the sitting room and Elizabeth's room, until Clifford said impatiently: 'For goodness' sake, darling, either sit quietly beside your mother or stay down here and give her a chance to sleep. Your present behaviour is guaranteed to make any invalid ten times worse.'

Depressed and fretful, Lisa saw the truth of his words and was persuaded to join him and Karen and Magda in a game of cards. At ten o'clock the game broke up. Clifford, who was leaving the following morning and wanted to make a very early start, went upstairs to make preparations for this, and Magda departed to set a light supper tray in the hope that Elizabeth, who had eaten nothing since lunchtime, might be tempted to take a little food before settling down for the night. There seemed little that Karen could usefully do—too many people fussing in and out of the sick woman's room would only be disturbing—so Karen decided to have an early night herself.

The hours of that night seemed particularly long and dark, and she was thankful to awake from the last spasm of fitful sleep and see the paling oblong of grey taking shape at the window. It was not long after six when she heard the faint sounds of someone astir in the house, and then the distant spurts of a car engine kicking into life, and she guessed that Clifford had departed.

She lay for a little while longer, then got up, shivering because the room was chill, and went to the bathroom, her thoughts a mingling of concern for Elizabeth and the knowledge that Nick would be home today. About five, he had said on the phone.

Karen paused in the act of drying herself, her eyes encountering themselves in the misty mirror, watchful, wary, above the bunched fluffy folds of pink towel, yet betraying that sentient, secret response that the merest thought of him could evoke. Abruptly she turned from the mirror and took down her wrap; he would doubtless be furious because she had not informed him about Elizabeth last night. But Karen had deemed it better not to. It could serve no useful purpose, only worry him, and she hoped with all her heart that by the time he arrived Elizabeth might be over the worst.

As Karen emerged from the bathroom Magda was coming out of the room across the landing. Karen stopped, apprehensive. 'How is she?' she asked anxiously.

Magda held up two crossed fingers. 'She's had a fairly good night, and she thinks she could manage some toast and marmalade. But pop in and see for yourself.'

On a wave of relief Karen did not hesitate. She tapped on the door and opened it, saying, 'May I come in?' before she crossed to the bed and looked down at Elizabeth.

Surreptitiously she crossed her own fingers behind her back. Elizabeth did look slightly improved, not so feverish, and when she spoke her voice, although still husky, had a little more strength.

'You're up betimes, darling. All well?'

Karen nodded, then impulsively bent to kiss the older woman, to be waved away weakly by Elizabeth. 'Don't catch my horrible germs—I've just been telling Magda that it would be better if everyone gave me a wide berth until I'm rid of this beastly bug. Timsy will look after me—she never catches anything!'

Karen smiled. 'Is there anything I can do for you?'

'No, darling.' Elizabeth eased herself into a more comfortable position. 'I've just been washed and tended like a baby, and Magda's bringing me some breakfast. Now go and have yours, there's a good girl.'

The motherly tones brought a smile as well as a sudden tendency to a lump in the throat to Karen; it was so long since anyone had talked to her in quite that way, and it was unexpectedly touching. She murmured, 'All right, I will,' turning away as she spoke, and at that moment there was the swishing sound of a car outside. Elizabeth's head turned sharply.

'Is that Clifford? Hasn't he gone yet?'

'I thought he left a while back. Perhaps he forgot——' Karen moved to the window and gave a small cry. 'No, it isn't! It's——' The words dried up in her throat as she drew the net curtain aside and looked down at the car below. Not Clifford's big white Merc. A dark red, more familiar car. Nick's car!

The door opened and Nick got out, tall and immaculate in an Italian styled suit of honey and brown flecks. He glanced up at the house, slammed the car door shut, and began to walk across the forecourt. Then he stopped suddenly, just within Karen's line of sight. A girl ran from the house, a girl still in her scarlet housecoat, her silver-gilt hair ruffled in the morning breeze and her arms outstretched.

It was Lisa. And she ran straight into Nick's arms.

Karen's hand fluttered to her throat and she heard Elizabeth say, 'What is it . . .?'

'It—it's Nick. He's come back earlier . . .' Her voice sounded as though it did not belong to her, and her stomach contracted painfully as though she had been punched. She could see Lisa's face across Nick's shoulder, aglow with a wild light that transformed it, the rose lips close against his ear and the slender hands moving convulsively round the back of his head. And Nick's own hands closing round the slender body arched against his . . .

Karen felt as though the room were reeling about her and she caught at the edge of the dressing table to steady herself. The last veil had fallen from her eyes. She hadn't imagined it. That crazy, incredible suspicion was true.

Lisa was in love with Nick.

CHAPTER EIGHT

AFTERWARDS, Karen could not remember the transition from Elizabeth's room to her own. All she knew was the sick aching anger that drove out all other thought and feeling, and left her weak and trembling. All she could see was the image of those entwined figures, as though they were etched in fire within her vision. How could Lisa embrace Nick in so wanton a way, a way that made a mockery of all her former show of coy affection and admiration for her adoptive brother? Had she no scruples, no conscience?

Karen clenched her hands until the pain of her own nails digging into her flesh transcended her anger. No use telling herself that Lisa's exhibition out there was the outcome of sheer panic and worry over her mother's condition. Or that it expressed only relief to see Nick and know his strength was there to lean on should further crisis arise. No, it was more than that, she thought bitterly. Those fallible human emotions and the one glimpsed on Lisa's face were as far apart as the poles.

And what of Nick?

Karen sank on the edge of her bed. If Nick had remained unaware he must certainly know now. He——

'Karen!'

She gasped as the door flew open. Nick stood there, his face a dark mask of anger.

'So there you are! Why didn't you let me know?'

Karen sprang up. 'Let you know? How dare you burst in here and shout at me as though I were one of your minions? After——'

'I suppose you didn't consider it important enough,' he cut in, slinging his briefcase and jacket across the other bed, 'or couldn't you be bothered? If Lisa hadn't phoned me last night I——'

'So it was Lisa! I might have known!'

For the first time since he had stormed in he stopped and looked at her, as though aware of her as herself and not a receptacle for his anger. 'What do you mean? You might have known?'

'You shouldn't need to ask.' Karen's mouth set in a tight line. 'Cast your mind back five minutes for the answer.'

The bitter, unguarded words slipped out before she realised they were free. Nick, seizing a casual, chunky-knit jacket from the closet, stared at her. 'What the devil are you talking about?'

'I'm talking about Lisa! I'm talking about her sneaking off to the phone after we'd all discussed whether we should phone you and decided the occasion didn't warrant it.' Despite her efforts at a semblance of control, Karen's voice was rising. 'And I'm talking about Lisa flinging herself into your arms just now for the whole world to see! As if—as if——'

'My God! So that's it!' Nick took a step forward, his eyes darkening and his mouth twisting with contempt. 'You mean you saw—you thought——!' he drew a rasping breath and a harsh laugh escaped him. 'It's too incredible to believe!'

'Is it?'

'Why don't you say it?' he gritted. 'You're accusing me of being in love with Lisa.'

The force in him frightened Karen, but pride kept her there, facing him. 'I didn't say that.'

'But you're implying it!' He balled one fist as though he itched to strike her. 'My God! That's rich, coming from you of all people!'

Karen recoiled. The words lashed her, to excruciate as no blow could. She turned away, dreading that he should see the betraying tears, but with a quick stride he forestalled the move and seized her arm, wrenching her round till he could see her face. For a long moment he searched her anguished features, the mouth set so tightly it was colourless, the averted eyes that refused to meet his, the quivering pulse at the throat, and then he released her so abruptly she staggered.

'My God! You're jealous! Wild, crazy jealous!'

She pulled the edges of her wrap close with shaking

fingers. 'Of you? And Lisa? Never!' Suddenly she swung round wildly. 'Since Lisa has summoned you so urgently, hadn't you better go and see Elizabeth—and set your mind at rest?'

'Is she awake?' he asked raggedly.

It afforded ill satisfaction to Karen to see that Nick was as shaken as herself. She said coldly, 'You'll probably find her having her breakfast—we aren't neglecting her the moment you turn your back. We love Elizabeth too much for that.'

Nick made no reply, but she saw the grim compression of his mouth as he zipped up his jacket and she could not help adding: 'I was in her room when you arrived—and I doubt if it's helped her peace of mind to know that you've driven up through the night with your foot flat on the floor—because you have, haven't you?'

His shoulders moved. 'Does it worry you?'

'It does when it was all unnecessary.'

'Well, I'm here now.' He shouldered past her with a brusque movement, then stopped. 'Listen, for Elizabeth, nothing matters as far as I'm concerned. Elizabeth is the only person who ever believed in me, who gave me a chance. She took me into her home and treated me like her own. I can never repay her—the debt is too infinite. But if ever anyone harmed her, I'd kill them!'

The vehemence of him filled the room like an invisible force. He looked long and hard at Karen, then moved to the door. There he looked back and added: 'For Elizabeth I would give my life. Because, in every way except the physical birth, she gave me mine.'

The clash with Nick left Karen utterly exhausted. With dragging movements she selected an outfit and slowly dressed, little caring that the beige sweater she had chosen was not an ideal match to the sage green wool overdress. Her skin looked pale and her hair lustreless when she gave a perfunctory glance at her reflection, but for the moment she was past caring what she looked like, and when, with a purely reflex action, she picked up her lipstick she looked at the gilt tube and dropped it listlessly back on the dressing table. What did it matter? What did anything matter?

There was no sign of Lisa when she went down to breakfast, a fact for which she was thankful; the less she saw of Lisa in her present mood the better. She was halfway through a slice of toast that tasted like sawdust when Nick appeared. He announced to no one in particular that when the doctor had been he was going to snatch a couple of hours' sleep before lunch. He had set off at midnight the previous evening, and had not wanted to disturb the household at half-past three in the morning, so had parked in a layby just off the Dellersbeck road and slept till six.

Timsy and Magda commiserated on this uncomfortable session of rest and assured him that if he felt tired there was no reason why he shouldn't have his lunch in bed and get his sleep out. Karen remained silent; she certainly did not feel inclined to join in with any pandering to Nick's creature comforts. And his next announcement did little to restore her peace of mind. Nick had decided to delegate everything to Lester Kirby, who had worked closely with him for several years, and take three weeks' leave.

'I reckon I've earned it,' he said.

Karen stayed silent. To respond with the delight that such an announcement should have evoked from her was totally beyond her power at that moment. She could think only of three weeks with Nick present every minute of the day—and night! And yet she had longed for his return! But with their relationship at its present state of impasse the very thought was daunting. Bitter resentment, dangerously near to hate, welled again in Karen's heart. If only Lisa would leave them alone! Before Nick had left the previous week they had been groping with reasonable success towards a tacit understanding and acceptance of the situation. Now, with a single stroke, Lisa had demolished that frail beginning.

The miserable day dragged on, fraught with fear that the atmosphere between herself and Nick must be crying its presence to the world. But Elizabeth's illness and the domestic round proved a distraction, and when the time she most dreaded inevitably arrived, when she and Nick were alone together in the privacy of their room, he lapsed into a curt silence that was almost a relief to Karen.

Anything, she told herself flatly, was preferable to the bitter, painful recrimination which seemed to be all Nick had for her now. And then, working in its strange twisted way, fate supplied a not very pleasant diversion; the bug which had attacked Elizabeth invaded the rest of the household.

Magda and Lisa wakened next morning with all the wretched symptoms. The seemingly invulnerable Timsy managed to stave off the onslaught for another day and then was forced to admit defeat. Two days later even Nick himself succumbed.

The doctor was a frequent visitor that week, dispensing large supplies of medicaments and informing them that practically the entire village had fallen victim to the epidemic, which was scant comfort to the sufferers. He also stipulated that at least forty-eight hours in bed was essential or unpleasant respiratory complications were liable to result, instructions which did nothing to assuage Nick's disgust at being stricken.

Only Karen seemed immune, and with the nursing and the extra housework which fell to her she was so tired by the end of the first week that she would almost have welcomed the ominous advent of a sore throat. But at least she had no time to brood on her own worries, and for the moment neither had Nick.

Clifford rang on the Thursday to say he was unavoidably held up and couldn't come to Dellersbeck that weekend. This upset Lisa, and even the arrival next day of a huge be-ribboned floral offering failed to cheer her. Lisa fretted about her hair, her skin, her dulled eyes—all the blemishing effects of infection—and refused all attempts to persuade her to eat.

'She's so listless,' Elizabeth said worriedly. 'It's over a week now and she just isn't getting better. And I don't know what she's living on.'

Karen looked at the tray she had just brought down from Lisa's room. Lisa had scarcely touched any of the dainty breakfast Elizabeth herself had prepared, drinking only the fruit juice and eating about two bites of one small finger of toast. She had looked so wan and pathetic, her oval face almost lost in the big white pillow, that Karen's conscience had rebuked her guiltily. For Lisa was even refusing to let Nick come in and see her. Had she made a dreadful error of judgment? Karen asked herself. Had the joyous greeting she had witnessed been simply that—unhidden affection at seeing Nick again? For the first time it occurred to Karen to wonder if she had forgotten to take into account the fact that Lisa's former modelling career had lent her an extrovert gaiety, a spurious way of demonstrativeness that was more facile than sincere. Could it be that in truth Lisa's 'darling!' to Nick meant little more than the 'thanks, love,' of a friendly shop assistant?

'She's far too thin. All this nonsense of staying slim,' pronounced Timsy, who had refused to stay in bed any longer and was now pottering round the kitchen, attired in an uncompromisingly masculine dressing gown of warm grey plaid. 'She's given up all that modelling business now, so why doesn't she let us build her up with good nourishing food?' With a mutter of exasperation Timsy plonked flowers back into a vase of fresh water and bore it away.

Karen began to clear the tray and Elizabeth, with the obvious intention of helping with the dishes, took a tea towel from the rail. Karen sighed under her breath, wishing that Elizabeth would go and rest but knowing it was useless to protest. In the couple of days since Elizabeth had been allowed to get up she had been restless and deeply preoccupied. Now, Karen noticed with a sense of shock the ravages the infection had left in the older woman. Already slender to the point of fragility, Elizabeth looked as though she had lost more weight she could ill afford to lose. Her cheeks were hollow, her eyes sunk in great bluish-grey shadows, and her hands almost transparent. With a sudden impatient movement Karen drew out one of the stools from beneath the breakfast bar and insisted that Elizabeth sit down.

'You can dry dishes just as well sitting as standing,' she exclaimed.

But for once Elizabeth's even temper deserted her. 'Don't you start, Karen, please,' she said wearily. 'Nick and Timsy and Magda are as much as I can cope with. All this protection and—and fussing over me. I'm beginning to feel smothered!'

'I'm sorry.' Karen bit her lip, and decided it was better to say no more. There was an unhappy little silence, then Elizabeth sighed.

'No, it's my fault. I must seem dreadfully ungrateful, but . . .' she paused, then looked up at Karen with an almost pleading expression, 'I'm so worried about Lisa.'

'Well,' Karen hesitated, choosing her words with care, 'I know it's difficult not to be concerned, but try not to worry too much. I'm sure she'll start picking up very soon, and the doctor did warn that this 'flu bug leaves a depression.'

'No,' Elizabeth sighed impatiently, 'it's not that—I know my daughter too well. She always took longer to get over her childish ailments, James used to say she loved to have the entire household dancing attendance on her. But this is something else, something deeper. Lisa's not happy.'

Karen felt a cold finger of warning touch her heart. She said slowly, 'Why do you think that?'

'I don't know. It's merely instinct.' Elizabeth polished a glass with movements that were too thorough. 'I've sensed it for some time now. I'm afraid that all isn't well in her marriage.'

Karen rinsed the bowl out, not looking at Elizabeth. 'Have you talked to Lisa?'

'No. You see, she's stopped confiding in me.'

'Perhaps there isn't anything to confide.'

'I wish I could be sure of that.' Elizabeth stood up and stared out of the window. Then she swung round abruptly. 'Karen, don't you see any change in Lisa? After being away for two years?'

After a moment of reflection Karen replied with perfect truth, 'Not really, but then perhaps I don't know Lisa well enough to be able to judge. Have—have you talked it over with Nick?'

'Oh, yes. He says I'm imagining it all, that there's nothing wrong with Lisa. And that if anything did happen he'll take care of it, of all of us, if necessary. But don't you see?'

Elizabeth's voice broke. 'This is all part of the protection! I haven't to be worried! I haven't to be told! But no one seems to realise how awful that is. Not to know! Just to —just to worry and wonder—and——' A great shudder racked her, and with a little moan she buried her face in her hands.

Karen ran to her, cradling the thin, trembling shoulders and trying to find words of comfort. Neither she nor Elizabeth heard the steps outside and a deep voice asking briskly: 'Is there a bowl handy? I've brought some grapes for—What the devil . . .?'

Nick dropped a bulging carrier bag on the table and crossed the room with three strides. 'Mother Beth, what's the matter?' He almost thrust Karen aside, to take Elizabeth in his arms and cradle her head in one hand with unbelievable gentleness. Over the silvery hair he stared at Karen. 'What happened?'

'She's worried about Lisa,' Karen said bluntly.

For a moment he directed a look of such accusation at her she recoiled, then Elizabeth was pulling herself away and dabbing at her eyes. 'I'm all right, just leave me alone for a minute . . .'

'You're going to sit down and tell me all about it.' Nick shepherded her firmly towards the door. He looked back over his shoulder. 'Make her a cup of tea, Karo.'

'Yes, of course.' Her mind in a turmoil, Karen filled the kettle. Elizabeth's fear was now her own. Was there any foundation for the suspicion that all was not well with Lisa's marriage? Karen had never cared for making snap judgments, and she felt she did not know Clifford well enough to form an accurate opinion of his character. During the months with Nick she had met Clifford on perhaps half a dozen occasions, no more, and while she had never felt particularly drawn to him she had not experienced any actual dislike of him. He was always courteous, if rather restrained, and when he entertained he was a most attentive host. As far as she could remember he had always deferred to Lisa if a slight difference of opinion arose, and never attempted to make fun of her at such times as the more breezy types tended to in a similar situation. And certainly Lisa wanted for nothing, in the material line. But as for love ... It was impossible to know a man until you lived with him, Karen thought.

The kettle belched steam, and hastily she filled the teapot. She added two extra cups to the tray—Nick would probably join Elizabeth and herself—and when she carried the tray through to the sitting room she was relieved to see Elizabeth sitting by the fire and looking a great deal more composed. But there was a deep furrow between Nick's dark brows as he came to take the tray from her. He murmured something about being back in a moment, and when he had gone Elizabeth gave a tremulous smile.

'You must think us a wearisome family.'

'Of course I don't.' Karen poured out tea, milking and sugaring it the way Elizabeth liked it, and placed it on the small side table to Elizabeth's hand. She said no more, sensing that Elizabeth was not yet ready to resume normal family conversation, and a few minutes later Nick returned, bringing the carrier bag. He set it down on a chair and delved into it.

'I've taken the grapes up to Lisa—she seemed pleased,' he said casually, 'and perhaps this will cheer you up a bit.' He handed a large package to Elizabeth and stood back, waiting for her to open it.

'Oh, Nick! You extravagant darling—you do spoil me.' Elizabeth held the casket of luxury chocolates and admired its attractive packaging. Then she reached up to kiss him. 'But what about your wife? Doesn't she deserve a special treat, after the way she's looked after us?'

'Did you think I'd forgotten her?' One corner of Nick's mouth twisted a bit as he took another package out of the carrier and turned to Karen. But he did not immediately relinquish his grasp, so that she had to draw near to him, and his free hand cupped round the nape of her neck. His kiss was warm and deliberate, almost as though he sought to reassure Elizabeth that she need have no doubts on the score of Karen and himself, and Karen's traitor heart began to race. With shaky fingers she undid the gift-wrapping, one part of her weeping secretly for the charade it all was, yet another part of her excited and touched at the unexpected gift. But he wouldn't have bothered if it hadn't been for Lisa and his mother; how could he leave you out? a small bitter voice taunted secretly.

It was a smaller box, but of white wood embossed with gilt lettering, and it contained an extremely exclusive selection of liqueur chocolates.

'You see, I haven't forgotten your favourites,' he said softly and mockingly as she began to stammer thanks. But it seemed he was not yet satisfied. 'Well, don't *I* get anything for that?'

There was no escape.

Karen had to put her arms round his neck and pretend wifely delight, submitting to the sudden coercion of his arms clamping round her waist. Their hold defied her to evade the disturbing masculine pressure of his body, a pressure becoming rapidly more intimate. It was as though some satanic genie in him urged him to test his strength against the breaking strain of her resistance. His mouth found her throat, his hand cupped her breast, and she whispered frantically: '*Nick!* Elizabeth's watching . . . !'

'So what?' But he released her, with the added indignity of a slap on her bottom, and eyed her scarlet face with a mocking scrutiny that was beyond Elizabeth's line of sight. 'You ought to know by now, my sweet, that I always extract payment in full for my gifts!'

'Poor Karen, you've embarrassed her,' Elizabeth rebuked. 'Really, you are a ruffian, Nick.'

'It's that South American heat—my blood hasn't cooled yet. Now who's going to open those chocolates?' he asked unrepentantly.

'I am—and that reminds me . . . do tell me more about Brazil,' Elizabeth exclaimed. 'We've hardly talked about——'

The shrilling of the phone in the hall silenced her. She made to get up, but Nick was looking at Karen. 'You're nearest—will you take it, darling?'

He could say the word so easily, she thought as she went to do his bidding. It was at moments like that she could imagine that nothing had changed, that love still lay unspoken in every gesture and casual exchange. Then she remembered the way he had kissed her and anger darkened her eyes. He knew she dared not resist and he had blatantly taken advantage of that fact. So much for his promise to keep to their bargain, she thought bitterly as she picked up the receiver.

The call was for Elizabeth, from Major Carson's German friend, Herr Lindner. Elizabeth's eyes lit up with pleasure as she hurried out to take it, but not so Nick's. He frowned.

'I hope Elizabeth isn't going to get involved in too much socialising. She's not well enough,' he said grimly.

Suddenly Karen lost patience. 'Don't you think you should let Elizabeth judge that for herself?' she demanded in a low voice. 'Or do you want to make her a prisoner of ill-health?'. Without giving him time to reply she surrendered to rebellion and went to put on an anorak and sturdy shoes. For the moment she had had enough of Nick.

She set off down the drive without any clear objective ahead of her, uncaring that the air was damp and cold and that there was a hint of fog. She was well wrapped up, and after a moment or so of deliberation when she reached the gates she turned to her left and set off purposefully to tramp the three-mile riverside walk that led to Dellersbeck Falls.

In summer it was a favourite and picturesque walk along a path beneath arches of intertwined branches through which the sunlight made a dancing play of dapples, and the river glided alongside, making its own whispering music. But today the river was swollen and sullen in colour, the trees were gaunt and chilled from winter, and the sky was a grey, lowering curtain above.

Karen met no one, and after the first mile she was feeling chilled and more despondent than ever. But stubbornness kept her going until she heard the distant roar that told her she was approaching her destination. The path began to widen, and a twist in it brought the falls into sight. There was a small clearing, and an ancient timber seat with the inevitable litter bin behind it.

Karen sat down on the damp, decaying board and stared

morosely at the hurtling tongues of water and the churning, white-foamed eddies beneath. It was not a very big waterfall, perhaps some fifteen feet high, but it plummeted sheer down a forked chasm worn deep in the rock face by the centuries of its own erosion, and halfway down it divided into twin cataracts of spume, one either side of a rocky shelf on which waterlogged moss and a solitary spindly bush fought to keep a precarious foothold.

Within a few minutes of her arrival Karen felt the chill dampness penetrating her clothing, but something in the endless swirling movement and the relentless force of the cross currents at the base of the falls kept her sitting there, caught in the elemental fascination old as time. It suited her sombre mood to surrender to it, letting the loneliness enfold her and isolate her from the demands of the world. She wondered idly how many had sat there before her, dreaming away the hours, seeking solutions to problems, perhaps tempted by despair and the lure of that wild stretch of white water below ... How many words of love, how many promises had been whispered here, pledged ...?

'Still sulking? Or just brooding?'

Karen started violently with shock. She had sensed no other presence, and the ceaseless sounds of the torrent had blunted all other sounds that might have warned of Nick's approach. She pressed her knees together, sitting up very straight and staring ahead. 'Neither,' she said coldly.

Nick seated himself at her side. 'What brought you here?'

'Why did you follow me?' she countered.

'For reasons.'

It was not a very satisfactory answer, and she clasped her cold hands tightly, determined neither to give in to the increasing cold nor move until she was ready, whatever objections he might make. Let him freeze, and serve him right, she told herself angrily.

'Elizabeth saw you set off.' Nick's voice was emotionless. 'So I thought I'd better make a show of catching you up. But when I saw you take the left-hand path along the riverside I had no option but to continue after you.'

'What option?'

He appeared to ignore the scorn in her voice. 'That.' He gestured.

She looked at the thick tendrils of mist weaving among the trees on the opposite bank, and the blurring outline of the branches. The atmosphere was undoubtedly thickening, but certainly not to the extent of obscuring visibility.

'So you thought I might get lost in the fog. How touching!'

'You're being childish. The local people have a healthy respect for fog. You might do well to do the same.'

Her mouth twisted bitterly. 'It's a pity it isn't thick enough to lose *you* in it!'

Nick moved, and inwardly she flinched, prepared for the sudden unleashing of his anger. But he merely folded his arms and leaned back.

'I suppose you're still sulking over my indiscretion.'

'I'm past sulking—I'm just weary. It was unfair! And you know it.'

'Perhaps.' His shoulders moved. 'But I enjoyed it.'

'That was more than I did!'

'You're not me.'

'Oh, you're impossible!'

'I'm not. I'm just a man, with a man's normal reactions to his wife's body. You're still attractive. I see no point in denying it, whatever happens.'

How cruel could he be? Karen tried to control her shivering and failed. She twisted round to stare at his dark, mocking visage. 'Listen,' she cried, 'you don't need to resort to pawing me all over in front of Elizabeth to convince her that all is still well. It's disgusting!'

Cynicism curled his mouth. 'I wouldn't have thought you so prudish, my sweet. Stop wasting your breath, for God's sake!'

'That has nothing to do with it!' she flashed. 'Elizabeth was as embarrassed as I was.'

'In a way, I hope she was.'

'What?' Karen stared at him, wondering if she had heard aright. 'You mean you—you did all that deliberately?'

'Of course.'

'Why? For heaven's sake!'

'For reasons which should be obvious.'

'Well, you certainly made your point,' she snapped. 'Don't ever dare do that again.'

'It shouldn't be necessary.'

'I hope not! Or I shall be tempted to forget my part of the bargain.'

'It was never a bargain,' he said coldly. 'It was a promise. And don't you start forgetting that.'

'You're not giving me much chance to!'

Abruptly Nick got to his feet, with a brusque movement that somehow suggested he had wearied of the wrangle. He moved to the brink of the path, where the bank dropped steeply to the river, and thrust his hands deep into the pockets of his jacket. His profile was etched darkly against the clammy grey shapes of the woodland as he said:

'I reckon that we've at least set Elizabeth's mind at rest regarding one of her constant concerns.'

'Us?'

He nodded.

Karen stood up, tautening her shoulders against the chill. 'I wasn't aware that she had any concern over us.'

'Until this moment, as far as I know she hasn't. And I intend it to stay that way.'

Karen took a deep breath. 'Then I suggest you stop being so despotic about reminding me about promises. Elizabeth will never learn the truth from me, if that's what worries you so much.'

'I can't help worrying! Damn it all, Karen ...' he swung round to face her, 'don't you realise that Elizabeth's forebodings as far as Lisa is concerned are well founded in fact?'

Karen's lips parted. She drew back a little. 'You don't mean ...?'

'Yes. It's quite true about Lisa. Her marriage is hanging together by a thread.'

'But I always thought ..,' Karen bit her lip. 'I mean, I thought she and Clifford had——'

'You thought wrong, then. Oh, he's given her everything she ever wanted, materially—luxurious home, money, clothes, jewels, position. Lisa could be a countess in a castle one day, if . . .' Nick stopped and shrugged deeper into his jacket. 'In all those respects Lisa made the marriage she always swore she would. But it's not enough.'

Karen tried to stifle a shiver. 'But I thought Clifford loved her. Oh, I know he's reserved, and a bit——'

'A bit of a cold fish?' Nick laughed shortly. 'I always imagined he might give that impression to a woman. But don't make any mistake about it. Clifford is not the demonstrative type, but he's crazy about her all right. So crazy he rages with jealousy if another man so much as looks at her. But it isn't enough for Lisa.'

No, Karen thought bitterly, it wouldn't be. No one man would ever be enough for Lisa . . .

'Their marriage was fated from the morning she walked down the aisle,' Nick went on slowly. 'They're completely incompatible. I'm surprised it's lasted so long.'

'Then why did she marry him?' Karen asked sadly.

'Because Lisa made the same mistake so many girls have made.' Nick turned abruptly and began to walk back along the path. 'She thought that money and jewels and luxury and a man prepared to lavish them all on her were enough. Until she discovered too late that something was missing. She didn't love him enough.'

CHAPTER NINE

NICK spoke scarcely a word during the three-mile tramp back to the house, and for this Karen could feel only relief. There was little left for Nick and herself to say to each other, and she had reached the stage where silence conferred a bitter safety free of the infliction of yet further wounds. Now, Nick broke his curt reserve as he glanced up at the hazy outline of the house and observed: 'This could last for several days.'

The dour prediction proved accurate. The mist that was rolling down from the moors settled like a white pall over the dale and persisted for three days. Occasionally it would thin and allow faint patches of brightness to percolate, only to close in again and enfold Dellersbeck and its occupants in a ghostly isolation during which life seemed to mark time.

Clifford arrived at lunchtime on the Friday and reported brilliant sunshine all the way up to York, which was scant consolation, but at least his advent with news of the outside world seemed to jolt Lisa out of her apathy. He brought with him a collection of large glossy holiday brochures, suggesting she might like to start planning their summer vacation, and Lisa regained a measure of her old sparkle as she curled up on the rug in front of the fire with the enticing vistas of faraway pleasure places spread around her on the floor.

His casual brainwave proved something of a diversion for them all. No one felt very inclined to go out driving or wandering around in the fog, and so the thought of holidays was doubly attractive in the circumstances. By the Sunday evening Lisa and Clifford had decided on the Seychelles, Magda had made a note of a particular package to Italy, Elizabeth had looked long and wistfully at an exotic and extensive itinerary which included Bali, Thailand, and Japan, and Timsy announced that she would be going to her sister in Southend as usual.

Only Nick remained aloof from the promise held out by the ad-writer's blandishments.

'But aren't you having a holiday this year?' Lisa asked.

'I'm having one now.'

Elizabeth looked up. 'Darling, I wouldn't consider this a holiday. What about Karen?'

'Karen knows that I've no objection whatsoever to her taking a break without me if she wants to.'

Karen's face was not the only one to register surprise at this statement. But before she could frame a suitable reply both Lisa and Elizabeth spoke at the same time, then stopped and looked at one another. Elizabeth smiled at her daughter. 'Go on, darling—I'm sure you were going to say the same thing.'

Lisa gave a crooked smile. 'I don't think I was, Mummy. You were going to exclaim in horror at the idea of Karen taking a holiday without Nick. But I don't agree. I think husbands and wives should take separate holidays. After all, they're together all the rest of the year. Oh, I know Cliff thinks it's a positively outrageous idea,' she flashed the same little smile at him, 'but then he's solid establishment through and through. Doesn't anyone agree with me?'

'It depends on whom you take the holiday with,' Nick said dryly.

There was amusement at this, except from Clifford. He tossed his brochure on to the coffee table. 'Then the next step is spouse-swapping, I presume.'

'Oh, for heaven's sake, Cliff . . .' Lisa's mouth tightened, but she did not look at his displeased face. 'We're getting back to the old double standard again. I never said a word about going along with anybody else, but that's the immediate reaction I get. Nothing about all the so-called business trips men make. And we know all about what happens on those! As for you, Nick . . .' Lisa paused and turned her head to look directly at him, 'you've certainly changed your out-look.'

'In what way?' His mouth quirked at the corners. 'I wasn't aware that *I'd* said anything outrageous.'

'It isn't what you said, darling, it's the way you said it,' Lisa giggled.

Nick shrugged. 'A very feeble innuendo, I'm afraid. Nothing to make a fuss about.'

'Oh, I'm not making a fuss! Just surprised. I expected you to side heavily with the establishment.' Lisa glanced at Karen, a curious expression in her eyes. 'You're a lucky girl, Karo! My brother sounds as though he'd joined the permissive society. Holidays out of bond now! Make the most of it before he reverts to normal!'

'I've already reverted!' Nick rose smoothly and swiftly from his chair, raising one arm threateningly towards Lisa before he switched on the television. He stood there, tall and dominant, one hand in his pocket while he waited for the screen to flicker into life before he selected the channel with the news.

It made a diversion, but not before Karen was aware of glances turning towards her and of Nick's own gaze encountering hers briefly, almost warningly. It was filled with sardonic irony, and a challenge she dared not accept.

Suddenly she felt unutterably weary. If only she could escape! Escape the undercurrents increasingly present, and the hostility she sensed more and more emanating from Lisa, escape the fear of Elizabeth perceiving the truth. Most of all she longed to escape the nerve-racking tension of the nights she was forced to spend with Nick. All through each day the dread of evening's approach was never far from her consciousness. The thought of those dark hours with Nick, still her husband, but now the silent stranger in the other bed . . . And all the time the constant fear that at any moment, with an unguarded word or gesture, a spark would ignite to set off the whole explosive situation. How long could she maintain control? For how long would Nick contain his . . .?

Karen sighed; perhaps it was as well that she could not know the answers. Foreknowledge might transform a galling situation into one completely untenable.

The new week dawned and brought release from the tenuous, depressing mist. Suddenly, not long after Clifford drove complainingly into its murky white fastness, the veil began to thin. The outlines of woodland came into view again, patches of sunlight glinted, and the mist became disintegrating swirls. By lunchtime it had vanished and there was scarcely a cloud in the sky. The sun beamed cheerfully, and suddenly it was spring.

Herr Lindner called, to be entertained to tea by Elizabeth and shown the new rose bushes she had planted. Lisa set off in her Saab to visit friends in Harrogate, where she would stay the night, and Nick sorted out tools to repair a side gate that was coming adrift from its hinges and replace a broken pane in the greenhouse. Karen's aid was enlisted to pass tools and hold things steady, and she sent up a fervent prayer that this unexpected interlude of tranquillity would not prove too shortlived; she desperately needed this breathing space to regain her equanimity.

When the mild fine weather gave every indication of settling down for a spell Nick suggested that they go out for a day's drive somewhere after Lisa's return.

They set off early in the morning, bound first, by Elizabeth's request, for Rievaulx Abbey; Elizabeth, Lisa and Karen with Nick in his car, and Magda and Timsy following in Timsy's small car. The countryside was beautiful, the young freshness of tender green burgeoning into life, golden splashes of daffodils everywhere, and the first daisies peppering the verges with white freckles. The Helmsley road was busy, the temptation of the sun irresistible to other families, despite the fact it was mid-week, but it was too early in the season for tourists and to Karen it seemed almost an intrusion to invade the idyllic miniature village of little stone cottages, some with thatched roofs, which clung to the sides of the steep winding road down into the valley.

A child's swing hung motionless in a garden, awaiting its owner's return from school, the sun-dappled river flowed alongside the narrow road, and a brown hen wandered unconcernedly in the car park, indifferent to the invading cars and the magnificent remains of the great Cistercian abbey which dominated the scene.

The time-worn stone of nave and transept rose from the greensward and made an awe-inspiring silhouette against the sweep of the hills behind, an enduring testimony to the skill of the stone masons who laboured so many centuries before, with faith perhaps the greatest of their tools.

Karen was susceptible to atmosphere, and Lisa's laughter suddenly ringing out seemed misplaced. Karen turned round and saw Lisa was now with Nick, walking across the cloister. Magda was out of sight, and Elizabeth and Timsy had gone to examine the shrine in the west wall of the chapter house. Karen took a step forward, then stopped. Lisa had appeared to stumble. Her cry was quite sharp, and Nick's arm shot out to catch her and steady her. Lisa laughed again, hanging on to Nick while she stood on one foot and rubbed at her other ankle. As they moved on Lisa kept within his arm, her head almost touching his shoulder, and he made no move to extricate himself.

Karen looked away and deliberately moved in the opposite direction. The sun still shone and the sky retained its unclouded blue, but she shivered. All pleasure in the day had gone. She stared blindly ahead, trying to tell herself she was foolish to read anything other than normal courtesy into the small incident. Nick had made the automatic reaction anyone would expect, and even if her suspicions about Lisa's real feelings had any foundation what difference did it make? *Your marriage is over!* Karen told herself fiercely. What does it matter who the woman might be who eventually takes Nick's heart? Karen closed her eyes, as though by the small action she could shut out all the pain and disillusion. But the pain was all inside her, nothing could assuage it—except the one succour that was denied. Abruptly Karen surrendered to the sick ache of bitterness and began to retrace her steps back to the car.

Nick took them all to lunch in Helmsley, and during the meal Karen found her attention persisting in returning to Lisa. There was something different about her, a subtle change that Karen could not define. Outwardly, Lisa wore her usual brittle gaiety, but it did not reach her eyes. They seemed to betray some restless inner fantasy wherein the real Lisa had taken wing. For a wild moment Karen thought she read a desperate worry in those remote blue eyes, then they surprised her own speculative gaze. Lisa's brows went up, almost with defiant challenge, and her glance slid away. Was it with guilt?

Karen bent her head. It was true; she might as well admit it, in the hope that by recognising a source of pain she might bring about an abreaction in herself and be freed from the torment of her own imagination. Freed of the envy of the power Lisa seemed to wield so effortlessly, drawing Nick's devotion, his protectiveness, his camaraderie—perhaps even his love. And yet she could destroy Lisa's power . . .

Aghast at her thoughts, Karen pressed her hands to her temples. Never, even in the darkest depths of misery, had that temptation ever presented itself. For in doing so she might destroy herself for ever . . .

'Are you all right, darling?'

Elizabeth's hand touched her arm, and the whispered concern brought instant shame. Karen swallowed hard, fighting down the sick feeling in the pit of her stomach, and forced a smile.

'Yes . . . just a slight headache. I—I'm all right.'

The others stopped talking, their attention concentrating on Karen, and she felt colour stain her cheeks. She stared down at her plate, knowing she could not eat any more of the rich dessert but picking up her spoon to make the pretence.

Magda leaned over. 'I've some aspirins with me. Would you like a couple?'

Karen nodded, realising it would be easier to accept the offer than make a protest which would only prolong her embarrassment.

'Would you rather we went home, darling?' Elizabeth asked, still concerned, and Karen shook her head with distress.

'No—it'll spoil your day. I'm all right, honestly.'

Hastily she swallowed the two tablets Magda handed over and gulped down some water, wanting only to allay the doubt that still lingered in Elizabeth's expression. She forced a smile and looked up, straight into Nick's eyes.

His gaze was direct and all-seeing, as though he penetrated

right through the shell of her pretence, and it was with great difficulty that she met those probing eyes. But he merely said, 'Are you sure you're okay, Karo?'

She nodded mutely, and, apparently satisfied, he gave the order for coffee. The awkwardness closed over and Karen gave an inward sigh of relief. She must learn to conceal her emotions in future, she thought grimly.

They did not linger very long over their coffee. Nick had planned a leisurely route over the moors, taking in Lastingham and Rosedale and then wending through the lovely stretch of countryside along the Esk Valley to the picturesque old town of Whitby at the mouth of the river.

It was nearing four when they reached Whitby. They had tea and thickly buttered scones in a little café by the harbourside, and then set off to explore the historic old port. It was fresh ground to Karen and she regained some of her composure in the fascination of exploring the narrow old streets that layered the steep hills on either side of the estuary, tier upon tier of tall grey stone houses with red-pantiled roofs, while above them all the ruins of the abbey was a stark crest against the skyline.

Elizabeth wanted to cross the bridge to the east side, where they wandered round the ancient market place and the quaint thoroughfares that clustered about the foot of the famous abbey steps. Here were the little shops that sold a wide diversity of merchandise—Whitby jet, freshly dressed crabs and oak-smoked kippers, oilskins and anoraks, home-made pies, antiques and curios, and of course the ubiquitous 'Presents from Whitby'; it was all there.

At last Nick glanced at his watch, then at Elizabeth as they reached the end of the lane of shops. 'Ready to turn back?'

'I think so—in a moment.' Elizabeth looked round, seeking her bearings. 'We passed a very nice shop a while ago. I'd like to buy a little memento for Karen while we're here.' She made off, the faithful Timsy in tow, and Nick glanced round with scarcely veiled impatience.

'Where's Lisa got to?'

'Into that boutique.' Magda nodded towards it. 'She's after

a white and orange jacket in the window. Norwegian knit—
it's gorgeous.'

Karen, waiting uncertainly, saw his mouth compress, as
though he were well aware of the time Lisa might take. He
started to speak, then stopped and abruptly seized Karen's
arm. He jerked her back from the edge of the kerb, heedless
of her small cry of surprise, and then she saw the big delivery
van coming unseen from behind. The horn sounded and the
vehicle mounted the pavement because the narrowness of the
road would not permit it otherwise to pass a car parked at
the far side.

The van edged along, its great bulk blotting out the light
and its side almost brushing Karen's skirt, and Nick's arm
closed round her, flattening her back against him. Dimly
she heard Magda muttering something about great big vans
like that shouldn't be allowed through tiny lanes, but it was
all a long way away. She could feel only the hard warm
pressure encompassing her and the rise and fall of his breathing against her back. Her own breath balled up in her chest
with the shock frisson that was surging through her body,
and the long moments of time seemed to stand still. Then
the brightness flowed back, and the pent-up breath ebbed
away as she recognised that frisson for what it was—sheer
intense pleasure of that sudden physical contact. Karen
swallowed hard, and then Nick's arm fell away and the
pressure was gone. He turned away, and she tried to get a
grip on her traitor senses and dispell the chill of bereftness.
She heard him say to Magda, 'Tell Lisa where we've gone,
will you?' and then felt the warmth of his hand thrust under
her elbow.

She took a blind, obedient step into the road, and Nick
said sharply, 'Just a minute!'

It was only a bicycle this time, but only Nick's curbing
grasp saved her. He stared down at her. 'What's the matter?
Are you all right?'

The safeguards of sanity and pride were reasserting themselves now and she said coldly, 'Of course I'm all right.'

'Well, look out, for heaven's sake. The street's no place
for daydreaming these days.'

'I wasn't daydreaming.'

'Well, whatever you were doing. You nearly walked into that cyclist.'

'I'm not a mind-reader!' she snapped.

'You don't have to be—just keep your wits about you in traffic.'

Suddenly her eyes were stinging with tears. Everything seemed to be going wrong this day. She shook her arm free of his hand and knew a wild urge to hit out at him. 'I didn't know if you were going to wait for Lisa or go after Elizabeth, and I didn't expect a great lorry trundling through on the——'

'Oh, forget it!'

'Well, don't talk to me as though I were a halfwit.'

'For God's sake! I never said you were!'

'And don't shout at me!' She broke into a run, but his long strides caught up with her almost immediately. He caught at her arm.

'I'm not—and keep your voice down,' he hissed grimly. 'If you must row, save it till we get back.'

'Oh, you're impossible,' she whispered fiercely.

'I could say exactly the same thing. What the devil's got into you today?'

'Need you ask?' she exclaimed bitterly, and slowed her steps. 'Look, there's Elizabeth.'

'Yes.' Nick slowed his pace, and added in an undertone that was iced with sarcasm, 'I'd take it as a favour if you'll endeavour to suffer my presence with reasonable civility until we get back to Dellersbeck—for her sake, if not mine.'

'Don't worry,' Karen returned, in a voice that matched ice for ice. 'I haven't forgotten. Unfortunately my acting talents are not as well developed as yours.'

She heard the sibilance of his indrawn breath and knew her shaft had struck home. But he remained silent, and she permitted his hand to continue to rest under her elbow, miserably aware that now there was no warm, unexpected delight in his touch, only the currents of animosity leaping and coursing along the channel of contact.

Elizabeth was standing outside the newly painted little

gift shop, whose windows had obviously just been lovingly dressed for the start of the holiday season. Colourful pottery, Continental and Eastern crafts and leather goods were attractively displayed, and on a miniature artist's easel stood a hand-lettered sign announcing that a full range of artists' materials and handicrafts was available inside. Karen gave an inward sigh, thankful that Elizabeth was in such rapt contemplation of the inviting array; a searching glance for her son and daughter-in-law might well have given her cause for disquiet. She turned now and saw them, and smiled.

'Isn't that Indian bag lovely?' Elizabeth pointed. 'Would you like it? Or shall we go inside and see everything?'

Karen hesitated, and Nick gave one of those wry half smiles that betrayed male resignation at the prospect of a lengthy feminine choosing session. He said, 'Yes, go on. I'll wait here for you.'

Unexpectedly Elizabeth shook her head. 'No, I want you to help choose something. Timsy will watch for the others.'

No presentiment came to warn Karen as she followed the determined Elizabeth into the shop. She thought only of the need to ensure that Elizabeth did not pick out an inordinately expensive gift, for the shop was undoubtedly a treasure store of extremely costly wares. The price of the Indian bag made Karen catch her breath when the salesgirl brought it forward, and she was thankful she had restrained any involuntary exclamations of delight at it or another that was similar. Painfully aware of Nick's silent, ironic presence in the background, Karen looked round secretly for something she could accept without a guilty conscience and at the same time know it would satisfy Elizabeth's affectionate and generous impulse. A sudden tragic flash of perception told her that Elizabeth had unconsciously wanted to buy keepsakes for herself and Nick, and her eyes misted over, so she scarcely made out the details of the delicately worked silver filigree trinket box Elizabeth had picked up. Then she saw Elizabeth pass on to a desk set of gold-tooled crimson leather and heard her exclaim, 'Perfect! I'll take that to start with.'

'Please . . .' Karen exclaimed desperately, 'just something tiny . . .'

Elizabeth smiled. 'I've just remembered—your third wedding anniversary will be here shortly. It is leather for the third, isn't it?'

Nick shook his head, and the salesgirl pulled a small chart out of a recess. She consulted it, and said with a smile, 'Yes, madam, you're quite right. The third is leather.'

The desk set was wrapped up, and still Elizabeth wandered round the shop. She selected a purse for Magda, another for Timsy, and the silver filigree box for Lisa, then turned to Karen. 'Now, darling, I do want you to have something *you* like, not something *I* like but which may not be at all to your taste.'

The salesgirl was hovering. It was plain that Elizabeth had made her day! She ventured, 'We have another studio upstairs, madam. Perhaps you may see something there . . .'

'Come on.' Once again Elizabeth led the way, up the wrought iron spiral staircase in the centre of the shop. At the top she said a little breathlessly, 'Oh, I am enjoying myself today.'

'Yes, you always did enjoy spending your money on your family,' Nick told her dryly. 'But please don't go too berserk!'

'I can't take it with me,' Elizabeth reminded him simply.

Nick was silenced. He stood back while his mother studied the shelves of glass and porcelain, and then homed to the centrepiece, a blue crystal bird.

They all looked at it, and there was little to say. It was delicate and exquisite, wingtips spreading, as though it were caught for all time on the verge of flight from its clear crystal bough. At last Elizabeth turned from it, a strange tenderness in her glance as she looked at Karen.

'There's no question now, is there? It's pure happiness, and I want very much to give it to you, my dear.'

She nodded to the salesgirl, and the blue bird was borne away to be packed. Nick moved towards the stairs, and then stopped as Lisa and Magda appeared below and began to wind their way up, Lisa saying excitedly, 'What gorgeous things! What have you bought, Mummy? Anything for me?'

'Greedy wench!' Nick hastily took the enormous carrier bag from her as it threatened to wreak havoc in a nearby display stand. 'You'll have to wait and see.'

Lisa pulled a face at him and began to explore. Indulgently, her mother and Nick followed her, and as the precious glass bird would probably take a little while to pack, in view of its fragility, Karen seized the opportunity to pick out a glass bell with a clear sweet chime that Elizabeth had admired. There was a bigger one, but Karen, hurriedly reckoning the money in her purse, knew with regret that she had barely sufficient to buy the small bell, and this was a token of love for Elizabeth that she wanted to buy with her own money, not Nick's. She took it to the salesgirl, who was hunting for a box large enough to contain the glass bird, and then turned to hear Lisa exclaim, 'Oh, what's through there?'

Karen, the bell safely in her bag, went towards the archway at the far end of the studio. Unsuspecting, she followed the others into the long picture gallery beyond, and then sheer horror jerked her out of her preoccupation. The picture-hung walls swam into a dreadful mist, all except one print in a white frame.

It seemed to grow, filling the whole gallery and staring accusingly at her. Karen could not move. She could only stand there in frozen horror, knowing it was too late to escape and not daring to look at Nick. From a long way away she heard Elizabeth's voice:

'I know there was an outcry from the purists, but I think it beautiful. Why shouldn't an artist translate Rodin into paint?'

'No!' Nick's voice was harsh. 'It's cheap and commercial. I——'

He stopped. Lisa had given a small choked moan. The next moment she crumpled up into a hunched posture and toppled to the floor.

CHAPTER TEN

THE salesgirl came running. Elizabeth gasped and dropped to her knees, and the two older women uttered cries of shock.

'Stand back! Get a chair, somebody,' Nick snapped, and the frightened salesgirl rushed to do his bidding. Nick knelt down and loosened the neck of Lisa's jacket, then the tight waistband of her skirt, and gathered her gently up into his arms. He carried her under the archway, to the main part of the shop, and set her carefully down on the chair the salesgirl had brought. He held Lisa close, dipping her head down, and gave a murmur of relief as she stirred and groaned.

'You're all right,' he whispered. 'Don't be scared, darling.'

'Here—I've got some smelling salts.' Magda held out the small bottle, and Nick uncapped it and held it to Lisa's nostrils. She groaned again and tried feebly to push the bottle away.

'What happened?' she asked weakly. 'Did I faint?'

'You certainly did.' He glanced up as the salesgirl came back with a glass of water. He urged Lisa to sip it, and after a few moments she drew a tremulous breath. 'Please—take me home, Nick. I—I feel'—she shivered visibly—'so sick and scared.'

'We'll get you home just as soon as you feel well enough to walk down there.' He inclined his head towards the stairs. 'Those damn spirals are too narrow, or I'd carry you down.'

Watched anxiously by the others, Lisa got unsteadily to her feet, her slender body leaning weakly against Nick, and let him support her carefully down the awkward descent. Karen gathered up the handbag and a parcel Lisa had dropped, and waited until Lisa was safely on the ground floor. Karen felt sick and shaken herself, and longed to escape from the shop which had seemed so full of attraction but now held nothing but ill-omen.

Downstairs, they found the owner of the business had arrived to close up for the night. She was a slim, pleasant-faced woman in her mid-fifties, and extremely concerned at what had happened. She wanted to make a cup of tea for them all, asked if they would like her to call a doctor, and finally, on learning that the party was some distance away from their cars, she insisted on driving Lisa and Nick and Elizabeth across town in her own car.

So Karen was left to make the return journey with Timsy and Magda. By the time they walked back to the Mini, and Timsy drove the forty-odd miles to Dellersbeck at a somewhat more sedate speed than Nick doubtless had, they were a full hour later in getting back home. Karen was silent most of the journey. The cold sick feeling refused to release its grip, and dread of meeting Nick slowed her steps when the moment could be postponed no longer. She walked into the hall, hung up her jacket, and went towards the wedge of light coming through the sitting-room doorway.

Nick was standing by the fire, his arm resting along the mantelpiece, and his dark, impassive features told her nothing of his inward mood. He said, in a voice that gave her no comfort, 'We were beginning to get worried about you.'

Karen let her glance slide away from his face. 'How is Lisa?'

'Asleep now, I think.' Elizabeth looked up tiredly from the fireside chair where she was slumped. 'She went straight to bed the moment we got in. Wouldn't have anything to eat or drink and flatly refused to hear of our calling in the doctor.' Elizabeth stirred restlessly. 'It's so worrying, the way she passed out so suddenly.'

Karen nodded. It was true. Lisa had gone out like a light, and she had looked dreadful when she came round from the faint. Deathly white, with her eyes like great dark pools in her face.

'And she'd seemed so bright today,' Elizabeth went on, 'as though she was getting over this bad spell she's been going through. I do wish she would let us arrange a thorough check-up for her.'

Nick straightened and sighed. 'You can't do any more

than suggest it. Lisa's an adult now, and you must realise it,' he added with a rueful smile to Elizabeth, 'even though I know it must be difficult for you to stand back and not interfere when your child grows up.'

'I suppose you're right.' Elizabeth flashed him a faint little smile that held irony. 'You've got all that to face, my dear.'

'Have we?'

He returned Elizabeth's glance, but Karen had caught the fractional hesitation before the 'we', and there was no mistaking the dark mockery in the gaze he directed to her above Elizabeth's head. His brows went up. 'Are you ready for the patter of tiny feet, darling?'

Karen felt a constriction tighten violently in her stomach. Suddenly she longed to strike him, to inflict on him a tiny portion of the pain he was able to inflict on her with those cruel words. Her hands clenched and her voice trembled as she forced herself to say evenly: 'At the present moment, no, and I doubt if you are either.'

Nick's mouth went into a thin line. But Elizabeth broke in, as though she sensed something of Karen's feeling, 'Are you so anxious to make me a grandmother, Nick?'

'Don't you like the idea?'

'Of course! I'd love to hold my first grandchild in my arms before ...' Elizabeth let the words trail away, and for a moment the room seemed cold and sombre. Then she sat up, forcing a smile. 'By the way, Nick, did you bring the things in?'

'No, they're still in the car. I'll go and get them.'

He went from the room and silence remained while he was gone. Karen felt the atmosphere was anything but right for the exchange of the gifts chosen so happily only a few hours ago, but she took the bell out of her bag and gave it to Elizabeth.

'Oh, my dear, what a lovely surprise!' Elizabeth's pleasure overflowed and she stood up to kiss Karen fondly. 'How fortunate I am to have a family who are so kind to me.'

It was difficult not to be kind to Elizabeth, thought Karen, swallowing the lump in her throat, and it was even more difficult to maintain a semblance of composure when Nick returned and without ceremony dumped the parcels and Lisa's carrier on the settee. Karen could sense his contempt burning into her as she unwrapped the exquisite glass creation, and she was near to tears of emotion and strain as she thanked Elizabeth.

'It's a myth, you know.'

Nick's voice at her shoulder made Karen start. She had not heard his noiseless steps across the carpet. He stood close to her, his breath stirring her hair, looking down at the blue bird she held safely in both hands. His mouth went down at the corners. 'Watch he doesn't fly away.'

'Nick, you cynical wretch!' Elizabeth rebuked. 'Ignore him when he teases you like this.'

Teases! If only she could! Karen was fully aware that every one of those words was calculated to hurt. She moved to the alcove at the side of the fireplace and placed the glass bird securely within its depths, beside several other of Elizabeth's treasured pieces. When she turned round Nick was standing by Elizabeth's chair, looking down at her with a slight frown.

'I think you should have an early night tonight—you're due for your check-up tomorrow, you know.'

Elizabeth's face closed. She sighed, then said resignedly, 'Another new specialist. Is it worth it?'

'Yes.' Nick's tone was flat. He hesitated, glancing at his watch, then said abruptly, 'Now I have to go out.'

'But why——'

He shook his head and bent to drop a kiss on Elizabeth's surprised, upturned face. 'Forgive me, Beth, I'm not in a very sociable mood as you've already noticed.' He straightened and looked directly at Karen. 'Don't wait up for me. I may be late.' A moment later he had gone.

Aware of surprised glances, Karen could only turn away. Suddenly she was too weary to pretend. If Nick wanted to take off into the night without any explanation other than that he did not feel sociable there was nothing she could do about it; she was the last person to whom he would be likely to defer. And secretly she could not pretend anything else than relief. Today she had had as much as she could take.

Magda prepared a light meal a little while later, but Elizabeth did not eat much and Karen had no appetite. Lisa was still asleep, her room in darkness, when Magda went up to see her, and shortly after nine Elizabeth gave in to persuasion and retired to bed with a sleeping tablet after exacting a promise that someone would make sure Lisa was all right and had something to eat before finally settling down for the night.

Karen had volunteered this, and mindful of her promise she went to prepare the tray promptly at ten o'clock. While she waited for the milk to heat Magda began setting out the breakfast things in readiness for the following morning. 'Will you be waiting up for Nick?' she asked suddenly as she sorted out cutlery. 'It's just that I don't like going off to bed until I know the place is properly locked up,' she added with a sharp glance at Karen.

'I—I'm going to have a bath and wash my hair as soon as I've done this.' Karen poured the milk into a beaker, avoiding the other woman's disconcerting gaze. 'He'll probably be back by the time I've finished. I should just go to bed, Magda, if you want to. It's been a tiring day.'

'You can say that again!' Magda shut the cutlery drawer with a bang. 'I wouldn't say no to an early night for a change. If you're sure it's all right . . .'

She hesitated, and at last, to Karen's relief, she said good-night and Karen was left alone in the stillness that instantly closed on the room.

A few moments later Karen put the tray down on the landing side table and tapped gently on Lisa's door. There was no reply, and Karen hesitated, then she thought she heard a sound like a soft moan and quickly she opened the door.

'Lisa . . .?'

'What is it?'

'Just Karen with a tiny supper. You must eat something.' Realising that she too was falling into the habit of cosseting Lisa, she picked up the tray and entered the room. In the dim light of the small bedside lamp there was a petulant flurry in the bed and a sulky, 'You can take it away again. I don't want anything.'

Karen looked down at the hunched shape under the clothes and the temptation to shrug and say 'Suit yourself', was strong. But she resisted it, and gently touched the top of the blonde head that showed against the lilac pillow. 'Lisa, what's the matter?'

'What's the matter?' Lisa flung the bedclothes free of her hands and stared up at Karen. 'Everything's the matter! I feel ghastly. I wish I were dead!'

'Oh, no!' Karen recoiled. 'It can't be as bad as that. Isn't there anything I can do? Shall I——?'

'There isn't anything anybody can do. Unless ...' Lisa twisted over and reached for the milk, slopping it over the beaker rim in her agitation. She gulped a mouthful, then cried, 'There isn't anything, I tell you. Just leave me alone, for God's sake!'

'But I can't.' Karen stifled dismay, knowing she must try to deal with this fresh crisis, if only to spare Elizabeth further worry. She got a tissue from the box on the dressing table and mopped up the splashes, then sat on the edge of the bed. 'You said unless ... Unless what, Lisa?'

Lisa gave a groaning sigh and sank back against the pillows. 'No, there's no way out. I might as well tell you— you'll find out soon enough. I'm pregnant.'

'Pregnant!' Karen's lips parted, and for a moment she experienced anti-climax. Her imagination had conjured up several disastrous possibilities that might account for the obvious distress affecting Lisa for some time, but this had not been one of them. 'But aren't you—glad?' she stammered.

'Glad! I'm shattered! A baby's the last thing I want,' Lisa said furiously.

'But your mother—and Cliff. They'll be thrilled.' Karen leaned forward. 'Oh, Lisa, it'll mean so much to your mother. Haven't you told her?'

'No.' Lisa's face was small and blanched. 'I—I wasn't sure, and I—I didn't want to believe it, but I'm sure now. I've missed twice.' Suddenly she crumpled and licked dry lips. 'Oh, Karen, I'm so scared. I've always been terrified of pain, and—and I'll lose my figure, and if it's a girl I'll have to go through it all again because Cliff wants a son. Because his older brother will never marry—he can't—and Cliff will inherit eventually and there'll have to be an heir. Oh, God! I wish I'd never married him!' She broke down, her shoulders jerking with the deep anguished sobs she could no longer control.

Karen forgot her own worries and reached out to draw Lisa into her arms. 'It'll be all right,' she murmured comfortingly, 'you're just scared now because it's the first time, and you've been ill with that 'flu bug, but it'll be all right ...' She rocked Lisa gently, trying to calm her, and shook her head when Lisa sobbed,

'But you don't know—you haven't been through it.'

'I know, but you mustn't upset yourself. For once you must think of the baby, and Elizabeth. Try to remember that this is the news she's longing to hear.' Karen eased herself free and looked beseechingly at Lisa. 'She loves you more than anyone in the world and this could give her something to hold on to, could even prolong her life.'

Lisa gave a shuddering sigh and groped for a tissue. 'I know. I've tried to tell myself that. Oh, Karen, I know I'm a selfish little beast—I always have been, but I can't help it.'

The admission surprised Karen, but she merely said quietly, 'Only saints are never selfish, and truly selfish people will never admit it.'

Lisa sniffed. 'Honestly, I do try, but I can't help it—people have always set me on a pedestal. Daddy idolised me, and I could never do wrong in Mummy's eyes. Everyone, my parents, Nick, Granny, and now Cliff, all loved me and protected me—but I couldn't live up to the Lisa they thought I was. Can't you understand? I'm not conventional in the way they are. I mean, I adore Mummy, but I just can't be like her, couldn't grow up the way she did, hidebound in the old outdated traditions—you know, classic twin-sets and pearls and a virgin until your wedding night. Then faithful unto one man until death do you part. All dewy-eyed over the little stranger in the cradle, and the word divorce something that had been censored out of the family dictionary.'

Lisa paused to draw an unsteady breath. 'Cliff's family are even worse. A divorce in the Earl's clan! It's unthinkable.'

Karen felt the chill of shock gripping her as the confidences poured out. Now that Lisa had started she seemed unable to stem the pent-up bitterness that must have been hidden deep in her heart for a long time. When at last she stopped Karen whispered: 'But does this mean that you and Cliff are going to part?'

Lisa's mouth twisted. 'How can we—now? With—this!'

'But I'm sure he loves you.'

'Loves me? He possesses me, tries to make me into what I'm not and never can be—the perfect wife first and a woman second,' Lisa said bitterly. 'The trouble is I haven't got the kind of courage I'd need to leave him and get my freedom, to live the kind of life *I* want and be *me*, not what my family think I ought to be. I can't destroy the illusions everybody has built up round me. Oh, God, I've tried, tried to be all the things Mummy and Daddy, and Nick, and Cliff wanted me to be . . .'

She sank back against the pillow, exhausted and wan but with a curious stillness, as though she had accepted at last the loss of her dreams. For long moments Karen was silent, then she sighed. 'I'm sorry, Lisa. I don't know what to say.'

'There isn't anything to say. I'm trapped. The way we all get trapped when we realise we have a conscience after all.'

The flat phrases struck an echoing knell in Karen's heart. It was true; Lisa, almost as much as herself, was caught in the web of circumstance, and at that moment she felt closer to her than ever before. She said quietly, 'It may not always seem as bad as this. When you've got used to the idea of the baby . . . promise that you'll tell your mother very soon.'

Lisa nodded, and almost automatically reached for one of the dainty chicken sandwiches Karen had made. She bit into it and murmured shakily, 'I feel better now I've told you.'

Karen nodded, and said hastily, 'Try to eat them all—I'll go and heat some more milk, this will be cold.' But Lisa put out her hand.

'Don't bother—it's all right.'

When Lisa had finished the milk and sandwiches Karen plumped up the pillows and straightened the rumpled bed-clothes, persuading Lisa to settle down for the night. But as she moved to pick up the tray Lisa said urgently, 'Karen ...'

'Yes?'

'There's just one thing. You won't tell anyone what I've told you?'

'Of course I won't.'

'Not even Nick—especially not Nick,' she pleaded.

'I promise.'

Lisa subsided at last and with a heavy heart Karen returned downstairs to wash the beaker and plate. The clock chimed eleven, sonorous and disturbing in the dark, silent house, and she quickened her drying movements on the utensils. Nick would be back any moment, and suddenly the dread she had been fighting all evening rushed back, driving out the dismaying implications of Lisa's confidences. She hung up the beaker and put the tea towel to dry, aware of the trembling that spread through her limbs. If only that gift shop had been closed ...

Karen gave a shuddering sigh. She would not wish ill on her worst enemy, but she would not have been human if she denied a heartfelt gratitude to Lisa. If Lisa had not fainted at that moment ...

Shivering still, although the house was not cold, Karen checked that the guard was in place before the dying fire in the sitting room and that all the doors except the main one were safely bolted before she went upstairs. Outside Lisa's door she paused, listening for a moment, but there was no sound and she moved on to her own room, her fingers hesitating before they closed round the door knob. Had Nick returned already, while she was with Lisa? But the big room was in darkness and chilled from a window in-advertently left open since the morning. That morning; how long ago it seemed.

Trying to close her mind to foreboding, Karen collected her shampoo and toilet things together, put her suit on a hanger, and made her way along to the bathroom. She felt too weary almost to be bothered, but the sea air had made her hair limp and so she went through the routine of lathering and rinsing, then sat on the edge of the bath, rough-towelling her long thick chestnut tresses and pinning them up into damp, sweet-smelling coils atop her head. As her fingers worked deftly she became increasingly aware of the silence in the big house. It pressed round her, forcing her to listen, and when the sound came she quivered and froze. But it came again, not the squeal of car tyres but the desperate scream of some small creature far out in the dark woodland. Some hapless little victim of a merciless predator, making its last hopeless struggle for life. Abruptly Karen turned on the bath taps, until the gush of running water blotted out those frantic, agonised cries.

So Lisa was going to have a baby. Karen tried to think of the joy this news would bring to Elizabeth, but she could think only of the promise Lisa had beseeched her to make. The things that Nick must never know . . . Abruptly Karen reached for her wrap and stared at the misted shape of herself in the bathroom mirror. The one last confidence, last secret, had been withheld; but what did it matter now?

Karen tightened the tie belt of her wrap and felt the tremors begin again. Her mouth tightened and she turned away from the mirror, knowing that this fear would not be exorcised until Nick had returned and the long hours of darkness gave way to a new dawn. With the deliberate movements of an automaton she made the bathroom tidy and then walked silently along the corridor. She opened the bedroom door and recoiled from the flood of light within.

'Nick . . .?' she whispered soundlessly.

The door creaked softly on its hinges, protestingly, and she took a hesitant step forward. Had she left the lights on? Then she saw the flat white oblong shape outlined against folds of rose nylon on the far bed, an alien shape that had not been there when she laid out her clean nightdress!

She stared at it with sick comprehension, her hand rushing to her throat, and Nick's voice said, 'Yes, it's for you. Why don't you look at it?'

She spun round. He stood in the open doorway, his dark hair untidy and his fists bunched in the pockets of his maroon towelling robe. He shouldered roughly past her and with a contemptuous flick of his hand flipped the white oblong over.

From its frame of cheap white plastic the reproduction stared up accusingly, the beautiful, damning picture that had changed her life. She shuddered and put her hands to her face, wanting to run, anywhere, to escape. But he was barring her way, his face implacable.

'Look at it!' he gritted.

'*No!*'

'Why not?' There was no mercy in his eyes. 'The world stares at it now. The world hangs it on its sitting room wall. The world can't be entirely wrong.'

Karen moaned softly. 'Please . . . not again! Not . . .'

'It's a bit late for shame.' The lines of bitterness were etched deeply round his mouth and accusation burned in his eyes. 'I think we should have it on *our* wall. Don't you agree?'

Karen strove to break free of the nightmare all this must surely be. She put out her hands imploringly. 'Nick, don't! I can't take any more!'

'And what about me? How do you think *I* feel? Seeing you there like that. Knowing all the time that you and Vince Kayne . . . For two years it's tortured me. Knowing, and wondering . . . How many times did you come from his bed to mine?'

She closed her eyes in agony, but he was insensate to all reason. He seized her by the shoulders, twisting her slender body till she faced him. 'Tell me!' he grated. 'Tell me the truth. If you can remember! And Stephan Esse! Was he there too? Out of the picture, but watching—and waiting. Did you sleep with him as well?'

Karen moved convulsively under his iron grip. 'I've already told you the truth! I was never Vince Kayne's lover. Never! Why won't you believe me? I only met Stephan Esse once in my life. I've never been unfaithful to you.'

'God! How can you persist with that blatant fabrication?' he stormed. 'How can you deny *that*?' He jerked his head towards the picture and his skin suffused with the depth of his anger. 'My God! Look at it! My own wife. Displaying her body for all the world to see. For every lecherous voyeur to gloat over! And yet you deny it? With two men who were noted for every vice in the book. You must think I'm a weak-minded fool!'

'No—yes! I do deny it!' she cried frantically. 'I can't explain it any more, but every word I say is true. The only man I've ever slept with is you. Oh, how can I make you believe me?' she whispered brokenly.

'Believe you!' He laughed in her face, and she caught the smell of spirit on his breath.

She turned her head away. 'You're drunk!' she said disgustedly.

'Am I?'

'Yes, you are!'

'Oh, no!' The twist of his mouth was a dreadful parody of a smile. 'I wish I were. Even you must admit I've never given you much cause for complaint in that respect.' Abruptly he jerked her against him. 'Maybe it's time I did.'

She recoiled from his mouth, moving her head frantically from side to side and fighting to free herself from his imprisoning grip. But her resistance acted like a goad, spurring him over the borderline of control. He caught her flailing hands in a way that brought a gasp of pain to her lips and pinned her helplessly.

'Oh no, you don't!' he grated, and the harsh undertone was infinitely more deadly than his previous blurting anger. 'I *have* been a fool—but I've come awake at last! Awake from a two-year nightmare in hell. The hell of wanting you and wondering what other man was having what should be mine. Mine!' he hissed. 'Yes, Karen, for two years I've dreamed of a moment like this.'

She stared at him mutely, her cheeks deathly white, and the harsh smile twisted his mouth again. 'Yes, Karen, it's time you paid.'

'Paid!' She moved convulsively, straining back against his arm. 'No, let me go—you're hurting me!'

'You deserve to be hurt! Oh, no—you're not going to cry your way out of my bed this time!'

His arms tightened mercilessly and his mouth curled with derision as he watched her teeth bite on her lower lip. 'You're not going to scream, are you, my dear faithless wife?' he whispered mockingly. 'You're not going to bring them running to find out the truth—unless you prefer an audience. I believe that was fashionable in the company you moved into,' he ground out bitterly.

Her eyes widened in horror. 'You're mad!' she whispered.

'Am I? I don't think so!'

She moaned softly, trying desperately to back away, and felt the edge of the bed cut into the backs of her knees. She stumbled, fighting him and her own lack of balance, and then the dark shape of him bore her down. She fell back, the material of her wrap dragging and straining round her, and then she felt the silk cord give way to his invading hands. The thin folds fell away, and the white glass ceiling light seemed to shine down like a spotlight.

For long moments his eyes ravished her nakedness, then a ragged groan escaped him and his mouth closed like fire on her breast.

Above his dark head Karen whispered desperately, 'No, Nick—not this way! Please—*not like this*——' and tried to move under his weight. But he was far beyond hearing, insensate to everything now except the force of desire and the drive of anger.

A thin red mist blurred Karen's vision, and the gall of heartbreak choked in her throat. He was too strong to fight, his limbs too forceful with determination, and desperately she tried to summon hate to numb her senses while he forced her body into submission. But hate would not come, only the agony of silent tears for a memory, for the memory of the sweet giving and taking of love that once he taught her; the love that was now a violation . . .

When at last he rolled off her and flung himself across the other bed she was too spent to move. She lay there, staring into infinity with grief-darkened eyes, and waited for the uncontrollable tremors to pass from her limbs. Only when the rise and fall of his breathing told her that he slept did she grope blindly to cover herself and stand for a moment like a trembling wraith, fearful of making a sound. But he did not stir, and she crept out to the bathroom, there to lave herself, as though she might wash away the pain of disillusion and the stirring fire of longing he had kindled in her traitorous flesh.

'Oh, God,' she whispered, when she lay taut and shivering between sheets that felt like ice. 'Make me stop wanting him. Make me stop loving him!'

CHAPTER ELEVEN

IT was near to dawn when exhaustion finally took its toll and Karen fell into a heavy sleep. She did not hear Magda's arrival with the morning cup of tea, nor the sounds of the household waking to another day, and it was not until the morning sun reached across the window, found a chink in the heavy curtains and sent its probing rays across her pillow that Karen stirred. She blinked, turning her head away in mute protest, and then jerked into wakefulness as everything flooded back.

She was alone. A cup of tea with a greyish film on its surface stood on her bedside cabinet and across the room the other bed was rumpled and empty. Karen grimaced and fought down a sense of nausea. She felt bruised and sore, her head ached, and her spirit felt beaten. The temptation to re-treat back into the warmth of her bed and seek oblivion was strong, but she forced herself into action; there was no escape that way.

For once she dressed and rough-combed her hair without her usual fastidious attention to grooming, until she glimpsed her wan reflection and shivered at the great dark shadows that bruised her eyes. God, she couldn't go down like that! She looked dreadful. With lacklustre movements she reached for the disguise of cosmetics, and then her hand stayed in mid-air as a tap sounded at the door.

Her stomach contracted, then relaxed. Did she really imagine that Nick would give her the courtesy of a warning knock? After . . . She looked at the door, wanting to ignore the summons without, then she shrugged and called wearily, 'Come in.'

It was Lisa. She looked almost as wan and dejected as Karen, and her thin hands clutching at the edges of her expensive chiffon négligé betrayed unease. She glanced be-hind her before she closed the door, and Karen stared at her.

'What's the matter—are you ill?'

Lisa shook her head and grimaced. 'No more than usual—I just threw up again. God, I wish I could . . .'

Karen took a step forward, alarm in her eyes. 'Lisa, you're not——'

'No, I'm not doing anything silly.' Lisa sank on the end of the bed and buried her face in her hands. 'I'm much too scared. Didn't you know, Karen? I'm one of those people who just goes on, hoping it'll turn out all right in the end.' She looked up and shook her head. 'It's not that—are you all right, Karen?'

Karen started. 'What do you mean?'

'Oh, I don't know.' Lisa got up and began to pace round the room. 'I—I heard you last night. And I wondered ... Was Nick devil-drunk or silly-drunk last night?'

'Of course not!' Karen tried to conceal her shock, and her face closed with a pride that was pitiful. 'You—you must have imagined whatever you—thought you heard.'

'I didn't,' Lisa said flatly. 'After you'd been in last night I lay for a while but but I couldn't go to sleep, so I got up and went downstairs. My stomach ached and I felt cold, so I thought I'd have some brandy and fill a hot-water bottle. Nick came in while I was down there. And I was scared.'

'You? Scared?' Karen folded her hands to still their trembling. 'Why?'

'Because I know Nick. I know that streak of violence in him.' Lisa stood at the window, her back to Karen. 'It always excited me. I used to try him, to see how far I could go before he cracked. But I always knew he would never hurt me—much. But you ...' Suddenly Lisa swung round. 'I was frightened last night, he was so quiet. But he was deadly underneath. He took the brandy glass from me and said, "Don't let me ever find you at this again, do you hear?" and he just stood there, until I backed away and left him. And then afterwards ... Karen, is everything all right?'

'Why shouldn't it be all right?' With difficulty Karen kept her voice steady. 'Yes, we had a bit of an argument last night. As you say, Nick has a streak of violence in him,' she added bitterly.

Lisa continued to stare at her, with something like fear in

her eyes. 'Are you sure? Because I——'

'Lisa, what's the point of this?' Karen's shoulders rose wearily. 'It's over.'

'Is it?' Lisa avoided her glance. 'I wish I was sure of that.'

'What do you mean?'

Lisa looked down at a trinket on the windowsill. She picked it up and weighed it in her hand. 'Karen, did something happen in South America?'

'Happen?'

'Because you came home, didn't you?'

'No, of course not!' Karen felt the recoil of shock. 'What are you talking about?'

'I saw you one morning, about a year ago.' Lisa replaced the trinket. 'You were going into Selfridges. I tried to catch up with you, but the place was so packed I couldn't.'

'You must have been mistaken.'

'No, I wasn't. You were wearing that red coat with the deep collar, and I called your name. You looked round, and then hurried into the store,' Lisa said flatly. 'Afterwards I tried to ring you, but those American people said you were out of the country. Then Mummy had a letter from you and Nick about a week later and it never said anything about you coming home. I nearly blurted out that I'd seen you, then something made me keep quiet. I—I didn't know what to do.'

Karen sank down on the dressing-table stool. Her mouth trembled and she fought for control. All the things she had often wished she could say to Lisa rushed round in her brain, but what was the use? It was all too late now. When she did not respond, Lisa came across the room and stood in front of her.

'Why?' asked Lisa. 'What happened?'

Karen looked up incredulously. 'For God's sake, Lisa! You mean you don't know?' Hysterical laughter welled up in her and she knew a sudden impulse to strike the helpless distressed innocence from Lisa's face. She mastered the impulse; the innocence was genuine enough. That was the ironic part of it. In flat tones she said: 'Yes, you might as well know. I never even went to South America with Nick.

But he insisted on the secrecy because he didn't want Elizabeth to know that we—that we were parted, and why we parted. We're only here together now because of—because of what the doctors said . . .' She let her voice tail off and shook her head hopelessly.

'Then this goes back to——?' Lisa's hand flew to her mouth. 'You mean . . .?'

'I mean it's all over. Our marriage is finished. Nick and I are through.' Karen picked up her lipstick and outlined her mouth with hard, uncaring strokes, as though with those flat statements she had brought the truth into the open at last and sounded the death knell of her own hopes and desire, her love and her happiness.

Through the mirror Lisa's shocked eyes searched Karen's face. 'Why—why didn't you tell me?' she asked.

'What was the point?' Karen met the scared gaze in the mirror. 'Could you—would you have helped?'

Lisa turned away. For a long moment she was silent, then she whispered, 'Was it—did Nick find out? Or did——'

'The picture in the paper.'

Lisa shuddered. 'You didn't tell him . . .?'

'No. I simply denied it. He wouldn't believe me.'

For a long moment Lisa was silent, then her shoulders slumped. 'Oh, God!' she exclaimed. 'What an unholy mess! What on earth are we going to do?'

'Nothing.' Karen stared unseeingly into the mirror. An unnatural calm had descended on her and she felt drained of all strength. She replaced the top on the lipstick and dropped it back on the glass tray. The sound seemed to shatter the silence, and Lisa gave a choked sob.

'Karen, I'm sorry,' she faltered. 'I wish there was something . . .'

Suddenly Karen could take no more. She stood up. 'It's too late for wishing. There's nothing anyone can do. Nick no longer loves or trusts me. And I—I don't think I could ever love Nick again.'

Uncaring now of Lisa standing helplessly in the room, she snatched up her jacket and bag, checking feverishly for money in her purse, and ran from the room. She hurried downstairs, pulling on her jacket as she went and praying she would encounter no one on her way. Let Nick make such explanations as he thought fit for her absence, she told herself bitterly.

A savoury drift of bacon came from the dining room as she passed, but it brought no enticement to Karen's appetite; breakfast was the last thing she wanted at the moment. All she wanted was to be alone for a while. Fortunately no one crossed her path, and she let herself out of the conservatory door and hurried along the side path, out of view of the dining room window. It was just after eight-thirty, the household was still at breakfast and Nick would doubtless be eyeing the clock as he prepared to drive Elizabeth to hospital for her appointment. In view of this it was unlikely that Karen would be missed for some time.

She had no set plan in mind as she walked into the village and boarded the nine a.m. bus, uncaring of its eventual destination. All she knew was an overwhelming need to get away from Dellersbeck and seek the anonymity of strange ground and strange faces where she had no need of pretence, until the acute edge of misery was blunted by time. She stared out of the bus window at the wide vista of verdant countryside as the bus wended its way through the little communities that dotted the long winding highway, and saw little of the passing scene. It was the same when she stepped down from the bus some fifty minutes later and stood uncertainly in the market square, her face pale and strained and the blankness of hurt clouding her eyes. She couldn't forget . . .

Karen wandered across the square, past the old town hall with its ancient clock tower, and into the High Street. A brash new supermarket reared incongruously between the pub and a row of worn grey cottages on one side, and across the narrow road a baker's, a chemist, a tiny shoe shop and a trendy fashion boutique rubbed shoulders more or less amicably. Karen stopped outside the display of cosmetics in the chemist's window, then moved on to the boutique, but there was no escape for her. Against the scarlets and pinks of tweed and jerseys, the flow of scarves and the glitter of gilt chains and beads looped artistically about branches of somewhat dried-looking staghorn coral she saw only Nick's face, the hate in his eyes, the harshness on his mouth, the bitterness and the anger and the scorn of him last night . . .

Karen closed her eyes, touching her forehead to the cold plate glass as she fought to repel the images, and a woman coming out of the boutique looked at her with concern. She stopped.

'Are you all right, dear?'

'Yes—thank you.' Karen forced a smile, but the woman did not look convinced.

'You look very pale—sure you're not going to faint or anything?'

Karen summoned another strained smile and shook her head. 'I'm always pale—but thank you.' She moved on, vaguely embarrassed yet touched by the woman's concern. She really must pull herself together if she looked as bad as that. With an effort she made her step more determined, trying to look as though she were perfectly in command of herself with a very definite destination ahead of her. But within a few minutes she had reached the end of the straggling High Street and the lost feeling closed around her again as she reached the crossroads. Listlessly she turned to the right, her steps slowing as they carried her towards the residential side of the town. Here were the gracious old stone detached residences built by the wealthy inhabitants of the last century, and further on the new bungalows with the picture windows encroaching out into the rural environment of farmland and woods.

When she reached the last bungalow Karen stopped. The sky was clouding over and the wind swept in unimpeded from the open countryside, blustery, and with a hint of rain on its gusty wings. She would have to turn back, even though the prospect daunted; back to the sadness of Elizabeth with heaven knew what sombre report from the hospital; back to Lisa in her flood of self-pity; back to Nick and his determination to control their lives—for a reason no one with an iota of compassion would dispute—and back to the charade she dreaded. It had never been easy, but now . . . Last night had stripped away all the frail skin of healing doggedly formed during the past two years and turned the knife in the wound. She finally knew just how much she had lost, how empty her future of everything except the pain of loss and longing. She thought of Nick's hands on her body for the first time in two years, of his body possessing hers once more, but without love, without tenderness, harsh with retaliation and undisguised carnal desire, and she was filled with sick torment at the memory.

She turned abruptly, her eyes blurred with unshed tears, and almost fell over a small toddler emerging from a gate with an exuberant puppy in tow. The child flashed a startled yet winsome look up at Karen from huge blue eyes with incredibly long lashes, and the puppy barked. A harassed young woman carrying an armful of washing just un-pegged from the line hurried down the path to retrieve and admonish her infant, and she shot Karen a curious, almost suspicious glance as she scooped the toddler into her free arm and shooed the puppy back into the garden. Then as she kicked the gate shut her frown relented and she exclaimed, 'I'm so scared he gets out into the road and gets run over.'

Karen murmured a suitable assent, held by that wide blue gaze and innocent child's charm, then began to retrace her steps, trying to shut out all the images of old cherished tender dreams awakened by the small encounter. Of a miniature edition of Nick in her arms, with the dark unruly hair and stubborn chin snuggling into her shoulder ... or the small feminine version of that determined mouth and intelligent brow, endearing, capricious, irresistible ... The cold weight of lead settled round her heart; how was she going to face and rebuild her future again, alone, without ...?

The rain was starting to fall as Karen reached the market square and discovered she had missed the bus and faced a wait of two hours for the next one. Thirst and despondency, if not hunger and the need for shelter, drove her into the little café at the far side of the square. It was warm, steamy, and crowded, but a middle-aged farming couple made room for her at their table and she ordered a pot of tea and the sandwiches of home-cooked beef that the friendly farmer advised.

She had not expected that she would be able to eat even a quarter of the sandwiches on the generously heaped plate the young waitress brought, but they were unexpectedly delicious and the tea strong and fragrant, and suddenly she realised that her body clamoured for food. It was now some eighteen hours since last she ate. Also, the taking of a meal helped to pass the time, delaying the moment when she must venture out into the downpour that now beat against the café window and sent the pedestrians outside scurrying about their business. But the café was full; it was lunch time and she knew she must soon make way for others. She finished her cup of tea, paid her bill and emerged as the clock struck the half hour.

Still another hour to wait, and across the square the bus shelter was already full of refugees from the elements. Karen prepared reluctantly to join them; her light jacket was scant protection for this kind of weather and she chided herself for her stupidity in venturing so far without sturdier attire. But that was her trouble; her emotions frequently overrode common sense, she told herself bitterly. And as for the subconscious wish that she could run away from everything ... but how could she? The circumstances in which she was trapped had not changed—except for the worse. Now it was going to be late afternoon before she got back to Dellersbeck, and while her resentful heart protested stubbornly that it cared nothing for what Nick thought—he cared nothing for her, did he?—at least she should have some consideration for poor Elizabeth, who had enough to worry about and would certainly be concerned at her prolonged absence if she——

Karen never saw the dirty polythene bag lying on the pavement.

A gasp was jerked from her as her foot skidded violently under her and her hands flailed the air as she fought to save herself from pitching helplessly into the gutter. But the road was coming up to meet her, and there was a squealing, rushing sound, and shouts, and then something hit her so hard she was thrown into the air.

She spun like a rag doll, sky and buildings whirled in a

crazy parabola, there was a confusion of noise and voices, a
thud that knocked every vestige of breath out of her body,
and feet all round her. In her mind she was still trying to
get back on her feet, even as she suddenly went limp and
inert, the road cold and wet under her face, and the roaring
starry blackness swept her into oblivion.

*   *   *

Merciful unconsciousness spared Karen the pain of being
moved and blotted out awareness of the circle of strangers
who gathered about her, of the distraught car driver, and the
young policeman who put a coat over her and pillowed her
head until the ambulance rushed to the scene. She remembered nothing of the journey to the cottage hospital, or the
casualty doctor making his examination, and the nurses
sponging the mud from her face as she was hurried to
X-ray.

When she opened her eyes it was to silence and a blur of
white and blue and green and yellow, which gradually re-
solved into white and cool blue walls and a folded screen
of cheerful lemon and green floral print at one side of the
bed. *Bed!* She was in bed, and there was something stuck
over her brow. She had a raging thirst, and an instinct that
told her not to try to move or she might regret it. She tried
to part dry, stuck-together lips, and a soft voice said, 'Good,
you're awake. How do you feel?'

Karen stared up at the fresh-complexioned young nurse
who stood by the bed, closing cool fingers round Karen's
wrist. Karen whispered, 'What happened? Where am I?'

'You're in a side ward of the Cottage Hospital.' The nurse
unhooked a chart from the foot of the bed, and added, 'The
doctor will be here in a moment.'

Consciousness was returning more fully now and it
brought no reassurance. Her head ached abominably, her
right arm agonizingly so, and the rest of her felt as though
it had been beaten. There was the feeling that a lot of things
had happened, but for the moment they all hovered beyond
the fringe of memory, and there was only the confusion of the
nightmare from which she had not yet awakened. She had

gone on a bus, and then into a café. And then . . .

'Now then, Mrs Radcliffe.'

The house doctor was tall and thin and dark-haired, with a whimsical, one-sided smile. He looked down at her. 'Not so worried now?' Without giving her bemused brain time to sort that out, he asked briskly, 'When did you last have food? Can you remember?'

'How did you know my name?' she whispered.

He was used to delayed reactions and smiled. 'I'm afraid we had to check your belongings. Just to put any valuables into safe keeping and to establish your identity, so that we could inform your next of kin in case they're worrying about where you got to.'

A rush of memory made Karen try to struggle up. She had a dreadful vision of the police arriving at Dellersbeck, and poor Elizabeth answering the door ... 'Please,' she exclaimed, 'I've got to make a phone call. I've got to let——'

'Take it easy. We'll see to that for you.' The doctor put a restraining hand on her shoulder and smiled. 'That would be Nick. Your husband?'

Nick! Karen subsided, and the tears squeezed between her eyelids. It did not occur to her to wonder how the doctor knew her husband's name was Nick; she only remembered why she had been running away from Dellersbeck that morning. Was it that morning? How long had she been here? What time was it? She tried to raise her arm to see her watch, and again the doctor shook his head. 'Will you stop worrying, young lady? Now what about that last meal you had?'

'It—it was,' she licked dry lips, 'at lunchtime. The clock struck half past one as I came out of the café. And—and then——'

'That's fine.' He glanced at his watch. 'We can get you down to the plaster room right away.'

Again Karen's dry lips parted and she whispered, 'Please, can I have a drink?'

'Not just yet, although,' he turned to the nurse, 'let her moisten her lips. You see,' he looked back at Karen, 'we've got to give you something to put you out for a little while, just until we reduce that Colles. Then you can have a nice cup of tea as soon as you're back in the ward.'

'Colles? My arm?'

He nodded.

'Is that all?'

'Isn't it enough?' He raised humorous brows.

She swallowed painfully. 'Will I be—all right?'

'Of course! Your head X-rays showed no damage there, and apart from the Colles and some bad bruising, you're still in one piece. We'll keep you in for a day or so, because of the concussion, and then we'll probably see you skipping out of the ward.' He paused, then added. 'From all accounts, you escaped quite lightly, young lady.'

'Did I?'

She subsided against the pillow and missed the somewhat thoughtful and rather puzzled glance he gave her. But he turned away, and a little while later the ward Sister came in, cool and professional, to note Karen's condition and tell her they were ready to set her wrist.

It was all over remarkably quickly. Little more than half an hour later Karen was back in the ward, drowsily sipping a cup of tea that tasted like nectar to her parched mouth. Perhaps it was the after-affects of the anaesthetic, perhaps shock, exhaustion or pain, but now she no longer cared about anything. All she wanted to do was sleep. But that was not to be for a while. Sister arrived, followed by a nurse for temperature taking, and then the young policeman who had first tended Karen at the scene of the accident came in, to ask her what she remembered of that disastrous few moments.

There was very little she could tell him, except that she had slipped and fallen, and he made notes carefully, obviously not wanting to distress her any more than could be helped. Then he asked if she had seen the car.

She shook her head, wincing with the unwary movement. 'Was that what hit me? It felt like a tank.'

He smiled faintly. Then a disturbing thought came to her. She said urgently, 'It couldn't have been his fault—I must have fallen right in front of him.'

'Yes. It seems as though you almost fell on his bonnet.

There was a polythene bag caught on your shoe—we think that was what sent you flying.' He stood up. 'That's how it happens, I'm afraid.'

He departed, and Karen closed her eyes, only to be aroused yet again by the arrival of the evening meal. Her eyelids drooping with weariness, she ate a little of the fish and potato, and all of the ice-cream, and was sound asleep long before the trolley stopped in the corridor outside for the gathering up of dishes. An hour later the nurse had to call her name twice before she began to surface, to hear a soft voice a long way away murmur, 'I don't think we should wake her,' and the little nurse repeating, 'Here's your husband to see you, Mrs Radcliffe,' in a brisk, cheerful voice.

Karen opened her eyes and saw Nick standing at the foot of the bed, Elizabeth beside him.

For long moments she stared at him, everything flooding back to her, and she wanted to cry out to him not to pretend, not to drag out the sorry charade of pity and devotion because it was expected of him and because Elizabeth stood there with unguarded shock and distress on her sweet face. Because she couldn't take any more . . . But he came forward, and it seemed her wish might be answered, for there was no regret or tenderness in his expression, only a closed, unreadable grimness that kept his features set like a taut mask as he came forward.

'Hello, Karen. How do you feel?' he asked, and bent down to brush her cheek with his lips in a purely token gesture.

She wanted to cry out, *Oh, I'm fine. I can't think what I'm doing here!* but Elizabeth had also come to kiss her, and she forced herself to say wryly, 'Not too bad—a bit achey. I'm still not sure how it happened.'

'My poor darling!' Elizabeth sat down at the bedside and looked at Karen with deep concern in her eyes. 'You might have been killed! When the police came we——'

'Oh, I know! I'm sorry!' Karen's fingers clenched with the agitation of distress. 'I was so afraid you'd——'

'What I can't understand is what you were doing over here

in the first place,' Nick interrupted grimly. 'None of us even knew that you'd——'

'Nick!' Elizabeth's tone was sharp with censure. 'This isn't the time for one of your inquests. Anyway, why shouldn't Karen feel free to go where she wishes? You don't expect her to be answerable to you for every move she makes!'

'I'm sorry.' His mouth compressed, and Karen watched Elizabeth relax, unknowing of how empty was the token apology, and reach for the bag Nick had put down on the floor.

She had packed the things she considered Karen would need; nightdress, toothbrush, a light dressing gown, talcum and other toilet articles, which she proceeded to stow away neatly in Karen's locker as she chatted away, plainly determined to lighten the mood. Magda and Timsy sent their love, and Lisa said how sorry she was and she would visit Karen the following evening—'That is if you're still here,' Elizabeth added with determined cheerfulness. Of her own visit to the specialist that morning Elizabeth was non-committal, shrugging away Karen's tentative enquiry. During all this Nick remained taciturn and seemed ill at ease, glancing at his watch a couple of times, as though he wished the awkward minutes would pass more quickly.

At last, in a silent lull, he asked, 'Is there anything you want?'

'No, thank you,' she said quietly. 'Elizabeth remembered everything.'

'Are they looking after you?'

'Yes. They couldn't be kinder.' She looked past his shoulder, determined to ask for nothing, nor to betray any sign of the pain and despair in her heart.

'There is a small private wing,' he persisted. 'I could arrange to have you transferred there.'

'I don't want to be in a private room,' she said flatly. 'I'm being moved into the main part of the ward tomorrow. Anyway, it's only for a day or so.'

'Is it?'

The flatness of his tone suddenly frightened Karen. Had he talked to the doctor? Was there something else wrong with her? Something they hadn't told her . . .?

There was another small silence, and abruptly Elizabeth looked at Nick. 'I think we should let Karen get some rest now. She looks utterly exhausted.'

'The visiting time isn't up,' Nick demurred.

'No. But look at her, Nick,' his mother said quietly.

It was not until the following morning that Karen glimpsed herself in her compact mirror and realised what Elizabeth meant. They had cut some of her hair close to the scalp in order to stitch the deep cut just above her forehead. There was an angry graze on her cheek, another above her right eye, and a huge bruise down her left arm, apart from the rainbow of purples and yellows that even now was spreading on the parts of her body concealed beneath the clothes. And of course there was the casing of dazzling white plaster that made her arm lie heavy with its unfamiliar weight. But Elizabeth had also discerned the aftermath of shock that lay behind the more obvious physical signs of the accident.

'We'll telephone in the morning for news, and I hope you'll be feeling a lot better by then, darling.' Elizabeth kissed her warmly, then gave Nick a meaning look as she straightened. 'I'll wait outside for you.'

Karen's heart contracted with bitterness. Elizabeth wanted to leave them together for those small, intimate exchanges of tenderness between husband and wife! Karen drew the covers closer up to her chin and stared blankly at the ceiling when Elizabeth went out. She had no strength for either defence, reproach or pretence, and she had no illusions left about Nick's true feelings concerning herself.

He stood up and walked slowly to the foot of the bed, not looking at her. 'All right,' he said flatly, 'I know there's nothing to be said.'

'No, there isn't,' she responded wearily. 'And if there were this is scarcely the time or the place to say it.'

'I realise that.' He sighed heavily. 'I'll go, then. Goodbye, Karen.'

The echoes lingered in the room long after he had gone, mocking and final. Nick had not bade her goodnight; he had said goodbye.

CHAPTER TWELVE

KAREN spent a restless, weary night that seemed endless. All her previous longing for sleep had gone, and even the sleeping pill which Night Sister gave her at two a.m. brought only three or four hours of dazed semi-consciousness that could not obliterate either physical discomfort or mental stress. In her stupor Karen seemed to relive all the unhappiness of her marriage and venture into the uncharted realm of the future, from whence scant promise beckoned. When morning brought the doctor he looked down at the feverish colour suffusing her cheeks and his smile faded.

'I hear you had a bad night.'

She tried to smile, and raised the plastered arm. 'I haven't got used to this yet.'

'You're going to be lumbered with it for a while, I'm afraid.' He checked her fingers for swelling. 'Does it feel too tight? We have to nick the plaster a bit sometimes.'

'No, I think it's all right.'

'Hm, let's inspect the rest of the damage.'

When he had completed the examination he drew the covers back over her and frowned. 'Anything worrying you, Mrs Radcliffe?'

There seemed a certain deliberateness in the question and she stared at him, then turned her head in a negative gesture. How could she tell him that her marriage lay in ruins? That each day she and Nick were together was by courtesy of deceit?

He said gently, 'Patients often have problems, you know, and we worry if those problems retard their recovery. Don't be afraid to ask for help if there's anything we can do about it.'

He was so concerned and gentle she could not speak for a moment. The sting of tears came into her eyes and she averted her face lest he should see. Somehow it hurt even more that a stranger cared in case she was scared or worried about something, and yet Nick could not bring one tiny iota of regret or concern.

'Hey . . .' the blur of the white coat leaned over her, 'we don't usually make our patients cry !'

She blinked hard. 'I'm not going to break your good record, Doctor.'

'Good. You're coming along fine, you know. We're going to move you into the big ward now. The company will do you good. You can get up after lunch, watch TV in the day room, if you like. All right?' With a smile he went on his way, and the nurse began to prepare for Karen's move.

As he had surmised, the companionship in the main ward did help. The camaraderie of hospital broke down most barriers with remarkable speed, and inevitably there was a live-wire among the patients. She was plump, blonde and noisy, and if her sense of humour was somewhat crude her unfailing cheerfulness could be relied on to raise a smile when gloom threatened. The saga of Jenny and her feller was endless, and before the day was out Karen had heard the medical histories if not the life stories of most of the other women in the ward as well. But there was plenty of aid and encouragement when she took her first unsteady walk down the ward. Although she felt stiff and sore she was secretly vastly relieved to discover that she still functioned more or less normally. It was just a matter of time.

Nick came again that evening, bearing flowers and fruit and accompanied by Lisa. Several heads turned as she walked slowly along the row of beds. She was immaculately made up, betraying no hint of the wan sickliness of the previous week, and she looked superb in a rich suede outfit of denim-blue trousers and tight matching waistcoat over an ivory silk blouse with full flowing sleeves. Nick was carrying her jacket, also of the blue suede.

She gave Karen a perfunctory kiss, and there was the conventional exchange of pleasantries. Jenny was holding court with her visitors at the next bed and there was so much noise that Nick gave an impatient murmur. After a few minutes he stood up. 'I'll leave you girls to talk. Okay?'

Karen nodded dully. She had not expected him to come, much less stay and make small talk when the absence of Elizabeth rendered this unnecessary. But Lisa did not seem very anxious to talk. She had reverted to the brittle, artificial manner of those first weeks at Dellersbeck, and Karen had the impression that she regretted those confidences made under the stress of discovering her unwanted pregnancy.

'Have you told your mother?' Karen asked at last.

'What?' Lisa blinked, then grimaced. 'Yes, I told her this morning. Your mishap and her own visit to hospital sort of monopolised things yesterday. And Herr Lindner landed over during the afternoon as well.'

'Is she thrilled?'

'About her German beau?'

'No.' Karen sighed, aware that Lisa was being deliberately obtuse. 'About the baby, of course.'

'You could say she was more thrilled than I am.' Lisa inspected her nail lacquer for chips. 'If I manage to get into this suit again after another couple of weeks I'll be very surprised. It's as tight as a drum already.'

'You'll be able to wear it afterwards. The baby isn't for ever,' Karen consoled, 'and suede stays in fashion pretty steadily.'

'Yes, except the cut doesn't.' Lisa looked round restlessly, her mouth tight with impatience. 'Where the devil has Nick got to?'

Karen could not answer this, and stole a glance at the ward clock. Although visiting hours were the high spot of the day for most patients she could not help wishing this one was over. At the best of times she and Lisa were scarcely on similar wavelengths, and at this moment Lisa was obviously itching to be away. While Nick ... Well, he'd made little pretence about his reluctance to spend any more time at Karen's bedside than bare convention demanded. If only we could all stop pretending, she thought sadly.

Lisa fidgeted with the strap of her bag, then leaned forward. 'Karen ...' she whispered, 'would you mind very much if Nick took me back before the hour's up? It's just,' she shuddered expressively, 'hospitals give me the creeps.'

Karen shook her head, and sudden weariness made her slide down under the bedclothes and turn her face against the pillow's stiff whiteness. 'I'm beginning to feel tired, anyway. Thanks for coming, Lisa.' She hesitated, then discovered she had no compunction about using her present misfortune to its limit. 'Why don't you look for Nick?' she suggested. 'He may be talking to Sister, or gone out to the car. Tell him there's no need to bother coming back here to say goodnight.'

She closed her eyes and sensed rather than saw Lisa's momentary hesitation before gathering up her bag and jacket and making her way towards the ward door. Determination kept Karen's eyes tightly closed, so that she did not catch the brief glimpse of Nick's tall figure reaching the doors at the same moment as Lisa thrust them open. Nor did she see Lisa's hand on his arm, urging him away, as he stared down the ward, and the sudden hard tightening of his mouth before he seized Lisa by the arm and hurried her into the corridor.

Karen hardly knew whether to be sorry or thankful next morning when the doctor decided, after a certain amount of deliberation, to keep her in for another twenty-four hours. She was feeling better, every movement had stopped drawing protests of pain from the bruised parts of her body, her ribs didn't hurt so much and her head felt less like a somewhat battered punchball. But although she was aware of the reawakening urge for return to normality there was still a secret sense of relief that the need for making decisions was to be shelved for another day.

The exuberant Jenny was discharged that morning, along with two other patients, and the ward seemed very quiet after they had gone. Karen made herself useful, taking on such small tasks as the staff nurse would allow, and trying not to think of the return to Dellersbeck the following day. If only there were some way she could escape! For she could not endure any more of Nick's contempt and his merciless disregard for her feelings. How he must hate her ... But try as she might Karen could find no solution, other than that of telling Elizabeth the truth. And that was impossible. Not for the first time Karen wished she had been more plentifully endowed with relations. But she was an only child, both her parents were dead, and several years previously her father's younger brother had emigrated to New Zealand, taking his family of four with him. Now there was only Aunt Helen left. And she had only one interest in life: her Highland farm where she raised a particularly élite strain of pedigree cattle. There would be little sympathy from Aunt Helen, and certainly no hope of faking an urgent S.O.S. summons for help from Aunt Helen to provide a convincing escape route.

As the evening visiting hour drew near Karen felt the old familiar tension coiling inside her like a spring. If only the clock could move forward an hour ... But when the ward doors were opened to admit the eager stream of visitors it was not Nick who escorted Elizabeth so protectively along the ward towards Karen's bed. Karen restrained a start of surprise as she recognised Herr Lindner. She had not expected to see him!

He greeted her, and drew a chair into place for Elizabeth. 'You are feeling more recovered, Frau Radcliffe?' he enquired, making a stiff little bow as he placed a transparent bag of delicious-looking black grapes into her hands.

'She *is* looking better!' exclaimed Elizabeth as Karen murmured her thanks. 'Any news about your coming home?'

'Tomorrow.' Karen could not help a stab of curiosity as she noticed the quick exchange of glances between Elizabeth and Herr Lindner. Glances which seemed to hold a satisfaction not entirely concerning herself. And Elizabeth had an air of suppressed excitement about her. What on earth had happened now? Karen wondered with renewed trepidation.

'That's wonderful!' Suddenly Elizabeth looked enormously relieved. 'Now, darling ... I was waiting until I saw how things were with you, but I think I'd better tell you now. I'm going to Germany on Friday.'

'*Germany!*' Karen gasped.

'I am hoping to take Elizabeth back with me,' put in Herr Lindner.

'But that's in two—no, three days!' exclaimed Karen, unable to grasp all this and wondering if delirium had set in as an unforeseen repercussion. 'Are you—is it a holiday?' she stammered.

'No.' Elizabeth smiled and glanced at her friend. 'Will you explain, Reinhard, please? I'm much too excited.'

'Certainly.' Again there was that rather special exchange of glances between Elizabeth and the tall German with the grave face. He turned to Karen. 'Please do not look so alarmed, my dear. I wish only the best for your dear mother. You may not know, but I lost my beloved wife five years ago when she suffered the same illness as Elizabeth. Then, as now, the doctors could offer little hope, and we could only watch helplessly as this dreadful scourge burned up all the precious life in her. Had she lived but a few years longer . . .' He paused, his precise tone faltering, then he went on: 'Near my home, which is close to the Austrian border, there is a very fine clinic where they believe they are at last in sight of a major breakthrough. It is a little complicated to explain, and many of the orthodox experts have reservations about the claims for this new treatment, although they are interested. But I have seen patients leave this clinic with new hope in their eyes and the promise of reprieve in their future.'

'But what is it?' Karen felt fear. Was Elizabeth being cruelly buoyed up with a promise of false hope? Even risking suffering while undergoing a treatment that would prove worthless? Would perhaps even shorten what precious time remained to her?

'Nothing to fear.' Herr Lindner shook his head. 'This is no place of quacks. It is of the highest repute, and its doctors are totally dedicated. They used orthodox drugs and treatment technique, but it is the way in which these are administered to the individual patient which has brought about quite remarkable alleviation.'

'They chart the time clocks and rhythms of the body,' Elizabeth broke in. 'Apparently no one has quite the same pattern—like fingerprints. There's still a tremendous amount of research to be done, of course, but they are convinced that this can have a very important effect in many ailments. Anyway, I've made up my mind,' Elizabeth said firmly. 'I've little to lose, and possibly a great deal to gain, and so I'm accepting Reinhard's kind offer. He will escort me there and visit me while I'm in the clinic, and he has very kindly offered his hospitality to Nick and Lisa and yourself if you wish to come to see me—as I may be there quite a while.'

Karen drew a deep breath. 'What does Nick think?' she asked.

'He isn't very pleased about it, I'm afraid,' Elizabeth said ruefully, 'but I'm not going to let him talk me out of it.'

'Your son is sceptical, my dear,' said Herr Lindner, 'and I quite understand his feelings. I too would be sceptical in the same circumstances. But it is your decision, and if you wish to think it over, or even change your mind, do not hesitate to do so,' he said steadily. 'I will understand.'

Elizabeth shook her head, and now the suppressed excitement had ebbed, leaving a brooding light in her eyes, 'No. This has come in the nature of a blessing. I've been wondering for a while now what was best to do. You see, it hasn't worked out the way Nick hoped.'

Karen looked at her wonderingly, half afraid, and Elizabeth gave a faint smile. 'It was a lovely idea, gathering us all together at Dellersbeck, and I appreciate it more than I can say. But it isn't fair to you all. Nick's too far from his office, it's a hopeless situation for poor Cliff, and it isn't fair to you. You see,' Elizabeth hesitated, then looked steadily at Karen, 'I know that all isn't quite as well between you and Nick as you'd both have me believe. I don't know what it is, and, beyond saying that if there's anything I can do you've only to ask, I wouldn't dream of interfering. But you should be in your home, organising your own lives, as should Lisa and Cliff, not living in this limbo-like set-up at Dellersbeck and marking time until I lose the battle with my enemy. Well,' Elizabeth drew a tremulous breath, 'I'm going to fight, but in my own way, and I'll feel a lot easier if I know my children have all gone home to set their own houses and lives in order. God willing, I shall hold my first grandchild in my arms. So, Karen, will you help me? Will you try to get Nick to understand? Because this is the way I want it.'

Karen nodded wordlessly, then leaned forward into Elizabeth's embrace. She swallowed hard, then whispered, 'I'll pray for you every moment you're away. That you'll come back well again. And—thank you, Elizabeth . . .'

She felt Elizabeth's arm tighten around her and knew that the older woman had understood the small, unspoken message. A few moments later it was time for the visitors to leave, and as she watched the slight figure of Elizabeth vanish into the ragged stream through the door Karen felt a strange sense of unreality possess her. It seemed her wish had come true in a way she had never expected. The strain and the anguish of the charade was almost over at last. By next week at this time she would be back in London—perhaps at Mrs Biggins', she thought with a flash of something like hysteria. But whatever she was she would be free of the impossible role she had played during the past few weeks. There would be letters to Elizabeth, of course, they would work out something so that no distress or worry would be allowed to hamper the new treatment. It should not be difficult to keep the truth from her for a while longer. Later, if she made the recovery they would all pray for, of course they would have to tell her. It wasn't a secret that could be kept indefinitely. As for Lisa . . . she must work out her own destiny . . .

Karen sank back against the pillows and stared at the misty bloom on the grapes which still lay on the bed. She opened the bag and pulled one free, savouring its sweet tangy juice. The main thing was that she would be free of Nick within a few days. Once back in London she need not see him at all. Anything which needed discussing could be done by phone. No longer would he be able to needle and torment her. She would be free!

That was what she wanted, wasn't it?

*   *   *

The sense of unreality was still there next morning when Nick arrived shortly before eleven, bringing a case holding her clothes. When she had donned the green slacks and the big loose white pullover he had brought she said her goodbyes and went out to where he waited impatiently.

He glanced at her rather closely as he took the case from the nurse. 'Are those things all right? I wasn't sure what to bring—because of that arm.'

'These are fine,' she said shortly.

'I dropped your other rig-out in at the cleaners yesterday. The thing you were wearing when ... I'm afraid they're in a mess, though.'

'It doesn't matter,' she said tonelessly. How could he talk as though nothing had changed? As though they still pretended. As though only four nights ago he had not flung all the same old appalling accusations at her, and in his rage lost control to the point of practically raping her. Did he imagine she had forgotten?

She walked out to the car, wishing she could be independent and refuse to drive with him. But there was so little time left. For the sake of it she might as well go along with him.

He saw her into the car, stowed her case in the back and got in, to drive off without speaking. Karen stared out of the window. It suited her not to talk, but about five miles on he stopped the car abruptly outside an old grey stone inn.

'We'll have a drink,' he said, opening the car door.

'I don't want a drink,' she said stiffly.

'But I do.' He came round to her side. 'Oh, come on, Karo. You look as though you need a stiff drink to hold you up.'

'Thank you.' Her tone was knife-edged with sarcasm. But she got out and walked ahead of him, determined not to give him the chance to touch her. Without asking what she wanted he brought a rum and Coke for her and Scotch for himself.

She stared through the window, determined not to look at Nick. It seemed impossible for them to be together without bitterness, so wasn't it better to be silent, no matter how unfair it was that way? For she lacked the strength to fight any more.

'Karo ...'

'No.' Without moving her head she said quietly, 'Just get

on with your drink, Nick. I don't want to talk, and I'm too weary for any more argument.'

'That sounds very final.'

'It was meant to.'

'Would it make any difference if——'

'No! Nothing will make any difference. You said yourself there was nothing left to say. Just accept that.' She stood up jerkily and set her glass on the table. 'I'll wait outside.' Before he had time to protest she went swiftly across the old inn parlour and out into the sunlight.

By the pub wall there was an ancient form with a single supporting bar along its back, and on this she sank, to sit there stiffly and watch a sleek black cat sunning itself outside a cottage across the road. Two sparrows swooped into a nearby hedge, to flirt and twitter, and the cat's tail twitched. It looked up, quivers disturbing the fur down its spine, and the sparrows took off noisily for the cottage chimney. The cat stayed alert and tense for a moment, then sighed back into its supine position on the cobbles. The scene was warm and timeless, and then Nick emerged from the inn and strode to the car.

He waited there, his face dark and set and his eyes full of anger, until she stood up and walked slowly across the grassy verge. The silence between them was like a tangible barrier during the rest of the journey. The familiar landmarks came into sight, and then the winding drive up to the house. Nick snapped on the brake and said abruptly: 'You know about Elizabeth?'

'Yes. She told me last night.'

'What do you think?'

Karen knew surprise that he should ask. But she betrayed none of it as she said carefully, 'I think she should go, and I don't think you should even try to stop her.'

'I see. And then?'

Karen shrugged and fumbled with the car door handle. 'I don't know. Because I don't know what you're asking.'

'You could try listening.'

'Don't you think I've listened enough?'

With that she went towards the house, to the warm,

affectionate welcome from Elizabeth and Magda and Timsy, and she was scarcely inside the hall before another car swept up the drive and Herr Lindner followed Nick indoors. There were flowers everywhere, and an extra special lunch had been prepared in honour of her homecoming. Only Lisa was missing.

'She went home this morning,' Elizabeth said in an aside while Nick obeyed her behest to get the drinks. 'I'm sorry you missed her, but on the other hand it's quite a long drive for her by herself, so I thought it best to let her make a reasonably early start. Actually it's working out well already. I know she's not really used to the idea of this baby yet, and when she suddenly announced that she wanted to tell Clifford the news herself and would I mind very much if she didn't stay on here till Friday I just went and helped her to pack. I must pander to her little whims, bless her, until she gets over this unsettling time.'

So Lisa had not wasted much time, Karen reflected as she sat down to the very tempting dishes Magda had prepared. But didn't it prove how much wiser Elizabeth was, and how courageous to make her own decisions against the advice and overbearing, even if well-meant, determination of Nick?

He was moody and withdrawn over lunch, and Karen wondered if it was because of Lisa's abrupt departure. Or because he so plainly had reservations about the charming Herr Lindner. But wasn't it natural? After being the principal male influence in Elizabeth's life ever since the death of her husband he was bound to resent this stranger who had suddenly assumed so strong a sway over Elizabeth's decisions. But did Nick have to betray his anger in its dark and moody guise? Perhaps Herr Lindner would not recognise it as such, but Elizabeth, who knew every nuance of her adopted son's nature, would certainly be aware of it and its reason.

And Elizabeth looked so happy.

She was responding subtly to Reinhard Lindner's charming courtesy and grave attention like a flower opening to the sun after the long night. Some strange alchemy of light was making her face glow, taking away the veil of years and revealing again the vivacious beauty of youth, and in a stab of perception Karen realised what was happening to Elizabeth.

Karen found she was whispering a silent prayer to herself as the lunch ended and they adjourned to the sitting room for coffee. It was said that love could work miracles; could this be the beginning of Elizabeth's own special miracle?

Wrapped in this engrossing speculation, Karen scarcely heard Reinhard remark on the warmth of the afternoon and ask Elizabeth if she would care to go for a drive. Elizabeth agreed, and then Karen heard her own name.

'Perhaps you and your husband would also like to accompany us?' Herr Lindner asked courteously.

'I'm afraid not!' Nick's tone was brusque. 'Thank you, Herr Lindner, but my wife must rest this afternoon. Now, in fact,'

Before Karen could protest she felt herself swept off her feet and carried to the door. High in his arms, she stared at his set face and exclaimed, 'Nick . . . what——'

'Don't argue!' he hissed in a low voice. *'Just don't argue!'*

He took the stairs effortlessly, as though she were a featherweight in his arms, and thrust the bedroom door shut with his foot before he deposited her none too gently upon the bed.

He was breathing more heavily now, half kneeling, half sitting on the bed, his hands still pinning her down. He drew a deep shuddering breath and his eyes burned down into her startled, almost frightened face.

'Why, Karen? Why?' he groaned.

Her mouth quivered. The hard pressure of him leaning over her intimidated, brought fear. She licked dry lips. 'Why what? Nick, let me up. I——'

'Why didn't you tell me?'

Weakness suddenly overcame her. She turned her head away, raising her hand to try to push him away. 'Please—don't start again, Nick,' she moaned softly. 'I—I can't take any more!'

'Nor can I. Oh, Karen . . . Karen . . . my darling heart . . .'
His hands came to cup the distraught, averted face and turn

it to his gaze. Then, unbelievably, he was cradling her against his shoulder, murmuring over and again, 'But why? Why? For two years ... two long endless years ... all because of a vain, selfish, promiscuous little ... I could kill her!' he ground savagely.

Karen trembled. Her senses were whirling as her brain tried to believe that Nick's disjointed utterances could have only one meaning. She whispered, 'What ...? Who ...? I don't——'

'Lisa!' he grated. 'Who else?'

'You mean ... you mean she *told* you?'

Nick looked down into Karen's disbelieving eyes, and scorn twisted his mouth. 'Yes, she told me—after I practically shook the truth out of her.'

Karen moved her head bewilderedly. At first she had the incredulous thought that Lisa had confessed. But that didn't fit in. She stammered, 'But how? How did you know—to ask her?'

Nick's mouth softened, and he pressed her back against the soft mound of the pillows. 'You talked. Or don't you remember?'

'I—I don't know what you mean. I promised Lisa I'd never——'

'Never tell me?' His eyes narrowed. 'God! Karen, how could you?'

She looked away, still bewildered and unknowing of what exactly had taken place between Nick and Lisa. Then he stood up and went to the window, to stare out.

'When I visited you in hospital—with Lisa—I went to find somebody who could tell me what was happening. You must realise, Karen, I was feeling pretty distraught. Elizabeth had just dropped her bombshell, and I was feeling rotten about your accident—I had a guilty feeling that my—behaviour had tipped you off balance and caused you to have that accident. When I spoke to the nurse she went all businesslike and said the doctor wanted a word with me. I had to wait a while, and when eventually he arrived he looked at me as though I were a wife-beater or something.'

Nick's shoulder moved, and the outline of him turned

from the light then swung back, almost as though he did not want to face her. He went on, 'Apparently you'd worked yourself into a terrible state while you were concussed, and again during the night. All about a picture, and Lisa, and how I hated you. You kept crying my name over and over again, as though you were trying to tell me something and I wouldn't listen. The doctor took all this in, and asked me if I knew what was worrying you so much. He looked at me accusingly, and said if you had something on your mind it could retard your recovery, and he hoped sincerely that I could set your mind at rest.'

Nick sighed and came back to the bedside. He looked down at her with troubled eyes. 'My first instinct was to ask you outright what it was, but Lisa was there, and she wanted out, and I realised it was impossible to talk to you there—it would have been too distressing for both of us. But all the way home I was thinking and wondering. Somehow I kept seeing your hair, the way it was falling round your shoulders as you lay there in hospital. The way you used to wear it when I first met you. And suddenly I was seeing Lisa's hair. Hers was always long and silky and brown, very like yours, and she was always very vain about it. Even as a child she would sit for hours in front of the mirror, brushing and admiring that mane of hers. I could never imagine her sacrificing it, yet she did, and had it bleached almost white into the bargain. I started asking myself why, and for the first time ever I realised how alike you two are in height and physical build. Then I remembered all the other little things about Lisa, things it never occurred to me to put together— she was simply Lisa, my adopted sister, and not for analysis. But there were all her affairs, the wild streak in her, the way she could never bear anyone to find her out in a misdemeanour, and suddenly there was a click in my brain and I was back to that housewarming we gave . . .'

Karen held her breath, afraid to break the thread of Nick's memory. His eyes had gone remote, far back in time, and there was something deadly in the quietness of his voice as he went on:

'Someone mentioned Vince Kayne that night, and Lisa got

all excited, saying she'd always wanted to meet him, and that chap Tony brought along—I can't remember his name—said he had a friend who was in Kayne's set. But I didn't take any notice at the time—you know what parties are like—and I never gave it another thought until . . .' Nick's hands clenched and his jaw hardened. 'Then I remembered all the wild stories about Vince Kayne and his artist trendies, all the publicity, the field day the press had after his death, and suddenly I couldn't believe the incredible possibility that came to me. Yet I knew! Knew there was something behind it all, and it had to be Lisa. So I challenged her, just blurted it out. And she turned as white as death, and gave herself away instantly by crying out that you'd given her away.'

'But I didn't!' The words were out before Karen could stop them, and Nick exclaimed sharply:

'You didn't what?'

'I—I told her I——' Karen bit her lip, still unable to make the damning confession sealed for so long in a promise.

'What did you tell her?' Nick demanded. 'That you'd keep her miserable, sordid little secret, even at the expense of our marriage? For God's sake, Karen, tell me the truth! Tell me what happened. How and why did Lisa involve you? Why did you keep silent?'

'I thought she told you.'

'Not why.' Nick's eyes were like stones. 'She said she never even knew that I believed you were the model for that picture, and Vince Kayne's mistress, and she wasn't admitting a thing. Then she dissolved into tears, said she'd never meant to cause any trouble, and she never dreamed the picture would become world-famous and copies of it be sold all over the world. She'd only posed for fun, because Vince had dared her and she couldn't resist his flattery, and he'd promised that he'd never sell the painting, and all she'd wanted was her watch back, and how could she know he'd get himself killed in a car smash the next day. Then she went into near hysterics, crying that all this was bad for her baby, and then she was out of the car and into the house. Every time I tried to corner her either Elizabeth, or Magda, or Timsy appeared, all dewy-eyed and protective at the thought of coming motherhood. Karen!' he seized her shoulders. 'Tell me!'

Karen felt weakness pervade her and trembling spread through her limbs. She still could not believe that somehow Nick had discovered the truth at last. 'There isn't very much more to tell. I suppose you've guessed that Lisa had a hectic affair with Vince Kayne, and he persuaded her to sit for the Rodin painting. She used to go in the afternoons, and the day before Vince was killed she'd accidentally left her watch in the studio. It was that lovely jewelled watch Cliff gave her, and she was in a terrible panic about it. Her name was engraved on the back, and she had visions of somebody going through Vince's things and finding it there. But she and Cliff were going to visit friends in Oxford and she was desperate. She hadn't time to go and collect it, and no excuse for putting off the visit, and if she waited until they got back home it might be too late. Also, there was the risk of Cliff noticing she was not wearing it. So,' Karen took an unsteady breath, 'she rang me and begged me to go and get the watch. She'd already phoned Stephan, who had a key to Vince's place, and he'd promised to be there all morning, then I was to take the watch to Elizabeth and ask her to keep it safe for Lisa till she got back, saying she'd left it in our bathroom the day before.'

'She had it all worked out, didn't she? A tissue of lies.'

Karen could not bear to look at his face. 'I got the watch okay, and a wrap and other odds and ends Lisa had kept there, but I never expected the press to turn up, or that photographer to be there as I was leaving. Actually, Stephan did his best to shield me, he knew I'd never had anything to do with Vince and I was only Lisa's sister-in-law. But they'd got wind of the affair, and with Lisa being married to Clifford, an earl's son ... Stephan's denials only made things worse. They blew up all the publicity about the dead artist and his secret mistress, and the mystery of the model in the painting. Even so,' Karen shuddered, 'I never dreamed that photo would be published, and that you'd recognise me and believe that I was the girl. When you stormed in that day, and accused me of—of being unfaithful, and—and——' Her voice broke and she put her face in her hands. 'I—I couldn't

believe it! I couldn't believe you could even think I'd ever—
that you wouldn't listen to me.'

'But why didn't you *tell* me?'

'Because I'd promised Lisa. She made me promise I'd
never tell anyone, not even you. Especially you. She was so
scared that——'

'Lisa scared! God in heaven!' Nick groaned. 'Do you mean
to tell me that because of that selfish, vain little bitch you'd
let me believe that my own wife ... Why, Karen? Why
loyalty to Lisa, of all people, before me? I don't understand.'

'Don't you?' Karen had gone very pale and her voice was
quiet. Suddenly she knew she had to be honest, no matter
what happened. She looked up at him. 'You were too ready
to believe the worst of me, Nick. You came home, furiously
angry, your eyes and your heart filled with suspicion. That's
why I walked out on you that day. Because you'd destroyed
my trust in you. You had none in me. My word was not
enough. You wanted explanations I was not free to give;
you refused to listen when I gave you my word of honour
that I'd never ever been unfaithful to you since the day we
met.' She sighed. 'Looking back, I know now I should never
have given that promise to Lisa, still less kept it. But at the
time I could think only that you didn't trust me, and there-
fore you couldn't love me.'

'Not love you!' He gave a rough groan. 'Oh, Karen!
Have you any notion of what I've suffered these past two
years?'

'Yes,' she whispered. 'Perhaps something like the anguish
and the agony I've been through.' Suddenly her mouth
worked and a spasm of sobs racked her. Nick gave a choked
murmur and reached for her, pulling her fiercely into his
arms.

'Don't!' he whispered. 'Try to understand. Karen—so often
in my life I was betrayed—before I met you, before Elizabeth
found me. And there was a girl, three years before I met you.
She let me believe in her, and there was somebody else all the
time. I began to wonder if there was anyone I dared ever
give my heart to. And I'd known you so short a time ... I
felt so bitter that day. I thought; you too ... And when you

stood there that day, telling me that there was nothing more to say, I wanted to hurt you; I wanted to vent all the hurt and bitterness of my own life on you ...'

Karen felt the rigor, like a fever, pass through his shoulders, and her hands tightened round him. She was remembering that first day at Dellersbeck, and Elizabeth's confidences, all that Nick had undergone as a small lost boy, and she began to understand.

'Karo ...' his mouth moved against her ear, 'can you forgive me for all the hurt, for letting my vile temper get the better of trust? For——'

'No, Nick—don't! I'm sorry too!' She clung to him, her arms convulsive about him, knowing only the need to have done with the past and feel his arms around her again without anger between them. 'If you only knew ... that day ... I couldn't believe it was really happening. I was supposed to be flying to South America with you the next day, and instead I was packing my case to walk out of your life. And you were letting me ... not trying to stop me ...'

'Because I thought you were guilty. That you didn't care, and that was why you were going ...'

'Oh, Nick,' she groaned, 'it's all been like a nightmare.'

'It's over, darling ...' His hands strained her closer to him, and her tears were wet against his face as he rained kisses on her brow, cheek, throat, and her own mouth sought blindly for comfort, tasting the tang of his skin and the warmth of his hard throat. Gradually the storm of passionate reaction began to ebb and Nick's fingers curled round her chin, tilting it till he could look down into her tumult-darkened eyes.

'Oh, Karen—my darling heart,' he whispered huskily. 'I can't believe I've got you back—say it's not a dream.'

'I'm trying to believe it too.' She looked longingly into his shadowed face, and reached desperately to hold him again. 'Tell me you do still love me ...'

For answer he caught her close, his mouth parting hers with fierce, possessive demand, as though he would draw her soul within his, till she could scarcely breathe. Long moments later he broke the kiss. 'Karo ...' he murmured urgently, 'I want you now, desperately . . . but I don't want to hurt you. The accident . . . your arm, and . . .'

She trembled. 'I want you, Nick. Hold me—I want to know that the nightmare's over, that we've found each other again.'

He held her, lying down beside her, restraining desire and gently touching her, kissing her and whispering all the small incoherencies of lovers, dispelling the last lingering doubt, until mental turmoil began to abate and desire sprang in her, making her body ache for the sublimity only the act of love could bring.

'You've too many clothes on,' he whispered shakily, and she laughed with the unsteadiness of emotions still hectically strained.

'Did that ever defeat you, darling?'

'Not really . . .' his hands were very gentle, his mouth tender. 'Do you realise it's two whole years since I last undressed my wife? Since I kissed her all over . . .'

Karen closed her eyes, the knowledge of love telling her that Nick was trying to erase the memory of that midnight hour four nights ago. And when at last she lay relaxed and fulfilled in his arms, his head a heavy, sweet weight on her breast, she knew her instinct had not played her false. For a little while he was silent, lazily gentling her, then his hand stilled its playing.

'Karo . . .'

'Mm?'

'There's something that worries me . . .'

'What?' She felt a flutter of panic.

'The other night . . . when I . . .' He raised his head and looked down, his eyes disturbed. 'I'm sorry, darling. I was so brutal.'

She shook her head. 'It doesn't matter now. Nothing matters now.'

But the shadow still darkened his gaze. 'I—I wouldn't like to think that we—that we made a baby. Not in lust and hate.'

A sigh trembled through her and tenderness curved her lips as she drew his head down to her shoulder and whispered against his hair. 'No, darling. I can tell you for sure that we didn't. When our baby does happen, it will be born of tender loving.'

He looked at her, and understood, and relief came into his eyes. Gently he drew the coverlet over her and whispered, 'Thank you, my darling, and now you must sleep. The dark side has turned now. Nothing can hurt us again after this, I won't ever let it . . .'

With her hand clasped in his and the healing peace of love in her heart at last, Karen obeyed . . .

*   *   *

Some six months later Karen and Nick gave a very special party.

Lisa was there, seeming at first glance rather subdued in comparison to her former self, although she looked as svelte and lovely as ever in long-legged evening pants of black velvet and a tight-waisted matching jacket over a blouse with cascades of lace at throat and wrist. But a second, more searching glance revealed a certain light of satisfaction, smugness almost, gleaming in her eyes and lingering in her smile. Today there had been a christening. Master Clifford Anthony James and Miss Emma Elizabeth Jane lay sleeping in their luxurious carry-cots in one of the bedrooms, no doubt exhausted by the excitement and all the adulation showered on their minute pink selves that day.

Lisa grinned somewhat maliciously at Karen. 'The situation has kind of reversed itself, hasn't it? Still, I'll be able to give you plenty of expert advice.'

Karen smiled. She was too happy to remember any bitterness. Elizabeth had come home, glowing with the joy of a woman once more in love and obviously radiantly happy as the wife of Herr Lindner. She refused to talk of her reprieve, of the cautious verdicts of the clinic doctors that held out fresh hope for her future. She could talk only of her new twin grandchildren, of the one that was yet to come, and of her new home in Germany with the man who had done so much to help all their hopes come true. Looking at Herr Lindner, his arm about his wife, Karen knew they need have no fears for Elizabeth. He would guard her, and his own new happiness, with devotion and strength and zealous care.

The party was breaking up now. Elizabeth went to steal a last proud goodnight glimpse at the twins, then remembered she had left her bag in the dining room.

'I'll fetch it,' Karen offered.

She went into the darkened room, switched on the light and picked up the bag, and paused to glance at the picture that hung on the wall.

It was in oils, and on a small gilt plaque at its base was printed: The Kiss, by Vincent Kayne, R.A., after Rodin. But the two naked lovers depicted here enwrapped in the great sculptor's immortal pose were far from Auguste Rodin's original conception. Gone was the stone, the plinth, the museum atmosphere. Here was warmth and colour that brought the lovers bang into the twentieth century. A crumpled pink counterpane covered the divan on which the lovers sat. Blue jeans and a shirt lay tangled on the floor where they had fallen, and a half empty bottle of wine caught a rich prism of light in its crimson depths. Behind the lovers an open window showed night and the garish red and blue of neon across the way—one could almost hear the roar of the city outside the still room where two lovers kissed for eternity.

The girl's face was in shadow, and for a moment she conveyed an impression of Karen; blink once, and the illusion vanished, leaving another strangely familiar, of another tall slender girl with brown hair that once flowed long and silken about her shoulders . . . But the artist's cunning was supreme. Attempt to pin down and define these impressions inspired by his eternal Eve and they were instantly lost, beyond recall until some trick of light and imagination evoked their mischief once more.

'Does it still worry you?'

Karen started as Nick's hands closed round her shoulders. 'I didn't hear you, darling—no,' she turned within his arms and looked up into his face, 'it doesn't bother me at all— except when I remember the frightening amount of money it cost. Nick, did you really buy it principally for an investment for me?'

'No, darling,' his voice was husky, 'I think I bought it so that I would never cease to give thanks for the gift I've been given. For you, my dearest heart. Because there is something imprisoned in that painting, and I pray to God it will always stay there.'

Her eyes were wide and luminous, questing as they searched his dark features for his meaning.

'The dark side of our marriage came early,' he said soberly, 'and it almost destroyed us.'

'But it didn't!' She framed his face with her cupped hands, smiling and trying to urge away the shadow of the past. 'Anyway, nobody notices it now—except Lisa, of course,' she added mischievously.

Nick's mood changed instantly and his mouth twitched. 'You're not afraid that she thinks I bought it because I cherish a deep, secret passion for her?'

'It never even enters my head!' Karen reached up to press her mouth to his. 'I know otherwise, my love.'

And there's still *more* love in

Harlequin Presents...

Yes!
Four more spellbinding
romantic stories every month
by your favorite authors.
Elegant and sophisticated tales of
love and love's conflicts.

Let your imagination be swept away to
exotic places in search of adventure,
intrigue and romance. Get to
know the warm, true-to-life
characters. Share the special
kind of miracle that
love can be.

**Don't miss out. Buy now and discover
the world of HARLEQUIN PRESENTS...**

Do you have a favorite
Harlequin author?
Then here is an
opportunity you must
not miss!